Death on Tyneside

Death on Tyneside

Agnes Lockwood Mysteries Book Two

Eileen Thornton

Chapter One

Agnes trembled with shock as she stared down at the gruesome corpse hidden behind a large bush. The face of the man had been lacerated mercilessly and was covered in dried blood. One glazed eye, hanging from its socket, lay over his cheek and appeared to be staring up at her. The hands, like the face, were also badly slashed. She wanted to turn and run away from the grisly scene, but at that moment, her legs wouldn't even begin to move. But her mind was working overtime. What on earth was DCI Alan Johnson going to say when he discovered that she become accidentally involved in yet another murder?

* * *

It was around ten o'clock on a rather chilly morning in March when Agnes Lockwood stepped out of the taxi. She looked across the road towards the River Tyne. Beyond, on the other side of the river, were the Sage building and the Baltic Art Gallery. Her gaze drifted a little further upstream, to where the Tyne Bridge towered above them all. She had been so looking forward to coming back to Tyneside and she certainly wasn't disappointed.

A movement close by caught her eye. The Millennium Bridge had begun to tilt upwards to allow a vessel to float beneath the massive structure. Some people waited for hours to see this spectacle, yet it was happening in front of her eyes right now. It was almost as though the bridge was raising a salute to her return.

Agnes smiled to herself as she took in the scene. How good it was to be back.

Her thoughts were interrupted when the taxi driver asked whether she would like him to take her suitcases into the hotel.

"You seem to have brought a great deal of luggage," he added, eyeing the three large suitcases. "It looks like you're planning a long stay here on Tyneside."

"Thank you, Ben. That is most kind." She smiled at the driver. "I'm not sure how long I'll be here, so I packed for all eventualities." She looked down at the suitcases. "Though I think I went a little over the top." She paused. "Would you leave them at the reception desk and tell the staff I'll be there in a few minutes?"

Agnes had met Ben, a young Asian man, on her last visit to Tyneside. She had hailed a cab one day and asked him to take her on a tour around the city. Since then, whenever she'd required a taxi, she had given him a call.

Glancing back across towards the river, she thought back over the years. She recalled how her mother had spoken fondly of her roots on Tyneside. Yet, to the best of her knowledge, her mother had never returned. Not even for a short visit.

But since visiting the area a few months ago, Agnes now understood her mother's dilemma. Perhaps she believed that, once back, she would have been reluctant to leave.

Agnes had found it difficult to pack her bags and return to Essex when she was last here, even in the knowledge she would be able to come back a few months later and stay as long as she wanted. The idea had been good; visit the area, before returning home to prepare for her flight to Australia where she was meeting up with her sons. But it hadn't been that simple. Once here, she had been loath to leave. Even while she was away on the other side of the world, her thoughts had kept drifting back to Tyneside... and to Alan.

Alan was an old school friend, now a Detective Chief Inspector with the Newcastle Police. They had met quite by chance on her last visit and it had been fun to catch up after all these years. They enjoyed each other's company and they'd had dinner together several times. She had even assisted him in a murder inquiry. Though she knew he hadn't really wanted her to get involved. She had missed him while she was away and had thought about him often.

"The receptionist is having your luggage sent up to your room. So there's no need to rush inside the hotel." Ben's voice broke into her thoughts.

"Thank you, Ben." Agnes reached into her handbag and pulled out her wallet. "Now, how much do I owe you?"

He grinned. "This one is on the house." He gestured towards the taxi. "I didn't turn on the meter."

"Ben, you can't give free…"

But she got no further as Ben held up his hands. "I insist. Anyway, as the meter was off, I have no idea what to charge. It's just good to see you back here on Tyneside… and before you say another word, you'll recall that on your last visit, you insisted on paying me for a ride, which never actually took place."

Nevertheless, Agnes opened her wallet and pushed a twenty-pound note into his hand. "Okay, agreed. The ride was free today. That," she added, pointing towards the note, "is merely a tip."

Ben smiled and shook his head as he climbed into his taxi. "I should know by now. I can't win where you are concerned. But," he added, waving the money in the air, "thank you very much."

Agnes watched as the taxi pulled away. Ben was a good man and she knew the money would be used wisely. During her last visit, she had learned that Ben and his wife had a son with health issues and most of their money went on trying to make his life more comfortable. But they were proud people and wouldn't accept charity. A large tip now and again was the least she could do.

Once the taxi had rounded the corner, Agnes decided to take advantage of having a few minutes to spare before checking into the hotel. She crossed the road and stood by the river, just as she had done on the first day of her last visit.

Back then, while she had been gazing down at the water, it had crossed her mind how clean it looked, compared to the way she remembered it. Heavy industry had dominated the quayside all those years ago, causing the river water to be murky. She had even wondered how many people may have died by simply falling in the river during those years. Or whether murderers might have dumped bodies here, in the hope they would never be seen again.

She closed her eyes and heaved a sigh. That day, when all these thoughts had fluttered through her head, it had never occurred to her things like that still happened. Yet, not long afterwards, she had discovered the body of a man floating around the Swing Bridge, only a short distance from where she was standing right now.

Pushing the thought from her mind, she swung around to face the tall, graceful building in front of her. It was time to check into The Millennium Hotel.

* * *

At the Newcastle Police Headquarters, Chief Inspector Alan Johnson put down the phone. "That was Chief Inspector Aldridge in Gateshead. He believes they've found their murderer."

Sergeant Andrews looked up from his paperwork. "The killer of the bodies found recently by dog walkers?"

Alan nodded. "Yes. You'll recall one was discovered on some spare ground near the golf course in Wrekenton, while the other was found in Saltwell Park."

"Well, good for them," Andrews exclaimed, thumping the desk. "It's good to get a result so quickly."

However, he couldn't help noticing that his boss was not looking quite so enthusiastic.

"It *is* good – isn't it?"

"Yes, it is," Alan replied, thoughtfully.

"But?" queried his sergeant. "I feel there's a 'but' in there somewhere desperate to come out."

"Oh, it's nothing," said Alan with a shrug.

"Nothing?" Andrews cocked his head to one side, as he spoke. "I feel there's something you're uneasy about."

Alan slapped his hands on the arm of his chair. "From what we've heard, it strikes me they've wrapped up this case a little too quickly."

Sitting back in his chair, Alan began to relay his thoughts, counting them off on his fingers.

"One, both bodies were found only a short time ago. Two, there were no clues left at the scene – the killer hadn't dropped anything that would lead the police to him or her. Three, there weren't any fingerprints and four, no DNA. Therefore they had absolutely nothing to go on – nowhere to even start an investigation."

He paused.

"Yet DCI Aldridge is convinced they've caught the man who committed the crimes."

"Did the inspector say why he had reason to believe they had the right man in custody?"

"No!" Alan stared down at the phone. "I just think he wanted to gloat that they had caught their man so quickly."

"Well, there's nothing we can do." Sergeant Andrews glanced down at his paperwork. "However, there is a bright side," he added, quickly looking back at the chief inspector. "At least it's been sorted before Mrs Lockwood arrived back on Tyneside. Otherwise, I think she'd have headed to Gateshead to help with the investigation." He paused. "When is she due back from Australia?"

"Not for another three weeks and two days," Alan replied, looking at his calendar. He had been marking off the days until her return ever since Agnes left Tyneside.

"Even then, I don't know whether she will come straight back up here. She may need a little time to settle down after the flight." He sighed. "You know what I mean. Unpack, and sort things out before deciding what to do next."

He fell silent. There was the possibility that seeing her sons again after such a long absence might make her decide to move over there.

"Anyway," he added, forcing a smile. "You're right about the fact she would have wanted to help DCI Aldridge with the case. He wouldn't have seen what hit him."

They both laughed.

At that moment, Alan's mobile phone began to ring. Reaching into his pocket, he was surprised to find the call was from Agnes.

"Can't you sleep?" He laughed into the phone. "It must be the middle of the night over there." *It's Mrs Lockwood,* he mouthed to his sergeant.

"Yes, I suppose it must be, but I'm not over there."

"Well, where are you?"

"I'm here."

"You mean you're back in England?" Alan sounded surprised.

"I mean I am here, on Tyneside."

"I don't believe it! I thought..." Alan looked at his sergeant. "Agnes is here on Tyneside."

"Why don't you take an early lunch and pop off to meet up with her?" Andrews suggested. "I can finish this paperwork. It doesn't take the two of us."

Alan nodded at Andrews. The idea had already crossed his mind.

"Where exactly are you? I'll come to see you."

Chapter Two

"I thought you were staying with your family for a few more weeks. I must have got the dates wrong."

By now, Alan had caught up with Agnes at the Millennium Hotel. They had ordered coffee and scones to be served in the drawing room. Since arriving, he hadn't been able to take his eyes off her. To him, she looked amazing.

She was wearing a dress he hadn't seen before. Though that didn't surprise him; she seemed to have countless outfits. It was the way this one graced her stunning figure that captivated him. She also had a new hairstyle. It was cut quite short, but it really suited her; made her look even younger and she was sporting a wonderful suntan.

At school, he'd had a crush on her and had been disappointed when her family left the area. However, he had never forgotten her and could hardly believe it when he saw her again at the hotel after all those years. She was fun, she was graceful, she took life as it came, and she was... amazing. Yes, amazing! He didn't care how many times he thought it. There was no other word for it.

"That was the plan," Agnes agreed. She smiled. "But I missed dear old England and I missed being here on Tyneside and..." Her voice trailed off.

"And?" Alan prompted.

She had been on the brink of adding how much she had missed seeing him during her time away, but had stopped herself.

"And, I just wanted to come back." Agnes finished her sentence.

She looked away. Why couldn't she come out with the truth? He was a good man, honest, hardworking and always looked smart, even when wearing casual wear. He was the sort of man who would look good in a pair of dirty overalls. Though today, as he was on duty, he was wearing a suit, a crisp white shirt and a tie and, despite not being able to see them at the moment, she felt sure his shoes would be well polished. Part of his army training, she supposed. Nevertheless, why couldn't she simply tell him the truth?

Glancing towards the door, she was relieved to see the waiter heading towards them with the coffee they had ordered. The short interlude while he set out the table would give her the chance to change the subject.

"Tell me what has been happening here in Newcastle while I've been away," she said, the moment the waiter left. "Didn't you get a medal or something for catching the thief?"

"No," Alan laughed. "Besides, I think it was you who actually put us on track to catch both the thief and the murderer."

"Then what else has been going on? Or has everyone been behaving themselves in my absence?"

"I have to say it has been very quiet since you left." Alan stroked his chin. "Obviously, there has been the usual trouble in the city centre at the weekends. But nothing the uniform division couldn't handle." He paused. "However, there have been a couple of suspicious deaths over in Gateshead, but it seems the DCI has apprehended someone."

"Oh, so they won't need my help?" Agnes smiled.

"It seems not," Alan replied, with a grin. "How long are you planning to stay? You never know, something else may arise while you're here."

"I haven't decided on the length of my stay, but I have come well prepared. Ben – you remember Ben the taxi driver?"

She paused for a moment to allow Alan to recall the name.

He nodded.

"Well, Ben was shocked when he saw my luggage at the airport," she continued. "He struggled to get my three large cases into his cab."

Agnes took a sip of her coffee. "I asked for my old room, here at the hotel." She shrugged. "I don't really know why. I suppose they're all the same. It's just I felt at home there, so why change it? There have been a few changes, though. I see the room now has a small safe tucked away in the wardrobe and the flimsy chain on the window has been replaced with something much more substantial. I doubt anyone could open the window wide enough to peer outside quite so easily now."

"Yes, I heard they were going to add a safe to each room once the dust had settled after the jewellery thefts," said Alan. "I didn't know about the window chain, though."

He paused, for a second.

"Agnes, would you like to have dinner with me this evening?"

"Yes. Thank you, Alan. I would like that very much."

* * *

Back upstairs in her room, Agnes threw her bag onto the bed. She was angry with herself. Why on earth hadn't she admitted to Alan that she had missed him while she was away? Why dodge the issue, when he was the main reason she had cut short her stay with her family? Yes, she had been truthful when she said she had missed England and Tyneside; but, for goodness' sake, she had missed him even more.

She had sensed Alan's disappointment when she hadn't included him in her reasons why she had cut short her visit to Australia. Though she had skimmed past the issue, she felt bad about it. She had wanted to tell him but panicked at the last minute. What if she had got it wrong a few months ago, when she first had the feeling he was attracted to her?

She looked at her luggage standing near the wardrobe; the cases were still waiting to be unpacked. She then glanced at her watch. It was still early in the afternoon. She had caught the first flight to Newcastle and Ben had been waiting at the airport to pick her up. Surely the unpacking could wait a little while longer?

She glanced towards the window. It was a nice, sunny day; tomorrow, it could be wet and miserable. Perhaps a quiet stroll would be good.

Her intention had been to take a simple walk along the quayside. However, when she stepped out of the hotel, she suddenly had the notion to visit the park at the north end of the city. She remembered going there as a child; it would be interesting to see how it had changed over the years.

* * *

Sergeant Andrews looked up when the chief inspector walked back into the office.

"Everything okay?" he asked. "Did Mrs Lockwood enjoy her stay in Australia?"

"Yes, I think so," Alan replied slowly. "Actually, now you come to mention it, she didn't really say very much about her visit with her family. However, she did say she was pleased to be back here on Tyneside."

"My guess is that she missed your company."

"Perhaps," Alan smiled.

He really hoped so, but only time would reveal Agnes's true feelings towards him.

Chapter Three

The taxi dropped Agnes off at the entrance to the park. She had taken the first cab in the taxi rank close to the hotel, rather than contact Ben. He might have felt inclined to give her another free ride and she wasn't having that.

Despite the chill in the air, she found a number of people in the park. Most were teenagers using the skateboard area. The local schools had broken up for the Easter break. She stopped to watch as they rolled up and down the slopes. The more self-assured travelled at high speed on the higher slopes, obviously loving every minute. Some of them were very clever, making it all look effortless. Others, not so confident, preferred to take things more slowly, staying on the lower slopes. Agnes decided that were she a youngster today, she would have been part of the latter group.

In her day, roller skates were the big thing. Someone had even let her borrow a pair one afternoon. But, once strapped to her feet, they seemed to take on a mind of their own. The wheels had started to move, taking her with them. The street they lived on had a slight slope, allowing the skates to gather speed. Why hadn't someone told her how to stop? She finally came to a halt when she crashed into a wall at the end of the road. She smiled to herself. Thinking about it now, it seemed funny, though at the time it had been quite frightening.

Moving on through the park, she came across the play area meant for younger children. She had been here numerous times as a child and was pleased to see it hadn't been forsaken for the more up-to-date entertainment.

Glancing at her watch, she decided to make her way back to the entrance. Alan was picking her up at seven o'clock and she still had to unpack her cases. Besides, the sun was going down and it was starting to get colder. However, she made a mental note to come back again another day; there were still lots of things she wanted to see.

She had almost reached the entrance, when she noticed several birds had gathered near one of the bushes. There had been two or three hovering around the bush when she passed earlier, but she had surmised they were enjoying the remains of someone's packed lunch. However, now a few more had gathered. Surely the sandwich, or whatever it was, would have either been eaten or carried away by now?

Agnes stepped a little closer to see what the attraction was. At first, she couldn't see anything and was reluctant to get too close, fearing the birds might fly at her – especially if they thought she was going to take their food. But when a couple of birds on the ground moved slightly to one side, she was able to see part of a shoe poking out from beneath the bush.

It looked like a trainer; in quite good condition, too.

"Maybe they'll come back to look for it," she mumbled, as she backed away.

However, as she continued walking along the footpath, her natural curiosity began to take over.

She stopped and turned around. Several birds were still there. Some were on the ground, while others hovered above the bushes.

At that moment, she made a decision, birds or no birds, she was going to have to go back and take a closer look.

* * *

"So what time are you meeting Mrs Lockwood this evening?" Sergeant Andrews asked, after Alan had told him he was taking her to dinner. "Fingers crossed something earth-shattering doesn't come up before then."

"I'm picking her up at seven, which reminds me, I need to book a table somewhere." He paused. "Perhaps it would be best if we dined at the hotel. Agnes is sure to be tired after her flight."

"Her flight? You mean she flew up here?" The sergeant grinned. "I know you told me she had missed being here on Tyneside, but it sounds as though she really couldn't wait another minute to get back here."

"Yes, I gather she took the first flight..." Alan's sentence was cut short when his mobile phone began to ring.

"You're kidding me, right?" Even as he uttered the words, the chief inspector knew he wasn't being fooled around. "You say you've found a body in the Exhibition Park? Where exactly in the park are you?"

Sergeant Andrews picked up on his boss's words. "A body – in the park? Who found it?"

Alan held up his hand, instructing Andrews to wait.

"We'll be right there."

"Get your coat. That was Agnes. She's found a body in the Exhibition Park." Alan grabbed the receiver of the phone on his desk and left instructions for the pathologist and his team to get over to the park. "We're already on our way."

"Mrs Lockwood certainly doesn't hang around," Andrews said, as he grabbed his coat and hurried towards the door.

Chapter Four

Detective Chief Inspector Alan Johnson and Sergeant Andrews found Agnes where she'd said she would be – near the tall bushes where she had located the body.

While they were talking on the phone, Alan had suggested she might like to move some distance away from the scene until they arrived, saying it might be too upsetting for her. But she had refused, telling him that some unsuspecting children might run into the bushes for a ball and come across that poor person lying there. "Seeing something like that could scar them for life."

Once Alan took a look at the body, he could see her point. The face and hands were very badly mutilated. Making sure he didn't contaminate anything, he leaned over the body to take a closer look. However, it was difficult to determine whether the cuts had been done by the murderer, or the crows and other birds still fluttering overhead.

"What do you think, Sergeant?"

Andrews shook his head. "That's something for the pathologist to figure out. But someone was certainly trying to hide the identity of the body. Look at the fingertips."

Alan took another look and saw that even the tips of the fingers had been burned away.

"I could have one of the officers take you back to the hotel," Alan suggested, when he returned to where Agnes was waiting.

He could see that she looked quite pale and her hands were trembling.

He placed an arm around her shoulder and glanced towards the entrance, just as two police cars turned in, followed by the pathologist's van.

"You've already had a long day, and now this," Alan continued, gesturing towards where the body lay. "Besides, it's starting to get colder."

Even as he spoke, Alan knew he was on a losing wicket. He had learned on her last visit that she was not one to step aside when there was a police inquiry.

"No, I'm fine," Agnes insisted, though she was still trembling. "I'm not tired and I'm not cold. You can see I am wearing a thick coat and scarf." She gestured to the heavy camel-coloured coat she was wearing.

Even though she was still in shock at finding the body lying behind the bush, there was no way she was going allow herself to be bundled off.

"Anyway, I found the body. Therefore I'm a witness," she added defiantly.

Andrews, who had been listening to the conversation, gave a hint of a smile as he raised his eyebrows. However, he remained silent.

"She's right," Alan said, picking up on his sergeant's amusement. "Mrs Lockwood is a witness as she found the body."

"Yes, I agree," the sergeant replied.

"You do?" Alan sounded surprised. "That's not like you. Why do you agree?"

"It's easier." Andrews grinned at his boss.

"You guys know I'm standing here right next to you, don't you?" Agnes chirped. She sounded a little more like her old self.

Alan coughed. "Okay, but please stand clear when Doctor Nichols, the pathologist, and the forensic team begin checking the body." He paused. "Did you touch anything before or since you phoned me?"

"Are you crazy, Alan?" Agnes retorted. "Of course not! I know better than to tamper with a crime scene. I took one look in the bushes and when I saw the body I backed off. Wouldn't anyone have backed away when they saw… that?" She pointed towards the spot where the body lay.

"Okay, okay." Alan held up his hands. "But I had to ask. Anything you might have come in contact with, we'll need to eliminate from our inquiries."

Agnes heaved a sigh. "I know." She thought for a moment. "That's my footprint," she said, pointing down to a small patch of flattened leaves lying in the earth at one side of a bush. "I placed one foot there and leaned forward to take a closer look at the shoe sticking out from the bush."

She looked at Alan. "But, I didn't touch a thing. I didn't even need to pull the bush to one side. From where I was standing, I could see… I could see… " Agnes was unable to carry on and tears filled her eyes.

"It's alright, Agnes. We really understand."

Even he, a hardened police officer and a former soldier, had been shocked when he had first laid eyes on the body. "Are you sure you don't want to go back to the hotel? I can take your statement later."

"No, Alan. I really need to be here." Agnes reply was slow and deliberate as she wiped away the tears. "I want to stay."

"Now, what have we here?"

Doctor Nichols's voice boomed out as he approached the scene. He was already wearing his protective clothing, though his mask was still hanging loosely around his neck. "Who found the victim?"

"I did." Agnes spoke before anyone else could say a word.

"Did you touch anything?"

"No. My only contact was to step onto the leaves to see what the birds were so interested in."

"Mm, birds," Doctor Nichols nodded. He looked Agnes up and down and smiled. "The number of times I have been called to a case because someone saw birds hovering over the scene of a crime would amaze you. I'll tell you about it sometime."

He looked back towards the bushes, where his team was waiting to proceed. "However, for the moment, I have a job to do."

Without another word, he strode off towards the bushes.

Agnes glanced across to where the pathologist was working. "He seems like a nice man"

Andrews shrugged. "Yes, he is and very good at his job, too."

"Do you really want to hang around here while Doctor Nichols checks the victim?" Alan said, changing the subject. "After that, the forensics team goes in once he gives them the nod. It could take a while."

"But what if someone needs to ask me something?"

"Like what?"

"I don't know…"

Agnes thought for a moment. She was determined to come up with some reason why she should stay.

"Like, for instance, what if they find a thread or a piece of material caught on one of the bushes? They could want to check it didn't come from something I'm wearing."

Alan couldn't argue with that – well, he could if he wanted to spend the time arguing when he knew he wouldn't win! Besides, it was too damn cold for Agnes to stand out here, and it was getting colder by the minute. The sun had already sunk behind the tall buildings which stood at one end of the park.

"Why don't we sit in my car while I take your statement? It will save time later – you haven't forgotten we are having dinner together?"

"Good idea," Agnes replied, tightening her scarf and pulling up her coat collar. "No, I hadn't forgotten," she added slowly.

"But, if you have changed your mind…" Alan sighed quietly, as though expecting the worst.

"No, I'm quite looking forward to catching up," Agnes replied, quickly. "However, would you mind awfully if we had dinner at the hotel this evening?"

Agnes wouldn't admit it, not even to herself. However, she had suddenly started to feel tired.

"Not at all."

Alan was relieved their meal together wasn't going to be postponed.

"Actually, I was going suggest we had dinner at the hotel tonight."

* * *

After Agnes had made her statement, Alan left her in the car, while he went back to join Andrews and the rest of the team.

Not long afterwards, Doctor Nichols reappeared from behind the bushes and headed towards them.

"The forensic team is checking out the scene before I have the body moved back to the laboratory."

He nodded across to where three people were trying to gather anything that would give the police a clue as to where to start looking.

"However, I have to say this is going to be a hard case to solve. So far, I've found nothing on the body to identify him. Of course, I'll be able to take a closer look when we get him back to the laboratory. There could be a tattoo, a birthmark or even dental records that would help. But on the surface, the murderer seems to have made sure there was nothing to identify the victim before dumping the body."

"Are you saying he wasn't murdered here?" Alan asked.

"No. That's the only thing I *am* sure about at the moment. There isn't enough blood at the scene. He was stabbed several times in the chest and also the neck. With cuts like that, there would have been more blood – lots more blood."

"What about his facial wounds?" Alan asked. "Did the murderer do that? Or was it the birds?"

"I'm afraid I can't say for certain at the moment. Some were very likely made by the crows, but others…" He paused, not wanting to commit himself. "I really can't say any more until I perform the post-mortem."

The chief inspector nodded. "Thank you, Keith. No doubt you'll be in touch."

"Are you thinking what I'm thinking, sir?" Andrews asked.

"I'm thinking Chief Inspector Aldridge might have the wrong man in custody," Alan replied. "And you?"

"The same," Andrews replied. He turned back to the pathologist. "What do you think? Can you see any resemblance in this case to the victims found in Gateshead?"

Doctor Nichols thought for a moment. "We know there were severe facial injuries to the faces of the victims, just as there are on this man." He gestured towards the body still lying in the bushes. "I understand there were also a few other stab wounds on their victims. The legs and arms had been cut in several places. However, you'll have to wait until I do a full examination before we'll know if there are any of these marks on this man."

"But there is the possibility the Gateshead Police got it wrong and the real murderer could still be out there?"

The voice came from behind. The three men swung around to find Agnes standing a short distance away.

Once she had given Alan her statement, he had suggested she stay in his car out of the cold. But now, seeing her standing there, he realized he should have known better. Agnes was not one for missing out on anything.

"We're simply thinking aloud at the moment." It was Alan who replied. "Doctor Nichols can't commit himself. It could be a totally different case altogether – maybe even a copycat killer. We'll have to wait until the pathologist sends us his report."

At that moment, someone behind the bushes raised their head and waved.

"I think they're ready to move the body." Doctor Nichols waved back at his man. "If anyone wants me, I'll be in the lab."

"And you know where we are," Alan called out, as the pathologist strode over to his van. "Don't forget, I need to know the moment you have anything that will help us find the killer."

By now, the body had been loaded into the van and the driver was all set to head back to the laboratory.

Doctor Nichols waved as he clambered into the van. "Got you!"

"So what happens now?" Agnes asked as she watched the van pull away.

"We wait," Alan replied.

Chapter Five

"We wait. That's it? Is that all you can say?" Agnes threw up her hands in despair.

It was later that same day and both she and Alan were walking towards the dining room at the hotel. Earlier, while enjoying a couple of drinks in the bar, they had mulled over the events of the day, ending with Alan repeating the statement he had made that afternoon.

"So, we wait until you hear from the pathologist? Surely there's something we could be doing, while he's doing the examination?"

"Something 'we' could be doing?" Alan questioned. "Who is this 'we'?"

"Us! You! Me! The police! For goodness' sake, Alan, you can't leave me out of this inquiry. I found the body. It was me who phoned it in. That poor man could still be lying there if it wasn't for me..."

"Okay, okay. I get it," Alan interrupted.

He suddenly stopped walking and pulled Agnes to one side.

"You want to be involved in solving this murder case. Hasn't it sunk in yet how close you came to being murdered yourself, the last time you poked your nose into a murder inquiry?"

"Alan, I know I very nearly got myself killed a few months ago." Agnes took his arm and they restarted their walk down the corridor. "But I got through that. Look at me. I'm still here – alive and well, and ready to be involved in this case. If the body had been found by someone else, then I might have stayed out of it. *Might,*" she repeated, wagging her finger at him. "But it wasn't. It was found by me. And now I want to see it through."

She stopped walking and swung around in front of him. "Alan, please, I *need* to see this through."

It was clear that her mind was set on being involved in this case and nothing he said would make her change it. Yet, despite her bravado that afternoon, he hadn't failed to notice that she had been terribly shocked at finding the mutilated body. He had also picked up on the fact she had also felt the cold creeping through her coat as the sun slid away. Nevertheless, he knew she would never admit to that, either.

"Yes, I know," he said, quietly.

He also knew he couldn't win. If he refused, she would only try to work the case on her own and goodness knows where that would lead. At least if he involved her, to a certain extent, he would know where she was and what she was doing. The best he could do was to make sure she didn't get into any real trouble – though, with a woman like Agnes, that was easier said than done.

"However," he said, "like I said, at the moment we have nothing to go on. Until we get an ID of the victim or fingerprints of the murderer, we are stuck."

"What about fingerprints of the victim?" Agnes asked. "If he was already in your system for something or another, surely you would be able to find out who he was."

"Yes, Agnes, we would. However, it seems you didn't notice that the victim's fingertips had been burned, leaving little or no trace of prints," Alan explained, patiently. "Unless, of course, Doctor Nichols is able to find a tiny area the killer missed. But then, even if that is the case, there might not be enough to establish who the victim is. At the moment, our best bet is the newspapers. Hopefully, once the news of a body found in the park is posted, someone will come forward to report a missing person."

Just then, they reached the dining room.

"Now, Agnes," Alan continued, as he held open the door, "can we please change the subject?" He laughed. "At least while we have dinner?"

Agnes smiled. "Yes, Alan."

During the meal, they talked about Agnes's trip to Australia.

"My sergeant was interested to know whether you had enjoyed your visit to the other side of the world. However, I couldn't really answer him. You didn't say much about it when we spoke earlier," said Alan. "Though I'm sure you enjoyed seeing your family again."

"Yes, it was great seeing them again."

Agnes went on to tell him about some of the things they had done while she was there.

"I had a wonderful time, but it is good to be back." She hesitated. "Don't misunderstand me… I really did enjoy my stay. It's just that I missed being here – on Tyneside."

"What did they say about you being caught up in a police investigation?" Alan continued. "I'm sure they must have been horrified to hear about your narrow escape from being shot in one of the Tyne Bridge Towers."

Agnes glanced away for a few seconds, reliving the terrible moment, which had happened only a few months ago. She had escaped by the skin of her teeth when David Drummond, a thief, and a murderer, pointed a gun at her head. In that instant, her whole life had flashed before her.

But, quite out of the blue, a man had turned up from nowhere and shot Drummond a split second before he pulled the trigger. Agnes knew she owed her life to that man, though she still didn't know who he was. He had disappeared as quickly as he had arrived.

She turned back to face Alan.

"I didn't tell them about that. I couldn't. I simply said I'd been able to furnish you with information about the thefts at the hotel."

"So the case was not reported by the Australian Press?"

"I guess not," Agnes replied, slowly. "You know, I never thought about it." She shrugged. "Maybe it was, and the boys missed it."

"Or maybe they had read about it and were waiting for you to mention it first?"

"Perhaps they were."

Agnes turned away and Alan could tell that she didn't want to discuss it further.

"Were they disappointed when you cut your visit short?" Alan asked, moving the conversation forward.

"Yes, they were. But I'll be going back later in the year as there is a new baby on the way. I'm going to be a grandmother again." She smiled. "Jason and his wife are having their second child."

"Do you know, I think that's the first time you have actually mentioned one of your sons by name."

"Gosh! Really?"

Alan nodded.

"I suppose I always refer to them as my boys as I never want to put one before the other," Agnes replied. "Jason is the eldest. He is thirty-two and his brother, William, is two years younger. However, age has never, ever come into it. They have always got on so well together they could almost have been twins."

They talked a little more before Alan looked at his watch. It was getting late and, though he knew Agnes would never admit it, she must be really tired by now.

"I think we should call it a day," he said.

Agnes would have loved to have said no. But she was starting to feel quite exhausted. She hadn't noticed it while they were talking. However, now the evening was almost over, she felt she needed her bed.

"Thank you, Alan. It's been a wonderful evening." She hesitated. "I missed you while I was away. We get on so well together."

"And I really missed you, Agnes."

"Even though I drive you mad with questions about the cases you're working on?" she grinned.

"Yes, Agnes – even then."

Chapter Six

Agnes slept soundly that night. She had been so tired, not even a tank running through the room would have stirred her.

When she woke, she felt quite refreshed and ready for whatever the day might bring. She showered, dressed, and set off downstairs for breakfast.

Larry, the young lift attendant who she met on her last visit, hadn't been on duty the previous day. But he was he was back at work this morning and looked as smart as ever in his uniform. The only thing missing was the hat, which came as part of the outfit. He had told her he hated wearing it. Once he checked in, he would place the hat in his locker for the rest of the day. The manager turned a blind eye unless there was to be a visit from Head Office. Then the hat had to come back out until the top brass left.

Larry genuinely looked pleased to see her again.

"I thought you might give this hotel a miss after what happened on your last visit."

"Not at all, Larry. I love it here."

He went on to ask how long she would be staying this time.

"I haven't decided," she replied. "Let's just say I have brought enough clothes to keep me going for a long while and, with the wonderful shopping centre a mere stone's throw away, I could be here for quite a while."

She held from back saying that Mr Jenkins, the manager, pleased she hadn't been put off after her last experience at the hotel, had given her a large discount and told her the room was hers at that price for as long as she wanted to stay. All he asked in return was that she didn't mention the previous incidents to anyone.

"It's not something we are proud of," he had said. "I would rather it didn't get around."

By now, they had reached the ground floor and the lift doors slid open.

"See you later, Mrs Lockwood. Enjoy your breakfast," Larry said, as she stepped out.

"Thank you." Agnes smiled.

The dining room was rather busy when she walked in. Despite it still being early in the year, there were quite a number of people staying at the hotel. Agnes wondered whether there might be something going on in the city. She recalled there was a racecourse at Gosforth, a little further north of Newcastle. Perhaps people were spending a few days here at The Millennium Hotel while the racing was on. But there could quite easily be a number of other reasons.

A waiter led her to an empty table set for two. He pulled out a chair and gestured for her to sit down. "Will your husband be joining you?"

"No. I'm staying at the hotel on my own…"

"Perhaps I could join you."

Both Agnes and the waiter looked up in surprise. Neither had noticed anyone approaching them.

"I haven't had breakfast yet and I am starving," Alan continued. "Would you mind, Agnes?"

"I would be delighted," she replied. She glanced up at the waiter, who was still looking a little bemused. "It's okay. I know this man, he's a friend."

The waiter nodded, though he didn't look convinced.

Agnes gestured towards Alan. "This gentleman is a chief inspector with the Newcastle Police."

"In that case, I hope you both enjoy your breakfast." He handed them a menu before moving back to the dining room entrance to escort another lady to a table.

"I guess he's new here. I don't recall seeing him before," Alan said, as he opened the menu.

Agnes glanced towards the waiter. "Yes, I think he is. He seems nice enough."

Alan didn't look quite so convinced. It had turned out that the last new waiter at the hotel had been an accomplice to a thief and a murderer. But he chose not to mention it at this time. Instead, he changed the subject.

"So what are your plans for today?"

"I haven't decided," Agnes replied. "I did think I might go shopping. But, as it is such a lovely morning, I might go back to finish looking around the park. I didn't see it all yesterday."

"Is that wise, Agnes?" Alan looked up from the menu. "I mean, after what happened yesterday, perhaps it would be better if you stayed away for a few days."

"Why? You don't think I'm going to find another body, do you?"

"No, it's just something Andrews said when we got back to the station yesterday and he could be right."

"What did he say?" Agnes asked, leaning across the table.

"He wondered whether the killer might have still been hanging around somewhere in the park while we were there. In fact, he did send a couple of plain-clothed detectives to take a look around to see if there was anyone lurking about near the crime scene." He shook his head. "But they didn't find anyone. Maybe we should have organized a better search at the time."

"But what has this got to do with me going to the park today?"

Alan remained silent, allowing Agnes to think it through.

"Hang on a minute," she muttered, suddenly seeing what Alan was getting at. "You think the killer could have been hanging around the scene when I found the body, and he might go back today on the off-chance I'll go there to take a second look."

Agnes laughed. "That's a bit of a longshot, isn't it? Surely anyone with even half a brain wouldn't wait around to see who happened to find the body of the person they had mutilated and then dumped behind a bush in a park. Anyone could have found it – even a child looking for a football."

"But it wasn't just anyone, Agnes. It was you," Alan said quietly.

"So it was me... what difference does that make?" Agnes still couldn't understand what the problem was.

At that moment, the waiter came back to take their order. Once he had disappeared back into the kitchen, Alan began to explain his fears.

"The last time you were here, your face appeared in every local and national newspaper. It was you who was nearly murdered for getting too close to a thief and a killer. If this person *was* still in the park and recognised you from your photograph, he or she could be worried that you might have seen something." Alan stared at her. "Your reputation precedes you."

"But I didn't see who put the body there," Agnes wailed. "I only saw people who were in the park enjoying themselves."

She shook her head as she thought back to the day before.

"There were some teenagers doing the skateboarding thing. I saw some mothers pushing prams or pushchairs..." Agnes broke off. "I really didn't give it much thought. It was only as I was on my way out of the park that I noticed more birds had appeared by those bushes. Even while I was dithering about whether or not to take a look at what they were so interested in, I didn't see anyone hanging around."

Agnes broke off and shook her head. "Why am I telling you all this again? I made a statement," she added.

"I know, Agnes." Alan reached across the table and took her hand. "But whoever did this terrible thing doesn't know you didn't see anything. If he was still waiting around in the park, for whatever reason, he could have seen you discover the body. If he picked up on who you were, he might really believe you saw something."

"That's why you are here this morning, isn't it?" Agnes said, suddenly cottoning on to the reason behind Alan's early morning visit.

"You didn't simply decide to stop by and have a friendly chat. You came here to warn me that someone might be looking for me?"

Alan nodded. "It suddenly came to me last night after I got home and I spent most of last night thinking about it. First thing this morning, I telephoned Andrews and shared my thoughts with him. I also told him I would be late."

"But what makes you believe the killer might have still been in the park?"

"The birds," Alan replied. "You said there were a few birds when you first passed the body, but there were more when you returned to the spot."

"So you think that when I passed the first time, the body had only been there a short while?"

"Yes," Alan replied.

He went on to explain the reasoning behind his concerns.

"I'm wondering whether the killer might have dumped the body only a few minutes before you arrived in the park. He could have been about to leave the scene when he spotted you walking along the path. At that point, he wouldn't have been sure whether you had seen him or not. Therefore, he might have decided to hang around to see what you would do next."

Alan paused to take a breath.

"By the time you reached the spot," he continued, "a few inquisitive birds had already flown down to take a look. Fortunately, you didn't take much notice at that point. But if you had, the killer might have believed you had seen him while he was disposing of the body."

"Oh my goodness, I never thought of that."

For a few minutes, Agnes was visibly shaken. But then she quickly pulled herself together.

"But this is all supposition," she said. "You're only guessing that the body had been there for a short time, aren't you?"

"No. Doctor Nichols now believes the person had only been killed a couple of hours earlier. Therefore, taking into account that the murder did not take place at the scene, I could very well be right in my assumption as to the timing of when the body was left there."

"Okay, so, if you *are* right and the killer was still there when I first walked past the body, surely he would have gone by the time I came back. Why would he continue to wait around?"

Alan shrugged. "Who knows what goes through the mind of a killer? Perhaps he gets a kick out of seeing how a person reacts to finding a dead body."

He hesitated. Had he gone too far? He only wanted her to be more cautious.

"Agnes, I'm not trying to frighten you. I simply want you to be aware that you need to be careful. What I mean is, try not to do anything to draw attention to yourself. For instance, don't speak to the newspapers. I'm sure they will want to talk to the woman who found the body, though I have instructed that no one gives out your name. Nevertheless, reporters have a way of finding these things out. Should one get through to you, simply tell them that you found the body and called the police. Don't tell them anything else."

"What else could I tell them, Alan?" Agnes sounded frustrated. "I don't know anything else."

"You know as much as I do," Alan replied.

Anything further to be said was put on hold as the waiter appeared with their breakfast.

"Enjoy your meal," he said, as he set down the plates.

"Thank you." Agnes tried to sound more enthusiastic than she felt. She peered at the name tag pinned to the waiter's shirt. "It looks delicious, Richard."

"So, you haven't heard anything more from Doctor Nichols?" Agnes asked, once the waiter had left. "Apart from the time of death, I mean."

"No, we haven't heard anything, which is not good news," Alan replied. "However, I'll phone the lab when I get into the office, unless Sergeant Andrews hears something in the meantime – though he would call me if there is anything significant to report." He paused.

"Agnes, please promise me you won't do anything without telling me first."

"I have to say, they do a really fine breakfast at this hotel. Don't you agree?" Agnes said, looking down at the plate of food in front of her.

"Don't change the subject, Agnes. I worry about you."

However, knowing he wasn't going to get anywhere further at this point, he looked down at his plate.

"Yes, I do agree. I'm really going to enjoy this."

* * *

Once breakfast was over, Alan left to go back to the police station and Agnes went up to her room.

Upstairs, she sat down on the bed and hugged herself. She wasn't really sure what she wanted to do today. The Eldon Square Shopping Centre was very tempting. But then so was the park. Her plan had been to go back to see the rest of the park today. However, Alan had sounded so convincing when he outlined his theory about the killer. Perhaps it wouldn't be such a good idea after all.

Yet, she really felt the urge to go there and, thinking back to their chat over breakfast, she hadn't actually agreed to stay away from the park. In fact, if she remembered rightly from the evening before, she hadn't promised she would stay away from the case, either.

Her mind made up, Agnes stuffed a few things into her bag, grabbed a coat and hurried out of the room; only pausing for a few seconds to make sure the door was properly closed behind her.

* * *

"How did it go?" Sergeant Andrews asked when the DCI entered the office.

"From Mrs Lockwood's expression, I got the impression she was shocked when I explained my thoughts on why the killer might have been watching her when she found the body."

"Did she agree to stay away from the park for a few days?" Andrews persisted.

Alan sighed heavily as he slung his coat over the hook on the stand by the door.

"No! Agnes is a law unto herself." He shook his head. "Have you heard anything from pathology or forensics?"

"No, not a word, which probably means they don't have anything further to tell us."

"Right, I'll phone the lab now."

Alan picked up the receiver.

"For heaven's sake," he muttered, as he stabbed the numbers into the phone. "This murderer is taking great pleasure in watching us run around in circles."

Alan listened carefully to what Doctor Nichols had to say. He made a few comments and asked a couple of questions. Nevertheless, for all that, there was still very little to go on.

"Nothing!" Alan said, slamming down the phone. "Well, nothing helpful, anyway. It seems Keith found similar cuts on the arms and legs of the victim. Presumably the same as those found on the victims in Gateshead. But so far there are no damn fingerprints, from either the victim or the killer. Nor any evidence found at the scene. The team seem to think the birds might have carried off any small clues – threads from clothing, hairs, whatever."

The DCI shook his head in frustration. "You know what I mean. The kind of thing we usually rely on. Even the wounds on the body were made with different knives, so we aren't looking for only one knife, but several. Some of the wounds were made by large blades, others by smaller."

Alan threw down the pen he was holding. He had been poised to make a few notes, but there was nothing worth writing down.

"What kind of person are we looking for here? We need to get into his head before he strikes again."

Alan picked up the phone and punched in the number of the Gateshead Police.

"I'm going to speak to DCI Aldridge again. Maybe he can tell us more about the murders in Gateshead," he said, while he waited for someone at the other end to answer. "Doctor Nichols hasn't been able to contact the pathologist who worked on the case. I gather the man is at a conference. But Keith left word that he needs to talk to him the moment he returns."

Alan turned his attention back to the phone when someone picked up. He asked to speak to the DCI.

"I suppose you've heard about the body found in the Exhibition Park?" Alan asked, when he was connected. "I need to know if there are any similarities between our victim and the bodies you found in Gateshead, because if there are, then I think you have the wrong man in custody."

He put the phone on speaker and replaced the receiver. It would save him having to explain it all to his sergeant later.

Andrews listened in on the conversation between the two chief inspectors. Despite the fact both victims had been murdered before being dumped and had received the same scars, Aldridge was loath to admit he might have been too hasty in charging the man they had in the cells.

"What is it with you?" Alan exploded. "It seems to me the killer is still on the loose, yet you are quite happy to sit back and charge the wrong man!" He glanced at Andrews and shook his head. "Believe me, you'll be laughed out of court."

Without another word, he ended the call.

"I agree with you," said Andrews. "The killer is still out there. But who is it and what is it he has against his victims? Are they people he has a grievance with? Could they owe him money and are unwilling to pay?"

"I would have thought that after the first body had been found, anyone owing money to this guy would have paid up immediately." He thought for a moment. "Do you think this might be a copycat killer?"

Andrews nodded. "Could be. If only our guys had found something at the scene, it might have helped."

There was a long pause.

"Get your coat," Alan said, suddenly leaping to his feet.

"Where're we going?" Even as he spoke, Andrews was grabbing his coat from the hook by the door.

"We're going back to the scene. We're going to do a little more poking around before it's too late."

Chapter Seven

On the drive to the park, Alan explained his theory.

"It was something Nichols said. About the birds picking up things and carrying them off."

He broke off as he was suddenly forced to brake hard to avoid hitting a young child, who had run out into the road. He waved at the mother, who had held up her hand to thank him for acting so quickly. Thankfully, he hadn't been driving very fast. Nevertheless, the boy had acted so hastily, the outcome could have been much worse.

Slowly moving away, Alan glanced in his rearview mirror to see the woman chastising the boy; probably more through fright than anger. But, in an instant, the woman changed her stance and pulled her son close, hugging him tightly.

In that split second, he thought back to the days when he was young. There hadn't been many cars on the road back then; his parents wouldn't have needed to worry about the traffic. But he swiftly changed his viewpoint, wondering what he would have been like if he had been a young father today. Very likely he would have reacted like that woman...

"You were going to say something about the birds." Andrews interrupted his thoughts.

"Yes, sorry." Alan recollected his thoughts. "It was something the forensics said about how the birds might have carried something away.

Any food would have been eaten almost on the spot, but what about birds looking to build nests?"

"Isn't it a little early in the year?" Andrews asked.

"Yes, for many birds it is. But crows and a few other birds tend to build nests at this time of the year if the weather is clement."

"You never fail to amaze me," Andrews remarked. "How would you know that?"

"It's just something I picked up over the years. Anyway, here we are," Alan concluded, as they swung into the park.

Luckily for the two detectives, it hadn't rained during the night, which meant that anything they might happen to find wouldn't have been contaminated.

"Right," Alan said, stepping out of the car. "We'll both begin the search where the body was found, though I doubt we'll find anything there. Forensics will have already checked that area thoroughly and they found nothing... not even a footprint, apart from the one made by Mrs Lockwood. Nevertheless, we have to start somewhere. From there, we'll split up and head off in different directions."

As he spoke, Alan opened the boot of his car and pulled out the boxes of latex gloves and evidence bags he always carried in there.

"Here," Alan said, handing some of each to Andrews. "Bag anything you think wouldn't normally be found in this area of the park."

The police cordons, warning people to stay away from the crime scene, were still in place. Andrews held one up so the chief inspector could pass underneath. The white markings, where the body had lain, were still visible.

The two detectives carefully looked around the immediate area, hoping to pick up something the forensics team had missed. But there was nothing to be found.

"Okay, this is where we need to split up," said Alan. "There are trees bordering the edge of the park. Starting from here, you head off in that direction."

He gestured towards the left.

"Meanwhile, I'll go this way. We both need to look carefully at the open ground. However, once we reach the trees, we must be even more thorough. Something picked up by a bird might have been dropped in that vicinity. Then we'll slowly continue to make our way through the trees and meet up again back here. Hopefully, we'll have covered the whole area between us. Do you have any questions?"

"Not about our search," Andrews replied. "But I can't help wondering why the killer disposed of the body here in the bushes, rather than in the trees. The bushes are quite thick at this point, yet the body probably wouldn't have been found so quickly if it had been left over there. Then, any birds hovering over the victim wouldn't have been so conspicuous."

"That's a good point, Sergeant."

Alan was thoughtful as he stared down to where the body had been found. A few moments later, he allowed his vision to trace across the ground, which led off into the trees.

"Of course!" The DCI uttered. He slapped his head, disgusted that he hadn't picked it up earlier.

"The murderer left the body in the bushes near the footpath because he didn't want to leave any footprints in the wet leaves or on any uncovered earth. Having already eliminated everything on the victim that might have given the police a clue as to who he was, why would he take the risk of leaving his footprints behind?"

Alan turned his head and looked behind where he stood. All that was visible were the large bushes.

"Stay here," Alan instructed, before stepping under the police cordon. Without looking back, he walked across to the far side of the footpath.

Turning around, he slowly moved across the path towards the bushes. As he got nearer, he shifted his feet from side to side a couple of times, before coming to an abrupt halt.

"Here! This is probably where he stood when he planned to hurl the body over the top of the bushes. He thought it wouldn't be discovered for a quite a while," he continued. "And it might have worked, if he hadn't been caught unawares by someone approaching."

"Mrs Lockwood?" Andrews asked.

Alan nodded.

"Maybe he heard footsteps in the distance and tried to dispose of the body too quickly, causing it to fall short of the goal, so to speak. After that, I imagine he simply wanted to run for cover before the person saw him."

"But there's one thing I don't understand," Andrews said, glancing up and down the footpath. "If he was carrying a man in broad daylight, how did he manage to get this far without being seen? Also, he would have to be a really strong man to even lift the body, let alone heave it over the bushes."

"That's two things, Sergeant," Alan replied. "However, we'll leave them both until we get back to the office. Meanwhile, let's start our search."

Andrews nodded and followed the DCI's gaze towards the trees. There was a lot of ground to cover.

"Wouldn't it have been better if we had brought a team of uniformed officers to help out?" Andrews asked. "When they search shoulder to shoulder, no evidence is ever missed."

"Money," Alan replied, without hesitation. "It's all to do with cutbacks. This is just something I suddenly thought of this morning when we were talking about what the pathologist said about birds. If I had taken the idea upstairs, we might not have had a reply until tomorrow. By then, any evidence we might find today could have been long gone." He sighed. "It's a sign of the times."

"I'll never understand how the so-called 'costing a job' works." Andrews made quotation marks in the air as he spoke. "The men are being paid whether they sit in an office, an incident room or whatever. Therefore, how does it cost more if a group of officers are searching a field?"

"I'm sure someone would be able to explain it to you, but for the moment, can we concentrate on the here and now?" Alan asked.

"Yes, got it," Andrews said. "As long as I don't have to climb up trees to recover evidence, I'm fine."

"If that's what it takes, Sergeant,"

"Have you seen how high crows build their nests?" Andrews protested. "They are usually at the highest point of the trees..." He paused when he saw the chief inspector grinning at him. "You're having me on, aren't you?"

Still grinning, Alan nodded.

But then the grin disappeared.

"Okay, fun's over. Let's do this."

Chapter Eight

When Agnes walked out of the hotel, she found Ben already standing by his taxi waiting for her. She had telephoned him the moment she made the decision to go back to the Exhibition Park.

Despite what Alan had told her, she felt she owed it to the dead man and his family to show the world that she wasn't afraid – and, who knows, she might also stumble upon something that would help find the killer.

She had thought of calling Alan to tell him of her plan. He could even have hidden somewhere close by, to watch out for anyone taking an uncanny interest in her movements. However, he would more than likely have tried to talk her out of it.

Besides, her mind was already made up. She wanted to do this.

Nevertheless, deep down, she knew Alan was right. It was a foolish idea. What on earth would she do if the man approached her? She glanced down at her handbag. At least she had something to help in an emergency. But, when push came to shove, would she have time to use it?

If anything should go tragically wrong, then Ben, her taxi driver, would be able to tell the police exactly where, and what time, he had set her down. At least it would be a start. Any other cab driver might not even give it another thought, but she knew she could rely on Ben.

He held the door open for her as she approached.

"The Exhibition Park, Ben," Agnes said as she climbed into the taxi.

"Are you sure you want to go there today?" Ben frowned. "There was something on the news last night about a body being found in the park. Maybe you should leave it for a day or two. Why not go to the Eldon Square instead?"

"That was yesterday, Ben," Agnes chirped.

She was relieved that she had left the scene of crime before the television crew and newspaper reporters had arrived, meaning she wasn't in the news. Not yet, anyway.

"But…"

"I'm sure whoever did it will be well away from here by now," Agnes interrupted. "I remember going to the park as a child. I just want to see how it is today."

"Pretty much as it was back then, I should think," Ben mumbled, as he clambered into the driving seat. "Though, I gather there have been a few new things for teenagers," he added, as an afterthought.

"I take it you haven't taken your son there?"

Ben started the engine and swung away from the hotel before he answered. "No. We're sure he would love it, but we are afraid it might be too much for him."

Agnes didn't reply. She understood the concerns Ben and his wife had about their son's health. The poor lad had suffered from a breathing disorder since his birth, which had led to other problems. Yet there were times when she felt they were being over-cautious. The boy still needed to have a life. However, on the other hand, wouldn't she have been just the same if it had been one of her sons?

"You've gone very quiet," Ben said. "It's not like you to stay silent."

"Sorry, I was just thinking to myself."

"What were you thinking about?" Ben laughed. "I bet you were thinking about the chief inspector. I'm sure he was delighted to see you back here on Tyneside."

"Yes, you're right. I was thinking about Alan," she lied. "We had dinner together at the hotel last night and he's taking me out somewhere this evening – though I'm not sure where."

"Perhaps he wants to surprise you."

"Yes, I'm sure he does."

By now, they had reached the entrance to the park and once she had paid the fare and had included a handsome tip, she stepped out of the taxi.

However, before she closed the door she leaned inside. "Ben, you are a lovely man and you care so much about your son. But, believe me, you should take him to the park now and again. He really needs to meet up with other children. Talk it over with your wife."

* * *

Ben kept his eyes on Agnes until she disappeared into the park, before turning his attention to the money she had placed in his hand. He pondered over what she had said and the large tip she had given him. It was almost as though she thought she might never see him again.

He scratched his head. What was he missing? Despite his advice, she had been adamant about coming to the park. Could it have been because of the body found here yesterday? It wouldn't surprise him. He knew she had been involved in helping the police a few months ago. Almost to the point of getting herself killed.

He should do something, but what? It was then that he thought of someone who could help. With that, he pulled out his phone.

Chapter Nine

Alan had almost reached the trees and was beginning to believe he and his sergeant were on a wild goose chase when he suddenly saw a tiny shred of material lying in front of him.

It was either navy blue or black. It was wet, which made it difficult to tell either way. He had been extremely lucky to spot it lying on a patch of dark leaves. Alan tried not to get too excited as he carefully picked it up between his gloved fingers and placed it in an evidence bag. It might amount to nothing. There was the possibility that it had been carried here from another part of the park, or even from the Town Moor, by a bird building a nest in one of the nearby trees. But, if luck was on his side, it could be something left by the killer when he dropped off the body.

Alan slid the bag into his pocket and continued on his search with renewed enthusiasm. Nevertheless, he knew that from now on, this would prove to be the most difficult part of the search. If a bird had dropped another piece of evidence while flying up to its nest, it could very easily have lodged in one of the branches above. Therefore both he and Andrews would need to look up above into the branches, as well as below, on the ground.

Alan stood up straight and arched his back to stop it from aching. All this bending over the crime scene wasn't doing him any good at all. A few years ago, he had hurt his back when he tumbled from a building while chasing a criminal and, though the doctors said it had healed, he still got the odd twinge to remind him of it. He would certainly suffer tomorrow.

Alan glanced across at his sergeant. Andrews didn't seem to be having any back problems at all. In fact, he had already reached the trees and was stretching up to untangle something from one of the lower branches. "What it is to be young," he mumbled, before he started searching again. Hopefully, between the two of them, they would have something to help with their inquiries. He would hate it if all this tramping around here had been for nothing.

He had only taken a couple of steps when his mobile phone rang.

"Alan Johnson," he said brusquely, not recognizing the caller's number.

"It's Ben. You remember me? I'm the taxi driver Mrs Lockwood uses."

"Ah yes, Ben. How can I help you?"

It had been a few months since Alan had last spoken to the taxi driver. But, as Agnes had used his cab whenever she needed a lift, he had given Ben his number should he ever need help.

"It's about Mrs Lockwood," Ben replied.

"What about her?" Alan asked.

"It's probably nothing. Maybe I shouldn't have called."

"What is it, Ben?"

"I dropped her off at the Exhibition Park and I'm a little concerned. On the news last night, we learned that a body had been found there yesterday. She could…"

"Yes," Alan interrupted. "I understand. Like you say, it's probably nothing. But thank you for letting me know. I'll get onto it."

"Agnes, you are an idiot," Alan muttered to himself. He closed his phone and shoved it into his pocket. "You're the most wonderful woman I have ever met, but there are times when you can be a real idiot."

"Who was it?" Andrews called out. "Is it news from forensics?"

Alan looked around where he was standing, making sure he knew where to continue his search before he made his way across to his sergeant.

"No. That was Ben, a taxi driver Mrs Lockwood uses." He glanced around the park as he spoke. "She's here."

"I thought she'd agreed to stay away today?"

"So did I. I really thought I'd got through to her, but she has a mind of her own." Alan paused. "You stay here and carry on with the search, while I go to find her."

He gestured across to where he had been standing when the call came through. "I was there, by that small yellow flower. Perhaps you could make your way around to that spot, though I hope to be back here before you get that far."

* * *

Alan hurried across towards the entrance where Ben said he had dropped off Agnes. Thank goodness the taxi driver was being so vigilant. Alan had made a few discreet enquiries about him and found that he was well liked by his peers in the city centre. It was then that he had decided to pass on his phone number, never really expecting to hear from him. But it seemed it had paid off.

He was still heading towards the entrance when he caught a glimpse of Agnes in the distance. She was walking in the direction of the lake. "Agnes, Agnes," he muttered to himself. "Thank goodness I've found you."

Though his eyes were fixed on Agnes, out of the corner of his eye Alan saw a man walking a short distance behind her. Could he be following her? Or was the man simply taking a stroll through the park?

Alan quickened his pace; either way, he wanted to catch up with her before the man got too close.

"I told you to wait for me!" Alan called out, when he had almost reached her. He was determined to let the man know that Agnes wasn't alone in the park.

He grabbed her arm and pulled her to a halt. "I thought I had lost you!"

Agnes was so startled when she felt someone tugging on her arm that she failed to hear Alan's words. She immediately began to grope around in her pocket for the pepper spray. But when she couldn't find it, she became frightened and was about to strike out with her fist when she turned and saw Alan.

"The tour bus will be leaving shortly," Alan said, as the man came alongside them. "You said you didn't want to miss it."

"What on earth are you talking about – tour bus?" Agnes gasped. "Oh, goodness me! I was so enjoying my walk through the park, I totally forgot the time," she added, suddenly realizing Alan's concern about the man who was now a short distance ahead of them.

She watched the man as he slowly continued walking towards the lake. From what little she had seen of him when he sauntered past, he hadn't struck her as being a prowler. He had looked more like a businessman taking the air before going back to some boring board meeting. Now, taking a closer look, she could see that he was tall, about thirty and clean-shaven. His light brown hair, though cut short, was slightly messed up. Though that could have been due to the breeze, rather than how he favoured it. He was also carrying a large briefcase.

However, her attention was drawn to the rather smart black overcoat he was wearing. It was buttoned up to the neck, probably against the chill. Nevertheless, what she couldn't help noticing was that it was the same style her late husband had always favoured. As she watched, his coat billowed slightly in the breeze, displaying a bright red lining.

Just then, the man turned around and peered at them both.

"I'd better get back before the bus goes off without me," said Agnes, loudly, hoping the man hadn't realized that she had been watching him.

"Were you following me?" Agnes protested, as Alan led her back to where he had left Andrews.

"No! I wasn't following you," said Alan, sharply. "Andrews and I were already here doing a search of the area where the body was found."

He had been about to tell her that he'd had a call from Ben telling him of her whereabouts, but decided against it. Agnes trusted the taxi driver. Telling her he'd heard about her movements from him might make her decide not to use his taxi again.

"I just happened to be taking a moment from the search, when I saw you and noticed a man walking some yards behind you." He paused. "I was concerned he might be following you."

At least part of his story was true.

A few moments later, they reached the area where Agnes had found the body the day before. Andrews was almost at the spot where Alan had been before he received the call from Ben.

Agnes looked back in the direction from which they had come and realised there was no way Alan could have seen her from this point. Either he had to have been looking for her, which meant he had learned she was here in the park, or he had moved some distance from this area to check on something else.

"Have you found anything?" she asked.

"I found something before I decided to stretch my legs," Alan replied, quickly.

He pulled the evidence bag out of his pocket and held it up. He hoped Andrews wouldn't contradict him by saying something about the phone call.

"I've found a couple of things, too," Andrews replied. He patted his pocket. "I hope forensics is able to get something from them."

He turned his attention to Agnes. "Nice to see you, Mrs Lockwood. Were you enjoying a stroll in the park?"

"Yes, I was," she replied. She glanced at Alan and narrowed her eyes. "But Alan caught sight of me and got the impression someone was following me, so my walk was cut short."

"Better be safe than sorry." Andrews looked at the DCI. "Why don't you take Mrs Lockwood back to the hotel, while I carry on here? I've almost reached the point you had got to before you left. You can pick me up in about forty minutes. Hopefully, by then, I'll have picked up any further evidence and we can hand it in later."

"Good idea," Alan replied.

After promising to be back shortly, Alan escorted Agnes across to where he had left the car. As they walked, neither said a word.

"Are we still on for dinner this evening?" Alan asked, once he had pulled out of the park.

"Yes, that would be nice."

"Agnes, I wasn't following you," Alan said. The silence was making him feel uncomfortable. "Like I said, Andrews and I were already in the park, checking the scene."

"Yes, I got that," Agnes retorted.

She heaved a sigh, suddenly feeling ashamed of her attitude towards Alan. Why was she behaving like this? She knew he was only watching out for her. Who knows? The man behind her in the park could quite easily have been the killer waiting for the right moment to pounce on her.

She recalled how, when Alan had grabbed her arm, her first thought had been that she was being attacked. At that moment, she had reached into her pocket for the pepper spray to defend herself, only to find it wasn't there. It had taken her a moment or two to realise it was still tucked away in her handbag. But, in those few seconds, she could have been murdered.

"Alan, I'm sorry." She hesitated.

For a moment, Alan thought she was going to change her mind about having dinner with him that evening. But before he could say anything, she continued.

"I'm sorry, I behaved foolishly today. I should never have gone to the park. I really don't know what came over me."

By now, they had reached the quayside and the hotel was looming up ahead.

"Forget it," Alan said, as he pulled up outside the Millennium Hotel. "Is there anywhere special you would like to have dinner this evening?"

"Why don't we have it in the hotel again?" she replied. "We can relax in the drawing room afterwards."

"No problem," Alan replied. "Will you book the table?"

"Yes, I'll book it for about seven-thirty. And by the way, dinner is on me tonight." She opened the door and leapt out of the car before he could protest.

"We'll talk about it," he called out.

"We just did!" She laughed. "And I had the final word," she added, before she closed the car door.

* * *

Back in the park, Alan returned to the spot where he had last spoken to Andrews. At first, there was no sign of his sergeant and, for a split second, Alan panicked. If, as he had first thought, the killer had come back to the park, might he have spotted Andrews probing around the scene all alone and…?

Alan was relieved when he caught a glimpse of his sergeant through the trees. He carefully picked his way across to where he had been when the call came in from Ben. After a brief pause to make sure he hadn't missed anything earlier, he continued to search the ground as he slowly made his way towards Andrews.

"I wasn't expecting you to go this far into the trees," Alan called out.

"I hadn't intended to," the sergeant admitted. "However, I found something rather interesting and wondered whether there might be something else lying around."

"What did you find?" the DCI asked, looking up from his search.

Andrews held up an evidence bag. "It's a cufflink. There has to be some DNA on that." He looked at the bag. "My guess it is expensive, too. I'm sure whoever lost this would be quite annoyed about it."

"A cufflink," Alan said thoughtfully.

It wasn't quite the sort of thing the DCI had expected. He had hoped for something more along the lines of a ragged old scarf, or a glove absolutely soaked in DNA.

"There have been murders committed by those who think themselves to be above the rest of us," Andrews said. "You've only to look back to a few months ago, when we discovered that an agent working for MI5 was found to be not only a thief, but also a double murderer."

Alan thought back to how the agent had fooled them all.

"Of course, you're right, Andrews. We can't afford to allow anything to slide past us. Did you find anything else?"

"No, not yet, but I am still…" Andrews paused, as a glint from something lying on the ground caught his eye. "Wait!" he called out, excitedly. "I've just found something else."

"Where, what is it?" Alan yelled, as he broke protocol and ran across the short stretch of unsearched ground to where his sergeant was pointing.

"Here!" Andrews pointed to the ground. "It looks like a tie pin."

He picked it up and took a closer look.

"It *is* a tie pin," he said, dropping it into another evidence bag. "And, unless I'm mistaken, it matches the cufflink I found." He held them both up.

"Well done, Andrews. Well done." Alan slapped the sergeant on the back. "Now, we need to get these items to forensics so they can check for DNA. Once we establish they don't belong to the victim, we can start showing them to the various shops in the city. Hopefully, one of them will be able to help us track down who bought them."

Alan paused and cast a glance around the open space behind them.

"Is there anything wrong, sir?" Andrews asked, as he slid the evidence bags into his pocket.

"I was just wondering whether the person these items belonged to might venture back to find them."

"Wouldn't he have done that by now?" Andrews clasped his gloved hands together in an effort to warm them. "I mean, if the guy believed he'd lost the items while dropping the body in the park, wouldn't he have come back last night, or even early this morning, to take a look around? He probably didn't see anything and assumed he hadn't lost them here."

"Yes, I suppose he would." Alan paused. "But what if he hadn't realised he'd lost them until sometime this morning?"

"Is that possible?" A puzzled expression spread across the sergeant's face. "Surely he would've noticed they were missing when he was undressing to go to bed last night."

Alan looked down at the ground and tapped a small mound of damp leaves with his foot. What Andrews said was true. Most people undressing for bed would be inclined to remove expensive items carefully. Unless…

Suddenly, he looked up at his sergeant and winked. "But, what if he was spending the night with a woman? Would he have noticed then?"

* * *

Once Alan dropped her off at the hotel, Agnes stopped to have a brief chat with the women behind the reception desk, before making her way up to her room. Inside, she tossed her coat and handbag onto the bed and moved across to the window and threw herself into a chair, idly gazing down at the scene below.

There were quite a number of people strolling across the Millennium Bridge; probably taking advantage of the early spring sunshine while they could. It was breezy today, but tomorrow it could be quite different, with the March winds blowing down the river at full strength.

As she sat there watching the people below, she reflected on her trip to the park. She shouldn't have gone there today. She had been foolish. Hadn't she learned anything from her experience only a few months ago? She needed to be more careful and not rush into things. She should have listened to Alan earlier that morning and gone shopping, instead of heading back to the very place where she had found the body.

She hadn't achieved anything at all and, as if that wasn't bad enough, she had dragged Alan away from the search he and his sergeant were pursuing. Heaving a sigh, she rested her chin on her hand and continued to stare out of the window.

Nevertheless, after about five minutes, she decided it wasn't like her to sit brooding on the past and she wasn't about to start now. The best thing for her right now was a stroll along the quayside. Plainly, she would need to make it up with Alan, but at the moment he was busy trying to solve a murder case. The making up would have to come later.

Agnes rose from her chair and was on the point of moving away from the window when someone below suddenly caught her eye. She hurried across the room and pulled open the top drawer of the chest of drawers. Grabbing the binoculars she had brought with her from her home in Essex, she rushed back to the window to take a closer look. Goodness knows why she had packed these, but as it turned out they were coming in useful.

Focusing the binoculars on the quayside below, she swept them to and fro until she found the person she was looking for. Her heart missed a beat. Short dark hair, clean-shaven and wearing a black coat; it could almost be the same man she had seen in the park that morning. But she was being ridiculous, surely; how many men in the city would fit that description?

Chapter Ten

Not wanting to be seen, Agnes took a step back from the window. Nevertheless, her eyes never left the man below. Could it possibly be the man she had seen striding past her in the park? Just at that moment, a strong breeze from the river lifted the hem of his coat and showed the shiny red lining.

Agnes's hand flew to her mouth. It *was* the same man she had seen in the park, after all. But what was he doing here outside her hotel?

Questions ran through her mind as she stood there watching him. Was it merely a coincidence he was now standing on the quayside outside her hotel? Or, more alarmingly, had he followed Alan's car when he had escorted her away from the park?

But why would he do that? Unless Alan had been right when he suspected the man was following her.

At the time, Agnes had thought Alan was being a little overprotective. As far as she was concerned, the man had simply been taking a break from a stuffy business meeting. But maybe Alan's concern had been justified. After all, as a DCI, detecting who was good and who was bad was his day job. He should know what to look out for. All the time these thoughts were running through her head, the man hadn't moved an inch from the spot.

Hoping she had got it all wrong, Agnes tried to convince herself that it wasn't the same man. After all, there must be other men with similar coats. But then, quite suddenly, he raised his head and looked up at the hotel. Lifting the binoculars back up to her eyes, she turned the dial in the centre slightly and peered down at him.

There was no mistake. It was definitely the man she had seen in the park; clean-shaven, short hairstyle, black coat with red lining. However, it was his piercing eyes that clinched it.

Just then, she noticed something else. Not something she had seen in the park; this was a thing she had only just picked up. But by the time she had refocused her binoculars, he had turned away and was walking towards the Millennium Bridge.

She watched him for a few seconds as he ambled across the bridge, trying to recall what had suddenly caught her eye. But, as she wasn't getting anywhere, she began to wonder where he was going. Wherever it was, he didn't seem to be in a hurry.

Forgetting all her earlier resolutions about not getting further involved in police business, she grabbed her coat from the bed and was about to put it on when she saw her reflection in the mirror. Perhaps it would be wise to wear something different. No point in giving herself away the moment he laid eyes on her.

She took a black coat out from the wardrobe and pulled it on. Satisfied that the man wouldn't realise she was the same woman he had seen in the park earlier that morning, she picked up her bag and hurried out of the room.

* * *

DCI Alan Johnson and his sergeant were back at the Newcastle Police Station. Andrews had handed the evidence bags over to the forensics team the moment they had arrived. Now, they could only wait to hear whether fingerprints, or any other DNA, had been found on any of the items.

Meanwhile, Alan was in the incident room informing the rest of his detectives of what they knew so far – which, to his mind, was precious little. Nevertheless, it was necessary to keep everyone up to date. The board, where new information was pinned the moment it came in, was empty apart from photographs of the murder victim and the area which had surrounded his body.

The detectives who had been scouring the missing person's lists and ringing other Police Stations in the area had not come up with anything, either. The reason could be due to the body only having being found a day earlier, which could mean the victim hadn't yet been reported missing. Also, as the victim's face was unrecognizable, it was likely to cause problems in identifying him. Unless there were any other marks such as tattoos or birthmarks to help.

"So we have nothing at all," Alan stated, stabbing his finger towards the board. "Surely there must be something the killer has missed? Someone out there must be able to help us."

"Why don't you ask Mrs Lockwood? I'm sure she'll be able to find out something." The voice came from a young detective at the back of the room. He laughed and looked around at his colleagues for support. However, no one joined him in his mirth.

"Morris!" Alan swung around to face the detective. "If you see this murder inquiry as some sort of a joke, then I suggest you're in the wrong job. You might want to find employment elsewhere."

"Sorry, sir." Detective Constable Morris shuffled his feet. "I just thought…"

"I know what you *just thought*," said Alan, emphasizing the last two words. "I'll see you in my office straight after this meeting."

"Yes, sir."

Alan looked at the rest of the group. "Has anyone any other suggestions or ideas as to where we should go from here?"

There was no response to his question.

"Okay," Alan said. "That's it for now. But if you get wind of anything, no matter how small or stupid it may seem, let me know and we'll follow it through. We need every scrap of information we can get."

Without another word, Alan stormed off down the corridor towards the office he shared with his sergeant.

"What the hell were you thinking, John?" Sergeant Andrews had arrived in time to hear the detective's crack at the DCI.

"I was only saying what everyone else was thinking," said Morris. "Bloody interfering woman! She seems to pop up wherever a body is found and the DCI allows her to get involved."

"You weren't here, so let me bring you up to speed, Morris. Mrs Lockwood helped us solve a case last year." Andrews paused, recalling how, at first, he had felt annoyed when she insisted on involving herself in a police matter. But he had been forced to swallow his pride several times when she had come up with answers.

"You weren't on this team back then," Andrews continued. "But no doubt you'll have heard it was she who figured out who the thief at the hotel was."

"Yes, I heard," said Morris. He looked down at the floor. "I suppose I should go and apologize to the boss now."

"Yes, you should. You aren't going to get very far as a detective with that attitude."

Sergeant Andrews watched Morris amble off down the corridor. Only when he saw the detective enter the DCI's office, did the sergeant go back to join his colleagues.

* * *

"I suppose you thought you were being funny," Alan growled, the moment Morris closed the door behind him.

"I can only apologize," said Morris, as he stepped closer to Alan's desk. "I don't know what came over me."

He eyed the chair in front of the DCI's desk, wondering whether he would be invited to take a seat.

"I do!" Alan snapped. "You thought you were being clever, trying to get one up on the boss."

Morris didn't reply. He simply looked down towards the floor. He knew now there was no way he would be invited to sit down.

Alan heaved a sigh. He never liked this part of the job and usually let things go; often pretending he hadn't heard when an officer made some wry comment. But Morris had really struck a nerve today. He had tried to score points by making fun, not just of him, but of Agnes. The one woman he had always admired.

"Okay, you can go," he said at last. "But in future, think before you open your mouth."

Morris turned to leave, but then stopped suddenly when a document on the DCI's desk caught his eye. "Will this go on my file, sir?"

Angry at Morris's outburst in the incident room, Alan had requested the detective constable's file be sent to him the moment he arrived in his office. His curt tone had made the office clerk leap to attention and the file had landed on his desk shortly after he had replaced the phone.

Alan had intended to make an example of him. But now he relented, as he thought back to when he was a constable. Hadn't he been a bit of a show-off at times, too? Though, to the best of his knowledge, he had never made fun of his senior officer.

"I haven't quite made up my mind," he said slowly. "Show me the real Detective Constable John Morris and then I'll decide."

"Yes, sir, thank you, sir," Morris said, before leaving the office.

* * *

Outside in the corridor, Morris closed his eyes and took a deep breath. He knew that if he wanted to further his career as a detective, he was going to have to stop larking around and get on with the job.

"You needed to prove you can do this," his father had told him when he first joined the force. "Not just to me or the men you will be working with, but to yourself."

His mother, the only daughter of a millionaire, had influence. Everyone wanted to please Mrs Morris. How he had got to where he was, was due to her being in the right place at the right time.

Nevertheless, he knew he wasn't going to get further promotion without being worthy of it. Detective Chief Inspector Alan Johnson had made that clear. Perhaps he was making a note of his stupid quip in his file at this precise moment.

Reflecting on the DCI's last words, he felt a little relieved. Maybe he had been given a reprieve. Now, it was up to him to let his boss see that he was capable of being a good detective.

Morris strode off down the corridor with a new frame of mind. Those few words with his boss had made him realise he needed to get a grip and start again. Up until now, his mother had played a big part in making sure his career took off. From the moment he told her he wanted to be a detective, she had made sure he hadn't failed any interview or exam.

At first, he had thought her influence was great. He had passed all his interviews with flying colours. Passing the exams had been a little more difficult; his mother had been restricted by the examination procedure. Nevertheless, he had passed each and every one, albeit by the skin of his teeth.

But he had to stop relying on her. From now on, he had to take heed of what his father had said and progress up the chain of command on his own – without his mother's interference.

He looked down at the suit he was wearing. It was cashmere. Very expensive, just like everything else in his wardrobe. When he became a detective constable, his mother had taken him to a shop in London and had ordered three made-to-measure suits and had bought expensive shirts and ties to go with them.

"You look the part," she had said proudly, when he tried them on at home. "You will not go unnoticed."

Since then, he had been transferred from his hometown in leafy Surrey to the Newcastle Police Headquarters, where his expensive suits and expertly cut hairstyle had not impressed anyone – especially his colleagues. Now, he needed to prove he was one of them; that they could rely on him for support during an investigation. Not someone who would worry about getting his suit scuffed or his hair messed up in a wrangle with a suspect.

He had hoped his quip in the incident room would help to break the ice… let the men see he was one of the guys, game for a laugh. Yet no one had laughed at his comment – no one had even smiled. Most had looked embarrassed.

By now, he had almost reached the incident room. He wasn't looking forward to rejoining the rest of the men. They would all be waiting for him to step through the door. Most likely, they would make a few wisecracks about how his days were numbered – if they even bothered to speak to him at all.

However, as he was about to push the door, it swung open and Sergeant Andrews stepped out into the corridor.

"How did you get on?" Andrews asked

"Okay, I think." Morris hesitated and shook his head. "Quite honestly, I don't know."

Andrews nodded knowingly. He had been called into the office once or twice early in his career and he had always come out of the interview not really understanding where he stood.

"You'll be okay," the sergeant told him, slapping him on the back. "You just need to stop trying to show off in front of your superiors," he glanced into the incident room, "and the rest of your colleagues. Now, get back in there and begin looking for something that will help us find the identity of the victim."

* * *

Once Morris had disappeared into the incident room, Andrews turned to look down the corridor towards the DCI's office and smiled. Alan had called him the moment Morris had left the room and told him what had transpired.

"I was going to make a note on his file," Alan had said, "but I had second thoughts. However, don't tell him that – not yet, anyway. Let him stew a little." There had been a brief pause before Alan had continued. "Tell the men not to be too hard on Morris. He might sort himself out if he's given a chance."

Chapter Eleven

Agnes was halfway across the Millennium Bridge when the man she was following suddenly stopped.

For a moment, she thought he had sensed there was someone watching him and fully expected him to swing round to catch whoever it was. Her first thought was to stop dead in her tracks. However, she forced herself to keep on walking. It would be a dead giveaway if he turned his head and found her standing stock still in the middle of the bridge with her eyes glued on him.

As it happened, he didn't look back. He simply reached into his pocket and pulled out his mobile phone. Now the phone was out in the open, she could hear it ringing.

Agnes breathed a sigh of relief as he lifted the phone to his ear and began to carry on walking while listening to his call. Unfortunately, she was too far behind to hear what he said, but at least he didn't know she was there.

At the other end of the bridge, the man crossed the quay and made his way up the stone steps which led to the Sage building. As he was the only person climbing the steps at the time, she hung around below until he was almost at the top before following him. Having got this far, she didn't see any point in drawing his attention to her now. Hopefully, if she climbed the steps fast enough, she would reach the top before she lost sight of him.

But when Agnes heaved herself onto the last step, there was no sign of the man. Trying to be discreet, she stood there for a moment as though she was taking in the scene around here.

He must already be inside the Sage, she thought, as she began to make her way across towards the entrance.

There were quite a number of people milling around inside, making it rather difficult to look out for one person in particular. Obviously, there was another attraction going on this afternoon. Nevertheless, she swiftly skirted around several groups of people as they all seemed intent on stopping her. It was almost as though the man had realised he was being followed and had phoned ahead to orchestrate the whole episode.

Finally, after dodging about for what seemed like an age, Agnes caught a glimpse of him. She moved a few steps to her right so that she could see him more clearly. From this new position, she could see that he was engrossed in a conversation with another man. Unfortunately, she couldn't see this new man very clearly due to people getting in the way, but she did see him take something out of his pocket and hand it to the man she had followed.

Whatever it was he had been given, he looked overjoyed to receive it. He leaned forward and clapped the man on the back. At that point, she was forced to look away for a fleeting moment, as a group of people pushed past her on their way to the café. By the time she looked back, the two men had disappeared. It seemed they had finished whatever it was they were doing and gone their separate ways.

Agnes made her way out of the crowded area towards the windows. She remembered from her last visit that there was a splendid view of the Tyne and its bridges from here. It was while she was gazing from the window that she glimpsed someone striding down the pathway below.

Standing on tiptoe and peering down, she was able to make out the man she had followed here. He was alone. Having acquired whatever it was he came for, he was making his way down the steep slope back to the Millennium Bridge. He had obviously left by the other door.

She shook her head in disgust. Why hadn't she thought of that?

Agnes turned away from the window and leaned her back against the wall. She was curious about what the other man had given him to make him so excited. Could it have been money? Was the man in the black coat a killer and had he come here today to get paid for murdering the man whose body she found in the park? And, come to think of it, where was the other man?

Agnes was beginning to get a headache with all the notions running through her head. She turned and looked back out of the window. There was no sign of the man now. He was probably already halfway across the bridge.

Nevertheless, Agnes decided she wasn't going to take any chances. She couldn't be sure that he hadn't spotted her behind him and was hanging around somewhere waiting to see whether she really was following him. With that thought in mind, she made her way across to the café and ordered a pot of tea and a very large sticky bun.

* * *

Back at the police station, the DCI and his sergeant had heard from the forensics team. They had found fingerprints on both the cufflink and the tiepin.

The downside was that the fingerprints weren't already in the system, which meant they needed to start a search for whoever had lost the items. Even then, the owner might have nothing to do with the murder. But they had to start somewhere. The upside was that they were rather expensive items. Therefore a jeweller's shop might remember who they had sold them to. It was a long shot, but they had to start somewhere.

They were still carrying out tests on the piece of cloth Alan had found. However, despite its ragged state, they had learned it had been torn from an item of clothing made from cashmere. Putting together the cloth and the items Andrews had found, they might have been from the same person.

By now, Alan was back in the incident room updating his team.

"As you can see," he said, holding up the evidence bags holding the cufflinks and tiepin, "they are very impressive items. I'm sure whoever lost them will be out there, hoping to find them as quickly as possible. Photographs of both items will be handed out to you all. I suggest you take them to every jewellery shop in the city."

Alan nodded to a uniformed officer standing in the doorway and the woman began handing out the photographs. He took one and pinned it up on the board.

"We can't assume that the items belong to our killer," the DCI added once the photographs were handed out. "They could have been lost anywhere in the park or even the Town Moor and picked up by a bird with an eye for shiny objects. But, at the moment, it's the only thing we have to go on."

"Surely only the more expensive jewellers would stock something of this quality," said one of the detectives, peering at the photographs. "None of the high street shops keep this sort of thing instore. You would need to go to London to even order something like this."

"Is that right?" Alan slowly turned around to face the detective. He lifted his left sleeve to reveal the rather expensive watch on his wrist. "My parents bought this on Northumberland Street. They told the jewellery shop manager exactly what they wanted and he ordered it for them. I recall my father telling me that the manager was very helpful. He was able to go back to the shop a few days later and pick it up, fully guaranteed. Therefore, detective, we can't rule out any jewellery shop."

He looked back at the team. "Anything else?"

Morris coughed.

"You have something to add, Morris?" Alan frowned. He'd had enough of this guy for one day.

"Can I see the originals?" Morris asked. He pointed towards the evidence bags.

Alan held out the two bags. "Yes, but you can't remove the items. Not yet, anyway."

Morris stepped forward and took the bags from the DCI and peered at the cufflink and tiepin.

"Are you familiar with either of them?" Alan asked.

"Yes, both of them, I think," Morris muttered.

"You *think*?" Alan was beginning to lose patience.

"I gave my father a similar pair of cufflinks," replied Morris.

"Of course you did." Alan didn't sound surprised. But he allowed the young detective to continue.

Morris turned the bags over and looked at the reverse side of both the tiepin and the cufflink. However, the inscription was too small to see clearly.

"I'm sure the forensic team has already magnified the writing on the reverse side of the items," he said, still staring hard at the evidence bags. "Did they send them up?"

Alan was rather taken aback. That was the last thing he had expected to hear from Morris. He suddenly felt quite small for his rather cutting remarks a few moments ago.

"Of course," Alan said, quickly gathering his wits together. He glanced at his sergeant and nodded towards the table.

Andrews distributed the photos, handing one to Morris first.

"Has anyone anything else to say that might help with the investigation?" Alan asked, while Morris pondered over the photo.

As no one replied, the DCI looked back at Morris. "What about you?"

"Well, I can tell you that the items were made in Germany." He looked back at the two evidence bags. "The markings are exactly the same as the ones I was given as a gift a couple of years ago by a German friend. He gave them to me when he came for a visit. He told me they wouldn't be available in the shops over here, as they were made by a small company – father and son, I think – and they didn't export their jewellery in a big way. Only if a jeweller ordered a set privately. I don't wear cufflinks, so I gave them to my father. My friend also brought my mother a rather lovely necklace."

"Does that mean you believe the killer is German?" Andrews asked.

"No, not at all." Morris quickly looked up at the DCI and Sergeant Andrews. "The items could have been bought by a British guy while on holiday. Or, like the DCI said, someone who might have ordered them from a shop somewhere in Newcastle."

Morris looked down at the photographs again. "But I do know they're expensive. Therefore I'm sure the guy will be pissed that he lost them."

Chapter Twelve

Agnes pulled up her collar as she made her way out of the Sage. It seemed to have turned colder since she entered the building. Or had it simply been very warm inside? Whatever the reason, she certainly felt the chill now she was back out in the open. She slowly made her way back down the steps and across the Millennium Bridge.

Without making it blatantly obvious she was observing them, Agnes gave a fleeting glance at each person as they passed by. For all she knew, the man in the black coat could be one of them.

Back on the other side of the river, she decided to pop into her favourite café for a glass of wine. When the weather was clement, she usually chose to sit at one of the tables outside. However, as she was feeling the cold today, she opted to sit inside.

Agnes sipped her wine as she thought back over the events of the day. So much had happened; it was hard to believe she had only arrived on Tyneside one day ago. Now, she couldn't wait to tell Alan that she had seen the man from the park here on the quayside and had followed him to the Sage. But, on second thoughts, she wondered whether it might be best to stay silent about the last part.

Alan would certainly not be very happy at the thought of her following the very person he believed to be trailing her in the park. Yet at the same time, she couldn't just tell him part of the story. After all, she had witnessed the man meeting up with someone else and, during the time they were together, something had changed hands. That could turn out to be important to the case. Alan needed to be able to trust her.

She thought back to when they had met up the day before. Was it really only yesterday? So much had happened in the last twenty-four hours, it seemed much longer. Yet, it was only yesterday when she had told him how she had missed being here. Though she hadn't felt able to tell him exactly how much she had missed being with him. Even last evening, she had fluffed around the issue instead of coming out with the truth? Why was that?

But that was a stupid question. Deep down, she knew why – it was because of her late husband.

Jim had been a wonderful husband and a great father to their two lovely boys. Now, she was afraid she might be betraying his love for them all if she were to get involved with another man.

She wrestled with her thoughts and, as she sat staring into space, tears welled in her eyes.

What would you think if Alan and I got together, Jim? Agnes thought, as she twisted the stem of her glass around between her fingers. *Would you feel I had let you down or would you give me your blessing? I need to know where to go from here...*

A shadow fell across the table and a familiar voice broke into her thoughts.

"Are you alright?"

Agnes closed her eyes. It was almost as though Jim had been listening in on her thoughts and had intervened by sending Alan to the café.

"Yes, Alan. I'm fine," she said, without looking up. "Why?"

"No reason," Alan said, sliding into the seat next to her.

A tear rolling down her cheek could not have gone unnoticed, but Alan didn't mention it.

"So, what are you doing here?" Agnes asked. "Stupid question," she added. "I guess you were looking for me. Why else would you be here?"

"I stopped by the hotel to see if you were okay. Once the girl on reception found you weren't in your room, I thought I would try here as I know this is your favourite spot on the quayside."

"You stopped by?" Agnes giggled. "Stopped by on your way to... where?"

"Okay, I skipped out of the office for a few minutes," Alan admitted. He shrugged. "I don't know why. I just suddenly had the urge to know you hadn't shot back up to the park the moment I left."

"No, I didn't go back up to the park. I didn't need to, because I saw the man you thought was following me. He was standing outside the hotel and I decided to follow him."

She paused, expecting Alan to leap in with some comment about how she should stay away from trouble or something to that effect. But as he didn't say anything, she continued.

"I followed him up to the Sage Building and saw him meet up with another man, but then I lost him in the crowd."

There was a heavy sigh from Alan.

Agnes couldn't quite tell whether it was a sigh of relief because she hadn't been able to get close to him, or a sign of despair that she even went out to follow the man in the first place. But, on reflection, they meant the same thing; he was worried about her.

She went on to tell him how she had stayed in the Sage; only leaving when she thought the man had well and truly left the area.

"Thank goodness for that," Alan said.

He looked up towards the bar and nodded.

"A large, very strong black coffee," he called out. Turning back, he said, "Agnes, if anything happened to you, I wouldn't know what to do."

Agnes grabbed Alan's hand. "Wait, that's not all."

"What else did you do?" Alan broke in. He sounded anxious.

"Nothing," Agnes replied.

She had been about to tell him the real reason for cutting short her stay in Australia, but she suddenly lost her nerve.

"I came in here and ordered a glass of wine." She gestured towards her glass.

For goodness' sake, what is the matter with me? Why can't I simply tell the man how much I really missed him while I was away? This isn't like me at all. I am usually so forthright – too forthright, sometimes.

Agnes picked up her glass and took a large swig. Setting it back down on the table, she turned to face Alan.

"What I am really trying to say, Alan, is that I missed you when I was in Australia." The words tumbled from her lips before she lost her nerve again. She could only hope they made sense.

"Yes, you said that last night," Alan replied. "But it's nice to hear you say it again,"

"No," she shook her head. "No, Alan, you don't understand. Yes, I missed dear old England, and yes, I did miss Tyneside very much, but the truth is… I missed *you*. *You* are the reason I cut short my visit with my two wonderful boys and their families in Australia. *You* are the reason I took an earlier flight back home."

Alan didn't say a word. He simply sat there staring at her.

"Well, for heaven's sake say something," Agnes said, before taking another large gulp from her wine glass. "Have I said the wrong thing? I always manage to get things wrong with you…"

"Do you mean that?" Alan asked, at last. "You missed me that much?"

Agnes gave a smile of relief. "Yes, I did, you idiot."

Before Alan could say anything further, the waiter arrived with his coffee and he began to fumble around for his wallet.

"Put that on my bill," Agnes said, with a grin.

The waiter nodded and placed the coffee on the table before returning to the bar.

"I couldn't wait for you to return, Agnes," Alan said. "In fact, I've been counting down the days to when you said you would be flying home." He paused. "Though I wasn't really sure you would come back to Tyneside. I had the idea you might decide to move to Australia. You know… to be nearer to your family. Or, even if you did come back to England, you could very easily have made the decision to stay in Essex. It must be very pretty down there in the springtime."

"Yes, it is very pleasant at this time of the year."

Agnes smiled as she reflected on the village where she lived. Near her house was a large village green with a pond at one side. It was all so very pretty and well kept. The Parish Council saw to that. Not far from there stood the railway station, giving easy access to London for commuters.

"But there is something about this area and you, which I really missed."

"I see. I come in second place!"

"No! I didn't mean it to sound like that. I meant…" She stopped abruptly when she saw the wide grin on Alan's face.

She punched his arm. "You knew exactly what I meant."

At that moment, someone walking past the window of the café caught

her eye.

"Good grief!" she exclaimed

"What is it?" Alan asked. He swiftly turned his head towards the window. "What have you seen?"

"*Who* have I seen, more like," she replied, quickly bending down to hide her face beneath the table.

"It's the man we saw in the park," she hissed, from somewhere under the table. "The man I followed earlier. He's out there. He's still wearing the dark overcoat. What's he doing now?"

A passing waiter noticed Agnes bending under the table and leaned down to speak to her.

"You have you lost something? Can I be of assistance?" He had a strong Italian accent.

"No thank you, I'm fine," Agnes replied.

"Don't worry, she's okay," Alan interrupted. "My friend is following a course of exercises." He pointed towards Agnes. "This is supposed to help her back problem. Her surgeon said it would do her the world of good to bend down from a seated position several times a day. It's one of those new-fangled medical ideas."

The waiter stood up and straightened his shirt. "Ah! Yes, of course," he said, as though he had read about such a procedure. "I hope it works," he added, before going to clear a nearby table.

"Has he gone?" Agnes said. "I feel like an idiot down here."

"Has who gone – the waiter or the man?" Alan asked.

"The man, of course," Agnes whispered. "I can see for myself that the waiter has gone."

"Yes, the man has gone. He went ages ago. He just walked straight past the café. He didn't even bother to look inside."

"And you didn't think to tell me!" Agnes regained her position at the table and smoothed down her hair, even though it hadn't moved an inch. "Where did he go?"

"He went over the bridge," Alan replied, sounding very relaxed about the whole thing. He took a sip of coffee.

"And you aren't interested in why he is still hovering around the quayside? Or even what he was doing here in the first place?" Agnes stared at Alan.

"Of course I am. While you were fumbling around under the table, I quickly rang Andrews and told him to get down here with a couple of detectives ASAP. With a bit of luck, the guy will come back this way, as he must have done earlier, and then they can follow him."

"Your back is good now, yes?"

Agnes looked up quickly to see the waiter who had spoken to her earlier.

"Yes, thank you," she replied. "The exercises seem to help."

"That is good," he said, then went to take an order from the next table.

Agnes turned back to face Alan, who, she could tell, was trying very hard to keep a straight face.

"You're enjoying this, aren't you?"

"Not really… well, maybe a little," he replied, before bursting into laughter.

"You…" However, before she could say anything further, she shook her head and started to laugh.

At that moment, Sergeant Andrews walked into the café and glanced around. He spotted the DCI sitting with Mrs Lockwood and strode towards them.

"Okay, what does this guy look like and did you see where he went?"

"He walked across the bridge." Alan gestured towards the Millennium Bridge. "This is the second time today he has crossed the bridge. Mrs Lockwood saw him earlier and followed him over to the Sage. He met someone over there before disappearing out the rear entrance. He's clean-shaven, has dark hair, rather smoothly cut and is wearing a black overcoat."

Alan looked at Agnes for confirmation.

She nodded.

"Is that it?" Andrews asked, glancing towards the window. "That description could fit a number of people out there." He nodded towards all the people milling across the bridge.

Alan turned towards Agnes. "Do you have anything to add?"

Agnes closed her eyes and thought back to earlier in the day. "His coat has a bright red, shiny lining. It was the first thing I picked up on in the park."

She sighed, opened her eyes and looked at the sergeant. He was staring at her as though waiting for something else. "But that's not enough, is it?"

Andrews looked at his boss and he shook his head.

"I can hardly strut around the quayside lifting men's overcoats to check whether the lining is red before I start following them."

Agnes suddenly thought of something else about the man. Something she had noticed when peering at him through her binoculars from the hotel window. She had been so engrossed in making sure it was the same face she had seen in the park, that she hadn't really noted this extra detail until it was too late. But now, that one tiny detail she had so very nearly missed could be very important.

"Wait!" Agnes set her glass on the table and closed her eyes again, desperately trying to recall the scene.

A few seconds later, she opened them and stared up at Sergeant Andrews. "He has a dark-coloured mark on the back of one of his hands," she stated, triumphantly. "I can't say for certain what it is. It could be either a tattoo or a birthmark."

"Thank you," said Andrews.

He glanced at his boss. "I take it you're leaving this to me?"

"Yes," Alan replied. "Except to say, make sure the men are spread out. If this man *is* our killer, we don't want him to get wind of the fact that he's being followed. Simply watch him. See what he does and where he goes and report back to me. This could be something, or it could be one big wild goose chase. So far, we have nothing on him."

Alan glanced at the detectives waiting outside. His eyes focused on one of them. "Is he a wise choice?" he asked, raising his eyebrows.

"I think so."

"Okay, sergeant. It's your call."

Andrews nodded before heading for the door.

"What was that all about?" Agnes asked, scrutinizing the men outside. "Who aren't you happy about being involved?"

"They are all fine men. It's just that one of them is new," Alan replied, still watching Detective Morris as Andrews gave them their orders.

"Aren't you supposed to be on duty?" Agnes asked, changing the subject. "Shouldn't you be out there with your men?"

"I have a few hours' leave due to me and I suddenly decided to take them this afternoon."

"When did you decide that?"

"The moment you told me you had missed me while you were away."

"Are you allowed to do that?" Agnes cocked her head to the right. "After all, you *are* working a case, aren't you?"

Alan followed suit by tilting his head to the left side.

"They owe me. Besides, my sergeant knows exactly where I am if he needs me. Andrews is a good man. He deserves to take the lead now and again."

"Then why don't you join me in a glass of wine?" Agnes asked, coyly.

"Because, you never know, I might suddenly be needed later today."
"So you really aren't off duty after all, are you?" Agnes replied.

Chapter Thirteen

Outside the café, Sergeant Andrews gave his instructions to the detectives. He stressed they were not here to make an arrest. They were simply to look out for the man in question and, should they see him, follow him as far as possible.

"If you get even a hint your cover is blown, call in to the station and get a new face to take over. Is that understood?"

The detectives nodded.

"You must understand that at this stage, we have nothing on this man," Andrews continued. "At the moment, we're just keeping an eye on his movements." Andrews paused. "Does anyone have any questions?"

As no one had anything to say, he split the men up. A couple of them seated themselves outside the café giving the impression they were reading their newspapers, while Andrews, accompanied by Morris, slowly walked across the bridge towards the Baltic Art Gallery.

They were almost halfway across the river before either said a word.

"I'm surprised you chose me." Morris was the first to speak. After his episode with the DCI, he had thought he wouldn't get the chance to help in a case for quite a while.

"To come on this assignment, I mean," he added. "You know – after what happened earlier, with the boss." He paused, having suddenly thought of something. "Does he know I'm here?"

"Yes, he knows, so don't mess it up," Andrews replied curtly. "Just keep your eyes open and if you see anyone who resembles the description we've been given, simply inform me – but for goodness' sake do it discreetly. Don't do or say anything that might let him know he's being followed."

Andrews walked a few steps, then stopped. Feeling guilty about his abruptness, he indicated to Morris to move over to the side of the bridge.

"Look, I didn't mean to sound so sharp," he said, not taking his eyes off the people walking past, "but you were an idiot back in the office. No one makes jibes at the DCI. The chief inspector could have had you transferred. Yet he didn't. He told me he had decided to give you another chance. And that's what I am doing now – giving you another chance. So don't mess it up."

"I won't." Morris nodded.

"Okay. Now let's get back to the matter in hand." Andrews glanced back towards to the café as he spoke. He hoped the DCI hadn't been watching. He might have got the wrong impression and thought they had stopped off to take in the views of the river from the bridge. However, with a bit of luck, he could have been chatting to Mrs Lockwood and missed their brief interlude.

Nevertheless, Andrews knew the chief inspector never missed anything. After working with him for the last couple of years, he had firmly come to the conclusion that the DCI had eyes in the back of his head.

* * *

"What do you mean, I'm not off duty?" Alan said. "Of course I am. I could be out there leading the detectives, but I'm here with you."

"Yet you have never taken your eyes off them," Agnes said. "Go on, Alan, admit it. Even when you are supposed to be off duty, your head is still out there with the men." She paused for a second. "Don't get me wrong. I think it's great. I would be the same. You say that once I get my teeth into something, I can't let go – but neither can you."

"You're right." Alan sighed. "I told Andrews I was leaving it to him. Yet, like you say, I'm sitting here in full sight of the detectives, watching their every move. How can I not be interested in what's happening?"

"So what do you think your sergeant was saying to the other detective, while they were chatting on the bridge?"

"I know exactly what they were saying," Alan replied. "But it's sort of personal, so let's just leave it there."

"Fine," Agnes replied.

Obviously, she wasn't going to get anywhere with her question. Therefore it was best to leave things be – at least for the time being.

* * *

Just as the two detectives had reached the other side of the bridge, Morris caught sight of the man wearing a black overcoat. He was walking in their direction.

"Don't look now, but I can see someone who fits the description of the guy we are looking for. He's heading this way," Morris said. "He came down the steps leading up to the Sage."

"Okay," said Andrews. "So tell me, what's he doing now?"

"He's still coming this way. I think he could be going back over the bridge."

"Right. Keep your eyes peeled. We're looking for a red lining inside the coat and tattoo or birthmark on one of his hands." Andrews paused. "Where is he now?"

"Almost upon us," Morris replied.

"I'm just going over there," Andrews said. He spoke loud enough for the man to hear. "I think I'll get a better photo of the Tyne Bridge. You wait here. I'll take one of you with the Baltic Gallery in the background. I could send it on to your wife," he added, holding up his phone.

"Yes, she would love that," Morris replied, quickly catching on that Andrews was seizing the opportunity to photograph the man.

As the man strode past, Andrews was able to catch a glimpse of a mark on the man's left hand. Morris, pretending to pose for the photo, saw a flash of red when the breeze lifted the edge of man's coat slightly. It was their guy – there was no doubt about it.

"It's him. We need to catch up with him," Morris said excitedly and would have broken into a run if Andrews hadn't caught his arm and pulled him to a halt.

"What the hell do you think you're doing?" Andrews hissed. "We're only here to watch this guy unobserved. You were just about to blow the whole thing!"

"I'm sorry. I got carried away." Morris hung his head. "It won't happen again."

"As sure as hell it won't!" Andrews snapped. He didn't have time to say anything further at the moment. He needed to get in touch with one of the detectives waiting on the other side of the river. He punched a number into his phone.

"Our man is on his way across the bridge," he said, as soon as the detective answered. "I'll send you a copy of the photo I just took. You can't miss him. He's alone and is the only person wearing a black overcoat. The mark I told you to look out for is on his left hand, though I doubt you will be able to see it from where you're sitting. Wait until you know which direction he is taking before either of you makes a move. Understood?"

"Understood," the detective repeated.

Andrews shut down his phone and nodded to Morris. "Let's go. I need to report back to the DCI."

Chapter Fourteen

Jones, the detective, who had taken the call, looked at the photo before slowly placing the phone back in his pocket. He couldn't see the bridge so clearly now, as several people had settled at the tables in front of him. Though it was still only March and quite cold, it was surprising how many people still preferred to sit outside and admire the view.

Jones knew better than to suddenly start bobbing his head around to scrutinize people as they streamed off the bridge. Everyone would wonder what he was looking at and turn around to see what it was. That was the last thing he wanted.

Calmly, he stretched across the table to where Smithers, a fellow detective, was sitting. He was giving the impression to anyone watching that his eyes were fixed on his newspaper – though, in reality, he was actually eyeing the people leaving the bridge.

"I've just had a call with some good news," Jones told him. "The flight will be landing shortly."

"That's great," Smithers said, looking up from his newspaper. "I guess we'll need to head off shortly to pick them up."

"Yes, but you'll have to take the lead. I haven't seen him for a long time. I doubt I would recognize him."

Smithers nodded, cottoning on that Jones couldn't see this end of the bridge. He and Jones had worked together for some time now and they had their own way of conversing while on a case. Anyone listening would simply believe they were having a casual conversation.

"I guess he'll be wearing the usual black coat?" Smithers said.

"Yes, that's what I was told. Probably the only person on the flight wearing a black coat."

"Yes, he always had a thing about black coats." Smithers laughed.

While they were talking, Smithers hadn't taken his eyes away from the people coming off the bridge. Though they were well wrapped up, none of the men were wearing overcoats. Most wore something more casual such as padded jackets or fleeces. But then he suddenly caught a glimpse of a man in a black overcoat striding towards the end of the bridge.

"In that case, I'll be able to pick him out quite easily." He laughed. "The man in black."

"Great!" Jones replied. "Let's go."

The two detectives waited until they knew which direction the man was taking. Once it was obvious he was moving away from them, they stood up and slowly made their way towards the end of the Millennium Bridge. By now 'the man in black', as Smithers had named him, was well ahead of them.

Still, not wanting to blow their cover, they continued to follow some distance behind. But once the man had rounded the corner, they gathered a little speed and the two men reached the edge of the café in time to see their target crossing the road.

"Right," said Jones. "Whichever direction he takes, I'll cross the road and follow him from behind, while you track him on this side. If one of us gets sidetracked, for whatever reason, the other carries on regardless. Okay?"

Smithers nodded. They had done this before; the job always came first.

However, both men were taken by surprise when the man in black didn't head off along the quayside. Instead, he headed towards the large building straight in front of them.

* * *

By now, Sergeant Andrews and Detective Morris had joined the DCI and Agnes in the café. On entering the building, Andrews had deliberately made it appear as though they had suddenly spotted some old friends while he and his mate had dropped in for a coffee.

"I guess Jones and Smithers are following him now, so it might be a while before we hear from them. The guy could be going anywhere," Andrews concluded, after bringing the DCI up to date.

However, he had hardly finished his last sentence when his phone began to ring.

"It's Jones," said Andrews when he saw the name showing on the screen.

The sergeant leaned away from the DCI when he became aware of what Jones was telling him. "Are you sure?" Andrews asked. "He actually went in there? I mean, he's not hovering around outside waiting for someone?"

The sergeant took a deep breath as Jones confirmed his statement.

"Smithers followed him inside to see what he's up to," Jones said. "We decided that if we both went in, it might look suspicious. Besides, if he comes out, I can take it from there and continue to follow him."

"I agree," said Andrews. "You guys know what you're doing. But keep me in the loop."

Andrews slowly closed his phone and looked at Alan. He could tell by the expression on the DCI's face that he was impatient to hear what was going on.

"The man in black, as the detectives have named him, has gone into The Millennium Hotel." He quickly glanced at Agnes, before looking back at the DCI. "Smithers followed him into the hotel to see what he was up to. He might simply be visiting a guest. If that's the case, Jones is waiting outside ready to continue following him." He paused. "They're a good team. They know what they're doing."

"Yes, I agree," Alan said.

He had often admired how well the two detectives worked together. It was almost as though each knew what the other was thinking.

He turned his attention to Agnes. She hadn't said a word. That was so unlike her. She usually voiced her opinions, whether they were asked for or not. There had to be something on her mind.

"Are you okay?" he asked gently.

"Yes, I think so," Agnes replied, slowly. "I'm just thinking it all through."

"Why don't you talk it through with us?" Alan asked. "It might help."

Agnes nodded, as she began to relay her thoughts. "When I first saw the man standing on the quayside earlier today, he was looking up at the hotel and I wondered whether he might have followed me back from the park. But then I dismissed the idea, thinking I was probably being paranoid."

She hesitated, as she thought about what she wanted to say next.

"But now, I am beginning to think my first thoughts about 'the man in black' were correct." Agnes made quotation marks in the air as she spoke. "Is it possible he watched me being dropped me off at the hotel and now he's in there looking for me?"

"If that's the case, then Smithers will be onto it," said Alan. "I don't want you to worry about it. Like I said, Smithers is a good man. He'll make it his business to hear every word the suspect says and –"

"Wait!" Agnes broke in. She laughed. "I'm sorry. I think I must have given you the wrong impression. I'm not worried about him knowing where I'm staying."

Agnes cast her eyes down to the floor, reflecting on what she had just said.

"Sorry, that was stupid," she said, looking up again. "Of course I'm concerned about my safety! But if this man *is* looking for me, then we'll know our suspicions about him are correct, which means we'll be justified in keeping tabs on him."

"*We?*" Alan ventured.

"Yes! *We!*" she replied sharply.

She coughed. She hadn't meant to sound so harsh.

"Sorry, Alan." She smiled. "I thought we had an agreement."

It was Andrews who broke the awkward silence which followed. "It's possible that our suspect was already staying at the hotel. He could well have taken the lift straight up to his room."

"Yes, it is," Alan replied, though he sounded doubtful about it. "All we can do now is wait until we hear from either Smithers or Jones before we start jumping to any conclusions."

* * *

Smithers followed the man into the hotel, taking care to stay well behind him. He stopped near a collection of leaflets, to give the impression he was interested in learning about the upcoming events in the area. However, he made sure the suspect was still in his line of sight.

Smithers had never been inside this hotel before. Glancing down at his attire, he suddenly felt out of place. Despite having one eye on their suspect, he hadn't failed to notice that other people milling around the reception area were smartly dressed. His grey coat and black trousers, both of which had seen better days, made him feel uncomfortable. Even his shirt, bulging through his unbuttoned coat, was slightly crumpled. But at least it was clean.

Since his wife had left him a few months ago, his clothes went unironed. Thankfully, he knew how to use the washing machine and dryer. However, the iron was still way down on his agenda.

On reflection, perhaps it would have been better if Jones had followed the man inside the hotel; at least he was wearing a jacket that matched his trousers. But it was too late for that now. He was here and he would have to make the best of it.

Out of the corner of his eye, he could see the man had reached the desk. It was time to move forward and eavesdrop on whatever he said to the receptionist. Grabbing a leaflet about one of the forthcoming shows in the city, Smithers ambled towards the desk.

Still not wanting to draw attention to himself, Smithers stood a few feet away from the man in black as he leaned across the desk to speak to the receptionist. Though the man kept his voice low, Smithers was near enough to pick up on most of the conversation.

"I was wondering whether you might have a room vacant tonight and maybe for the next couple of nights," the man asked.

"I'll check," the receptionist replied and turned towards the computer.

After tapping a few keys on the keyboard, she looked back towards the man and smiled. "It seems you're in luck. We have a vacant room on the third floor."

"Excellent," the man replied. "I was afraid you would be fully booked. The city is quite busy at the moment."

"Yes, actually we're quite busy. There are a number of events in the area at the moment," she replied, glancing back at the screen. "May I have your name, please?"

"Harrison. Richard Harrison," he replied, without any hesitation.

"And may I ask the reason for your visit?" The receptionist looked up as she spoke. She laughed. "Silly question. I expect you're here for the racing in Gosforth Park."

The man gave a hollow laugh. "Ah yes, you're spot on."

The receptionist looked back at her screen as she typed in the information.

Smithers, a seasoned detective, quickly guessed the man was lying. The laugh and the slight touch of relief in the man's voice at being furnished with a reason for his visit, gave him away.

Smithers smiled to himself. Yes. Mr Richard Harrison, if that was his real name, was good, but he hadn't fooled him. Whatever the actual purpose of the man's stay in the area, it wasn't for the race meeting.

Smithers watched as the receptionist handed the keycard to Richard Harrison.

"I'll call for a porter to take your luggage," she said.

"It's still in the car at the other end of the quayside," he said, a little too quickly. "I'll get it later."

"Very well. Enjoy your stay and should you need anything, there is always someone on the desk."

Harrison nodded and moved away towards the lift.

"Sorry to keep you waiting," the receptionist said, looking towards Smithers. She smiled. "What can I do you for you?"

"I was going to ask you about a room," he replied. "However, I got the impression the man in front of me took the last one."

"Let me check," she said, turning back to the screen.

* * *

Standing a short distance from the hotel, Jones was keeping a close eye on the door; though no one would have guessed. While he was waiting, he had looked at his watch a few times and had pretended to make a couple of phone calls so anyone passing would think he was waiting for a colleague who was late.

Yet, despite all that, he was all set to follow the man in black should he suddenly appear through the door. His partner would soon catch up with him, though he would stay some way behind. They had done this so many times before, they had it down to a fine art.

As it turned out, it was Smithers who emerged from the hotel.

"So what kept you?" Jones said loudly, for the benefit of a couple of people who were standing nearby. He pointed at his watch

"Sorry," Smithers replied, catching on to the charade. "I got talking." By now, they were some distance away from the hotel.

"The man booked a room," said Smithers. "He called himself Richard Harrison."

"That's a shame. I was getting used to calling him the man in black," Jones replied, with a grin. "Never mind. So tell me what you found out."

Smithers went on to explain what had transpired at the reception desk.

"I ended up booking a room at the hotel."

"You didn't!"

"I did! I had to have some reason for hanging around for so long and booking a room was the only option." He paused. "Besides, it's one way of keeping tabs on our man."

"You're going to have to smarten yourself up a great deal if you're planning to spend a few nights in such a posh hotel." Jones laughed.

"Oh, I didn't book it for me – or you, for that matter."
"Well, who the hell *did* you book it for?"

Chapter Fifteen

"*Morris*? Why Morris?"

By now, both Smithers and Jones had joined the DCI and the others in the café. Smithers had just finished telling his boss what had happened in the hotel and how he had ended up booking a room.

"It's a great idea to book a room," Alan said. "But, I repeat, why did you book it for Morris?"

"I was thinking on my feet and it suddenly came to me that Morris would blend in with the other guests at the hotel. You only need to look at how he's dressed today to see that." As he spoke, Smithers gestured towards Morris, who was still wearing one of his expensive suits. "He even talks like one of them."

Since the episode with the DCI earlier that day, Morris hadn't had time to return to his flat and find something more in keeping with the rest of his colleagues.

Alan glanced at the young detective and nodded. That part was true. Morris certainly fitted the bill of a man who might stay at The Millennium Hotel. Yet the DCI was still sceptical. What experience did this naive detective have out there in the field?

"But he's new to us. Morris doesn't understand the way we work. Wouldn't it be better if you or Jones stayed in the hotel?" Alan paused and looked at Andrews. "What do you think, Sergeant?"

The sergeant leaned his head on one side, while he thought through what the detective had said.

"I think Smithers could have a point," he said. "If he were to suddenly appear in the hotel, then Harrison might recall seeing him in reception. It could set Harrison wondering whether it was just a coincidence, or if he had he been followed. There is also the possibility that Harrison had spotted him and Jones together near the bridge. Therefore, to my way of thinking, Morris is a good choice."

Andrews began to list a few further reasons for his train of thought.

"For a start, he's new to the area so no one outside the force will recognize him. Also, as Smithers has already pointed out, he'll blend in, which is imperative in an undercover operation."

"Okay, I'll go along with it," said Alan, reluctantly. He turned back to Morris. "But don't mess this up. Keep an eye on this man, Harrison, but, at the same time, don't give him the slightest hint that you are watching him. Do you think you're up to it?"

"Yes, sir," Morris replied. "I'll do my best."

"You'll do more than that, Morris," Alan said. "You need to give this assignment everything you've got," he said, in a softer tone. "It's essential we, the team, know whether this man, Richard Harrison, is responsible for the murders of the bodies found in the parks, both here in Newcastle and in Gateshead. Therefore I stress," Alan stabbed his finger on the table, "it is imperative you keep me or Sergeant Andrews," he gestured towards the sergeant, "informed at all times as to what is this man is up to. Even if you think it's something really trivial, we need to know. *We* will decide what is important – not you. Don't you dare let us down by going off on your own tangent and maybe missing something vital, which," he paused, "could mean getting someone or even yourself murdered! Is that understood?"

"Yes, sir." Morris glanced down at the table for a moment. But he looked up sharply as the DCI began to speak again.

However, this time he was giving out orders to the other detectives.

"Smithers, Jones, get back to the station. Andrews, you get Morris back to his flat and, while he's packing his case, explain the ins and outs of undercover work. I'll catch up with you later."

* * *

Agnes had remained silent while Jones and Smithers gave their report to the DCI. They had eyed her warily when they first sat down. Smithers had stroked his chin, his eyes flitting from her to the DCI as though questioning whether he should proceed with his report with a member of the public present. It was only when Alan had told him to go ahead that he began informing them of what had transpired in the hotel reception.

Agnes had been surprised to learn that Richard Harrison, as he called himself, had suddenly decided to book a room. When Jones had phoned Andrews earlier to say their suspect had entered the hotel, it had crossed her mind that he had gone there on the off-chance of seeing her in one of the public rooms.

However, looking at it from a different angle, it may not have been a sudden decision on Harrison's part. What if Smithers had got it wrong and Harrison had been planning to stay there all along? But, if that was the case, hadn't he left it a little late to book a room? What would he have done if all the rooms had been taken? It would be interesting to see whether he actually did have any luggage. Maybe it would be a good idea if she were to look out for him dragging his suitcase into the hotel. That was the only way she could be certain he had planned to stay at the hotel.

She grimaced. Did she really want to spend the next few hours sitting within sight of the reception area simply to see whether Richard Harrison returned with any luggage? Besides, even if he did, he might simply have gone home and packed a case – assuming he lived nearby. She shook her head in frustration.

"You're very quiet." Alan broke into her thoughts.

Agnes glanced at the empty chairs at the table. She had been so deep in thought, she hadn't heard the detectives leave.

"Yes. Sorry," she said. "That's not like me at all, is it?" She paused. "I was simply thinking everything through. Though quite honestly, none of it makes any sense."

"I could always find another hotel for you," he suggested. He placed his hand on hers. "Agnes, you aren't fooling me. Despite your bravado earlier, I could tell you were concerned about this man. You don't have to stay at the Millennium. There are lots of other hotels in the city and, quite honestly, I would rather you moved somewhere else."

"Yes, I am a little concerned." Agnes swallowed hard. "Well, a lot concerned, actually. The fact he is staying on the floor beneath me doesn't help. Nevertheless, don't you see? Only by me staying on in The Millennium will we find out whether this man really was following me. If so, he will approach me at some point and then we'll know what it is he's after.

"If, on the other hand, he simply decided to stay at this particular hotel on the spur of the moment, he won't be interested in me at all. He'll probably walk past me without showing any sign of recognition. After all," she added, hoping to sway the DCI, "you now have one of your detectives staying there. He'll know what to do should a situation arise."

She was about to end there, but another thought popped into her mind. "I've just thought of something else. Assuming Harrison *did* follow the two of us back to the hotel, he'll have seen us heading across towards Sergeant Andrews in the park, rather than hurrying off to pick up the tour bus you mentioned. From that, he could have put two and two together and twigged that you're both detectives. Maybe it would be best if he didn't see the two of us together until we have a better understanding of who he is and what he's really up to."

Alan remained silent as he thought it through. He couldn't argue with her. She was right on all fronts.

"Alright," he said after a long pause, "on condition that at the first sign of trouble, you leave that hotel. Agreed?"

"I gathered from the way you spoke to Morris, that you would rather have had a different man staying at the hotel," Agnes said. "Why is that?"

Alan noted how swiftly she had moved on to another subject. He would have liked to insist on his condition, but he knew he wouldn't get anywhere. Agnes was a law unto herself. Yet wasn't that what he had always admired about her? Even at school, she'd had a mind of her own.

"Morris is new and, before you say a word, I normally haven't anything against new officers. It's just that this one is rather cocky and thinks he knows it all and…"

"And he rubbed you up the wrong way," Agnes piped up, before he could finish. She laughed. "Best get used to it, Alan. That's the way the world is going these days. Most of the kids of today think they know it all."

"Not just the kids," Alan said.

"Cheeky monkey," she said, with a grin.

Chapter Sixteen

Agnes sorted through her clothes in the wardrobe, trying to decide what to wear for her meal with Alan. In the end, she chose a rather smart, royal blue dress. The colour suited her perfectly and it fitted like a dream.

Undecided as to whether to wear a brooch or a necklace, she decided to wear them both.

Why not? she thought, as she stood back and looked at her reflection in the mirror. *They look good together.* Glancing at her watch, she saw that it was almost time for Alan to pick her up.

After a brief discussion that afternoon, Alan had thought it would be best if they went to a restaurant some distance from the hotel.

Once that had been settled, they agreed to meet outside the hotel at seven-thirty. Alan said he would wait in a taxi around the corner from the hotel – well out of sight of the window of Harrison's room.

Fortunately, with a little diplomacy and smooth-talking, Smithers had managed to find out from the receptionist which room she had given Harrison. From there, he had manoeuvred the conversation around to where it was situated and what view it had of the quayside, by making up a cock and bull story about how his friend Morris would prefer a room overlooking the River Tyne.

Agnes looked at her watch; it was time for her to make her way downstairs. Taking a deep breath, she stepped out into the corridor and, after making sure her door was firmly closed, she made her way towards the lift. The sign above the doors told her the lift was on the ground floor. With a bit of luck, it would be empty when Larry brought it up to the fourth floor.

"Good evening," she said as she stepped inside, "ground floor, please." It was then that she noticed a light in the lift was now showing that it had also been called to the third floor; the very floor where Harrison had been given a room.

"I'm rather late, Larry," she said, looking at her watch. "Could you take straight down before stopping off for the next guest?"

Larry looked at her. "Are you in trouble again?"

"Could be," she said.

"No problem." Without any hesitation, he pressed a button which would override the system and swiftly send the lift to the ground floor.

"Brilliant! Thank you," Agnes said, as the lift came to a halt. "I owe you one."

Once she stepped out of the lift, Agnes hurried towards the main entrance, only pausing for a second to see whether the man in black was hovering around the reception area. Fortunately, there was no sign of him. Outside on the pavement, she quickly made her way around the hotel to where the taxi was waiting and leapt in.

"For goodness' sake, Agnes," Alan exclaimed, as she settled down beside him. "You didn't even stop to make sure this was the right cab. You could have jumped into a car sent to trap you!"

"Don't get into a state, Alan," she replied, calmly. "I could see Ben sitting in the front. Besides, I know the number plate of Ben's taxi off by heart."

Ben didn't say a word as he started the engine and headed off towards the city centre. Nevertheless, even though it was dark, Alan could see the huge grin on Ben's face through the rearview mirror.

Alan had chosen what he understood to be a rather quiet, up-market restaurant on the outskirts of the city centre's heaving night-life.

"It's a good thing I booked a table," he mumbled as they stepped inside. "It seems there are a number of people who prefer to eat in quieter surroundings. I also thought it would have been more stylish..."

Agnes had noticed Alan's swift glance at the other diners before looking down at his own outfit. Though he hadn't gone to the extent of wearing an evening suit, he was very well turned out and was even sporting a bow tie. She guessed he was feeling a little overdressed.

"It's wonderful," she said, "thank you for bringing me here. And, might I add, you are looking extremely smart this evening."

"Thank you," he replied with a smile.

Alan didn't say anything further until they were seated and had been handed the menu.

"Agnes…" He hesitated, as though wondering whether to continue.

"Yes?" she asked, lowering the menu.

"Did you really mean it… you know, when you said you had shortened your stay with your family because of me?" He voice was hesitant. "What I mean is, we didn't really get a chance to talk about it as Harrison suddenly showed up outside the café. After that, everything seemed to go haywire and the subject was left… hanging, if you see what I mean. Once I got back to the station, I couldn't stop thinking about it and wondered whether…" He took a deep breath. "What I mean is…"

"I know what you mean," Agnes interrupted. She leaned across the table and placed her hand over his. "Yes, I meant every word. I really missed you, Alan. Since bumping into you again, my life took on a new meaning. I don't mind admitting, Jim was my life. When he died, part of me died with him. But then something happened when I came back to visit my hometown. Yes, it was wonderful to be back, but it was only when I met you that I realised I was alive, in the here and now."

She paused.

"The problem was, I thought I might be betraying Jim, which was why I kept my distance on my last visit. I believed that by spending some time in Australia I would get over you. I'd come back to England and settle down in my comfortable lifestyle in Essex. But it didn't work out like that. I shortened my trip and, once back in the country, I headed straight here to see you. Even so, I held back from telling you how I really felt. Somehow, I couldn't…"

She paused and looked away.

"But today, just before you arrived at the café, something happened," she continued. She looked back up at Alan. "Something which told me Jim is fine with our relationship." She paused again. "However, I'd rather not talk about it, if you don't mind. That is between Jim and me."

"That's okay, Agnes." Alan reached across the table and placed his hand over hers. "Please understand, I would never ask you to betray anything between you and your late husband. If you are happy and truly believe he is okay with us, then I am grateful to him." He smiled. "Now, would you like to talk about something else?"

"Yes, please," Agnes replied, swiftly.

"May I take your order?"

Neither had noticed the waiter walking towards them.

"Can you give us a few more minutes?" Alan asked

"Certainly, sir," the waiter replied, moving on towards the next table.

She gave Alan a devious smile, before looking back at the menu. "Tell me, have you found out anything further about Richard Harrison since we spoke this afternoon?"

* * *

Morris slowly unpacked his case in his room at the Millennium Hotel. He knew he was only a few doors down the corridor from Agnes Lockwood's room; the very woman who had got him into trouble with his boss. Though, if he was honest, that had been his own fault. He had tried to be clever, but the DCI had not been amused.

However, he was concerned about being in such close proximity to the woman. Random thoughts tumbled through his mind.

Had the DCI told her about his remarks in the incident room? If so, he should apologize and get it over with. But what if his boss had kept quiet about it? She hadn't given anything away when he met her in the café that afternoon. Apologizing for something she knew nothing about would bring the whole stupid episode back out into the open.

Morris had hardly been able to take it in when Smithers had suggested him for the job. He knew this undercover job was a great opportunity to prove he was capable of being a good detective. Nevertheless, delighted as he was at being given this case, he secretly wished it didn't involve Mrs Lockwood in any shape or form.

He sat down heavily on the bed and gave a large sigh. But, after a few minutes' reflection on the instructions his sergeant had drummed into him while he was packing his suitcase, he leapt back to his feet. Andrews had stressed that he shouldn't speak to Mrs Lockwood unless they happened to casually bump into each other in the hotel.

"It is important you give the impression to everyone at the hotel that you don't know each other," Andrews had told him. "In other words, you have never met, nor have you ever heard of, anyone called Agnes Lockwood."

At the time, he had nodded blandly while listening to the sergeant drone on about undercover work. For goodness' sake, he knew all that! He had been told about undercover work and what it entailed during his training. Did Andrews think he was a complete idiot?

Therefore, why was he acting like the new boy on the block? Why was he worried about what Mrs Lockwood might or might not say? If she was half as good as the DCI said, she wouldn't even glance in his direction unless they happened to be thrown together. He needed to get a grip and give his full attention to the job at hand.

With that thought in mind, Morris continued to unpack his case.

Chapter Seventeen

Both Agnes and Alan were enjoying their evening. The food was delicious and, despite the large number of diners, it was quiet in comparison to some of the other restaurants they had dined in. While there was music playing in the background, it wasn't turned up to full volume and they were actually able to hear themselves speak without having to raise their voices too loudly.

All too soon, the evening was over. Alan had arranged for Ben to pick them up from the restaurant at about ten-thirty.

"Don't worry if you're a little late," he had told Ben. "We understand and will be quite happy to wait until you arrive."

Nevertheless, Ben was at the restaurant on time. He popped his head through the door to let Alan know he was there, before disappearing back outside.

"Perhaps I should have given him a later time," Alan said, as he called for the bill. "The evening has passed too quickly."

There was a definite chill in the air as they stepped outside the restaurant and made their way across to the waiting taxi. Yet, for all that, it wasn't quite as cold as it might have been for the time of the year.

"Back to the hotel?" Ben queried, once Agnes and Alan were both seated in the back of his cab.

"Perhaps you could drop us at the bottom of The Side – near Bessie Surtees house," Agnes suggested, before Alan could say a word. "A walk along the quayside would be good."

"It would?" Alan asked, pulling up his coat collar. He didn't sound quite so enthusiastic. "Don't you think it's a little too cold for strolling around the quayside?"

"No, of course it isn't." Agnes hid a smile.

"Okay, Ben, you heard the lady."

Ben nodded and before very long, he pulled up a short distance from Bessie Surtees House.

"Is this okay?" he asked.

"Yes, this is fine, Ben," Agnes said, stepping out of the taxi. "Take care of yourself."

"I will," Ben replied.

Alan handed him the fare and a tip before Ben shot off to look for his next fare.

"Why here?" Alan asked, looking around at the restaurants and clubs.

He clutched the collar of his coat and hunched his shoulders, trying to keep warm. It was even colder down here on the quayside than it had been outside the restaurant and that had been bad enough. He made a mental note to wear a thick scarf in future.

"Because I wanted to see whether the ghost would reappear now that I'm back," Agnes replied.

"The ghost? What ghost?" Alan stared at her.

Agnes gave him a playful punch. "Come on, Alan. You remember, don't you? A ghost appeared up there at the window. It happened just as we found the body on the pavement a few months ago." She pointed towards the window above the plaque on the wall.

Alan remained silent.

"I definitely saw someone up there, Alan. They were closing the window at the time. But we later learned there was definitely no one in the building at the time." Agnes clapped her hands. "Therefore, it must have been a ghost."

"It was a trick of the light," Alan replied.

"So, you're telling me that a trick of the light pulled the window shut?" she retorted.

"Could be!" Alan grinned.

After a further glance at the window, she hooked her arm through his and they began to stroll along the quayside.

"Okay, Alan. But one of these days, you'll find I was right."

"One of these days, I *might* find you were right," he corrected.

They passed a number of people as they slowly made their way towards the hotel. From the sound of their jubilant voices, they appeared to be in good spirits.

As they passed yet another rowdy group, Agnes sighed. "What it is to be young."

"We're not old, Agnes. I guess there's still plenty of life left in us yet," Alan replied. His eyes seemed to be focused on a crowd of people walking towards them.

"Then why are you looking so serious?" she asked. "Don't tell me you're going to arrest them for being happy. They aren't doing any harm."

Following his gaze, she realised he wasn't really looking at the group of people after all. His eyes were fixed on a man some distance behind the joyful throng.

The man was alone. He was leaning against the rail at the edge of the quay and appeared to be lighting a cigarette. However, as they drew closer, it became obvious that the man's attention was focused on something or someone on the other side of the road.

"That's Detective Morris, isn't it?" Agnes said. "Do you think Harrison is over there somewhere?"

"Don't look around." Alan spoke quietly, though there was a ring of urgency in his tone. "If Harrison *is* out there somewhere, we don't want him to know he's being watched."

Agnes glanced back towards the crowd of revellers they had passed only a few short minutes ago. However, by now, the group had almost reached the Tyne Bridge and, as far as she could tell, no one else was heading their way. A swift scan in the opposite direction told her that, for the moment, no one was coming that way, either. She had hoped there might have been another collection of happy people they could have blended in with. But obviously they were on their own.

"Nor do we want him to see me with you here and now," she whispered. She guided him towards the edge of the quayside.

"Agnes! What the hell are you doing?" Though Alan kept his voice low, she could tell he was angry.

"For goodness sake," Alan continued, "Morris might have followed Harrison out here. I need to get you back to the hotel as quickly as possible without him seeing you. If Harrison realizes you are really staying here, he could..." Alan stopped sharply, unable to say the words.

"He could kill me! Is that what you were about to say? He could kill me." Agnes shook her head. "Don't you see, Alan? If he sees you take me into the hotel, he'll know for certain that I'm staying there. How long will it take him to find out which room I'm in and that I'm staying there alone? Once he knows all that, what's to stop him from finding a way to kill me in my room?"

"Okay, okay," Alan said, holding up his hands. "I give in. So what do we do now? In other words, what's your plan?"

"Plan?" Agnes grinned. "What plan? I don't have a plan. Who could plan for a situation like this?"

Not wanting to turn her head, she glanced at Morris out of the corner of her eye. By now, he was puffing on his cigarette and had half turned towards the river.

"Perhaps Morris only came out for a cigarette after all," Agnes continued. "Maybe he thought he saw something but made a mistake, or perhaps you were too quick to jump to a conclusion." She shrugged. "But are you willing to take that chance?"

"Okay," Alan replied. "You're right. There is no way I would gamble with your life. Therefore, what do we do now? Any suggestions?"

"I suggest we call Ben and ask him to pick us up right now and take us both to a quiet hotel elsewhere in the city."

Chapter Eighteen

Alan was the first to awaken the following morning. He looked across the bed towards where Agnes was lying. Her eyes were closed and she was breathing evenly. She was still asleep.

Last night, when she suggested they should both stay in a hotel somewhere else in the city, he had hardly been able to believe it; that was the last thing he had expected to hear. But she had meant it and, once Ben arrived on the scene, it had been her who gave him the instructions. "I'm sure you will know of a hotel with a room to spare – despite the racing season."

To his credit, Ben hadn't batted an eyelid. Perhaps he had expected something like this to happen. Maybe he already thought they were sleeping together; that being the case, last night would not have been a surprise to him.

"If you would you like me to pick you up tomorrow morning, just give me a call," he had said, as he set them down outside the hotel.

Alan looked at his watch; it was almost seven a.m. He would need to get dressed shortly and call Ben. *But what the heck,* he thought, gently placing his arm across Agnes, *the office can wait a few more minutes.*

As he lay, he thought about the night he had just spent with Agnes. It had been one of the most wonderful times of his life – and so unexpected. A few months ago, he would never have believed he would ever meet up again with the girl he'd had a crush on at school all those years ago – let alone sleep with her. Yet it had happened. He had been delighted when she came back north after returning from Australia, but he really never thought it would come to this...

"What time is it?" Agnes said dreamily, breaking into his thoughts.

"A little after seven," Alan replied, removing his arm from around her waist to check his watch. "Sorry, I didn't mean to wake you. I need to get dressed and call Ben to take me back to my place to change for the office."

"So early?"

"Early? This isn't early. I'm usually at my desk by seven-thirty." He paused when he saw her smiling at him. She was fooling him around. "But come to think of it, I'm due to a couple of hours off. I could be a little late this morning..."

* * *

It was almost ten o'clock by the time Alan walked into the office.

Once Ben had dropped him off at his home to change, he had phoned the station saying he would be a little late.

Truthfully, he hadn't felt like going in at all. He would rather have spent the day with Agnes. But there was a murderer to catch and, if this Harrison character had anything to do with it, he wanted to make sure he was caught as quickly as possible – especially as the wretched man was staying at the same hotel as Agnes.

He recalled how, earlier that morning, he had tried once again to talk her into moving into another hotel. He had even suggested the one they had spent the night in. It was clean, a short distance out of the city and certainly not as well-known as The Millennium. But once again, she had refused. Agnes could be very stubborn at times.

He frowned as he remembered how his ex-wife had had a tendency to be stubborn, too. When they were courting, they had got on very well together. It was only after they were married that things began to change. There had been times when her stubbornness really rubbed him up the wrong way, causing them to argue over the most trivial of things.

Yet Agnes couldn't do any wrong in his eyes. No matter how stubborn, awkward or argumentative she could be, he loved her all the more for it.

At that point, he had stopped buttoning his shirt and had sat down on the bed. He loved her. There, he'd said it. Well, he hadn't actually put it into words, but he'd thought it and quite honestly, that was the first time he had admitted it, even to himself. When she went off to Australia, he had feared she might not return to Newcastle and he would never see her again.

Alan dragged himself back to the present. He was on duty and, wherever else he would rather be, he needed to focus on his job. The first thing on his agenda this morning was to contact Morris. He wanted to know whether he had simply strolled outside for a smoke last night, or if there had been a more case-related reason for him to be standing out there in the cold.

He was about to pick up his phone, but stopped when Sergeant Andrews appeared. Maybe he had already heard from the undercover detective.

"Have you heard from Morris?" Alan asked.

"No. Not a word. Would you like me to give him a call?"

"I'll do it," Alan said. "I happened to catch sight of him last night when I was taking Mrs Lockwood back to the hotel. I wasn't sure whether he was simply out there for a smoke, or if he was following our guy. If he *was* trailing him, he was doing a good job. He must have seen Agnes and me, but he gave nothing away."

Alan thought for a moment. "Actually, even if he wasn't trailing our man, he did well by not appearing to recognize me. You never know who is watching."

He picked up his phone and began to punch in the number of Morris's mobile. Once that was done, he looked back at Andrews.

"But I'm surprised he hasn't checked in this morning. You did tell him it was part of the job, to keep in touch at regular intervals?"

"Yes, I explained everything to him while he was packing," Andrews replied.

Alan nodded and held the phone closer to his ear.

At first, there was no reply but, just as he was about to hang up, Morris's voice came down the line. Alan put the phone on speaker.

"Hello, Kate."

Alan glanced across at Andrews and raised his eyebrows.

"Who the hell's Kate?" Alan said, looking back down at the speaker.

"It's so good to hear your voice, Kate."

"I take it Harrison is close by?" Alan said, realizing that it was an awkward moment for Morris.

"Yes, that's right."

"Where are you?" Alan asked.

"I'm in the dining room at the hotel, having breakfast. And, yes, I know it's a little late to be having breakfast, but I decided to take a stroll along the quayside earlier."

"You were watching our man?"

"Yes, that's right and I still am."

"Okay," Alan said. "Leave it there, but don't forget to phone in when you get the chance."

"Yes, I will, Kate. 'Bye for now."

The line went dead.

"I guess we'll just have to wait for his call," Andrews said, with a sigh. He looked back up at the DCI. "By the way, did you enjoy your meal last night? I recall you were trying out a different restaurant – somewhere away from the city centre.

* * *

In the hotel dining room, Morris stuffed his phone back into his pocket. He hadn't been sure whether to answer, not wanting to draw attention to himself. However, as people were turning their heads at the sound of his fun ringtone, he thought he had better answer it.

Earlier, it had crossed his mind to turn off his phone before entering the dining room. But he had forgotten. Therefore when he answered, he'd had to think on his feet, so to speak. Thankfully, DCI Johnson had picked up on the fact the timing was awkward. But 'Kate'! He closed his eyes and shook his head. Surely he could have come up with something better than that. He was going to have to ask his colleagues for help about coded messages while out in the field. But more importantly, he needed to change the damn ringtone.

He was enjoying his breakfast when he saw Agnes walk into the dining room. She stood near the door for a few moments until she was able to catch the eye of one of the waiters.

"Am I too late for breakfast?" she asked.

"Not at all, madam," he said.

Morris watched closely, as the waiter led her to a table only a short distance from where Harrison was sitting.

"Thank you," she said, as the waiter pulled out a chair for her.

Morris was very impressed with the way Mrs Lockwood had walked to her table and sat down without giving a single clue that she recognised Harrison.

She can't have missed seeing him – he was in her direct line of vision as she approached her table, he thought.

Morris was also impressed that she hadn't given a hint that she knew him, either, which was remarkable, to say the least. Most of the people he knew would have given the game away the moment they saw the suspect, let alone the detective watching him.

Suddenly realizing he was still staring at her and that he was the one most likely to let the cat out of the bag, Morris turned his attention to the waiter, who was still standing by her table.

"I'm sorry but, when you have a moment, could I have another pot of tea, please?" he asked. "The bacon is a little salty this morning,"

The idea was to lead Harrison into believing he had been waiting for an opportunity to call the waiter. The added remark was simply to ease the tension a little.

"Of course, sir," the waiter replied in a dull tone. "I will also inform the chef of your complaint."

"Toad!" Morris muttered to himself, as the waiter strode off towards the kitchen. *Can't anyone take a joke any more?*

Nevertheless, his ruse seemed to have worked. Harrison gave him a sympathetic smile before turning back to his own breakfast.

But then another thought struck Morris; Harrison hadn't really taken any interest in Mrs Lockwood when she was led to the table near him. Either he was darn good at hiding his innermost thoughts, or he was totally innocent.

Being this close to the suspect, Morris was tempted to keep his eyes on him for the rest of the meal. The man might do something to give himself away. But then he thought better of it, as he would very probably give *himself* away! Nevertheless, before turning away, there was one thing he noticed… but before he could give it any further thought, the waiter arrived with his fresh pot of tea.

"Your tea, sir, and chef apologizes for the bacon. It seems we have a new supplier. Hopefully, once he has a word with them things will get better."

"Thank you," Morris replied.

He was tempted to add that he hadn't really been complaining, but decided to leave it there. Why dig himself a deeper hole?

At that point, Morris saw Mrs Lockwood call the waiter across to her table. He heard her place an order for the full English breakfast. "And a large pot of tea, please," she added.

"Very good, madam."

Once the waiter had disappeared, Morris saw Agnes open the newspaper she had been carrying when she walked into the dining room.

She's a very attractive lady, Morris thought, as he watched her leaf through the pages. *It's little wonder that the DCI couldn't resist allowing her to meddle in the case last year.*

Morris was still watching her, when, out of the corner of his eye, he saw Richard Harrison preparing to leave. Could he be going back up to his room to collect something, or would he walk straight through reception and out onto the quayside?

Morris was in a dilemma. He needed to know where Harrison was going. But at the same time, he knew he couldn't leap out of his seat and follow the suspect.

Harrison stood up and began to walk towards the door. Though Morris was giving the impression he was focusing on his breakfast, he was still keeping an eye on him. Yet, he wasn't sure what he was going to do once Harrison had left the dining room. If he was seen out in the reception area, Harrison would know that he was being watched. If he stayed seated, he would have no idea where the suspect had gone.

Suddenly, Morris noticed Agnes was looking at him. Though her hands were still resting on the newspaper in front of her, she seemed to be discreetly pointing at something. For a moment, he wasn't sure what she was getting at until he realised she was directing his attention to the large mirrors on the walls.

There were several mirrors placed in different parts of the public rooms. He had noticed them before but hadn't really taken them seriously into account until now. Depending on the angle of the mirror you were looking at, you could see various reflections of the reception area.

Why the hell hadn't he seen that? And he was supposed to be a detective! Morris scolded himself as he continued to watch Harrison ambling towards the main entrance. Wherever the man was going, he certainly didn't seem to be in any hurry.

His eyes still fixed on the mirror, Morris sat back in his chair. He decided his best option was to wait until Harrison was safely through the door and out onto the quayside before making a move. There was always the chance that he might suddenly remember he needed something from his room and start heading back towards the lift.

Once he was sure Harrison was clear of the building, he rose to his feet and left the dining room.

* * *

Meanwhile, the DCI was frustrated at there being no further news regarding the murder of the body found in the park. So far, everyone on the team had drawn a blank.

Not one of the jewellery shops in the city centre had a record of anyone placing an order for the cufflinks and tiepin like the ones found in the park. This meant they would need to look farther afield.

Doctor Nichols had failed to find anything further to help the investigation. Although the last paragraph in his report had set minds in motion

The heart, liver and kidneys had all been stabbed several times by the killer. It could be likened to a frenzied attack, except it appears the killer knew exactly where these organs were located. It could be that the other random stabbings to the body, including the slashes made to the throat and face, were simply to mislead the police.

Did that mean the killer could be a doctor or a nurse? Or was it someone who had looked up what they needed to know on the internet?

Alan had hoped someone would have been reported missing by now. Yet no one had come forward. At least, if they knew the name of the victim, they would have somewhere to start the investigation instead of twiddling their thumbs. He had instructed the officers at local police stations to inform him immediately if a member of the public even hinted that a friend or relative was missing.

Normally, the police tended not to take these matters too seriously until a person had been missing for almost forty-eight hours. Very often, the 'missing' person turned up the next day, with a monstrous hangover. But this was different. There was a body lying in the morgue without a face and he needed to know who it was.

Yet there was another reason why this case was top priority – a more important reason as far as he was concerned. He needed to know whether the man he saw in the park was the killer – especially as the man in question was staying under the same roof as Agnes.

Sergeant Andrews was watching his boss. He knew he was troubled about this case, but today he looked even more disturbed. It wasn't hard to understand why: the main suspect was staying at the same hotel as Mrs Lockwood. However, they did have a detective on the premises, although Morris wasn't the first person either of them would have chosen for the job.

"Did you enjoy your evening?" Andrews repeated the question he had asked a few minutes earlier. "You said you were going to a restaurant away from the city highlife."

"Yes, thank you. Sorry, I started thinking about the case and forgot you were there. We both enjoyed the meal. Actually, you should try it sometime. I think you would like it. It was quiet and relaxing."

Andrews pulled a face. "Quiet is not really my thing."

"No, don't get me wrong. It was busier than I thought it would be, but there wasn't loud music blaring out all evening. The music was soft and at least we could talk over it."

"I'll think about it," Andrews said.

Alan looked at his watch. "I wish Morris would get in touch with us. All this waiting around is driving me nuts."

Just then the phone rang.

"Johnson," Alan said into the mouthpiece.

"It's Morris here."

"First of all, Morris, where are you?" Alan quickly set the phone on speaker.

He had learned over the years that it was wise to find out where his men were when they rang in. One officer had been cut off one day and Alan hadn't known where to start looking for him.

"I'm in the Baltic Art Gallery. Harrison met up with a woman at the entrance. At the moment, they are both upstairs looking at the various displays."

Alan was about to say something, but Morris continued speaking. "There aren't many people in here at the moment, so it's a little difficult for me to keep him in view without him seeing me."

"Were you following him last night when I saw you on the quayside?" Alan asked.

There was silence.

"Are you still there?" Alan asked, desperately trying to stay patient.

"Yes. Sorry, sir. Harrison has moved into another room. About last night, yes, I followed him outside. He slunk off into the shadows, but I could still see him. He met a woman. That's when I turned away. It was too dark for me to see her clearly, but I think it's the same woman he's with now."

"So what happened next?" Alan didn't want to sound as though he was hounding the detective, but he needed more information before Morris shut down his phone.

"Nothing happened. Harrison was still talking to the woman when I turned and glanced back in their direction.

"What's Harrison doing now?" Alan asked.

"They've started walking… hang on a minute." There was a pause.

"What the hell is he doing now?" Alan yelled.

"They were walking towards where I'm hiding," Morris said in an undertone, "but they stopped to look at something else."

Morris paused for a second. "Look, I'll have to hang up. I need to get into another room before he sees me."

"Okay, but keep us up to date."

Chapter Nineteen

Once Morris had disappeared from the dining room, Agnes couldn't help thinking about the case. Alan had made it plain that he wanted her to stay away from the investigation.

"That's Morris's job," he had told her. "Leave it to him."

However, she hadn't actually agreed to sit this one out. Instead, she had changed the subject; not wanting to make a promise she knew she wouldn't keep. Surely there was something she could do – even if she were only able to supply the police with the odd scrap of information?

She glanced across to where Harrison had been having breakfast. The waiter hadn't yet cleared the table and when she saw his used cutlery lying on the plate, she suddenly had an idea.

Agnes looked around the dining room. Thankfully, most of the guests had now left. There were only two tables still in use and the people at those were engrossed in their newspapers. The waiter serving this area of the dining room had disappeared into the kitchen. However, he could reappear at any time to clear away the two tables near her. She needed to act swiftly, though discreetly, if her idea was going to work.

Once she was safely outside the dining room, Agnes gave herself a thumb's up. She'd done it. No one had noticed her removing the used cutlery from Harrison's table. Using a clean tissue from her handbag, she had managed to pick it up without adding her prints.

Now, all she needed to do was to get the evidence to Alan. Surely his team would be able to pick up the fingerprints from the knife and fork. Though, on reflection, they might have to eliminate the prints of the waiter who had set the table earlier that morning. Why was everything so complicated? Still, she couldn't think of everything.

By now, Agnes had almost reached her room. It was time to start planning what she was going to do after her visit to the police station. It was raining heavily this morning. Maybe it would be a good day to visit the Eldon Square shopping centre.

She had planned to go back there after her first visit a few months ago, yet she had never got around to it. Besides, Alan would be pleased to know that she was staying well away from Richard Harrison today.

The sudden thought of Alan drew her mind back to the previous evening.

Even now, she couldn't believe the idea to spend the night together had come from her lips. The idea had floated through her mind when they were standing together on the quayside. But she hadn't expected to hear herself say it out loud. It wasn't the sort of suggestion that came from a lady. On the other hand, perhaps it was in this day and age. This was the twenty-first century. Anyway, before she'd had time to think about it, the offer was out in the open.

However, there was something else she was going to have to think about over the coming days and weeks. She needed to tell her two sons the truth about Alan. When she was with them in Australia, she had only spoken of Alan in his official capacity: the detective in charge of a murder case.

But now that things between Alan and herself had moved to another level, both Jason and William ought to know. There had never been any secrets in the family and she didn't want to start now.

Thinking about Alan reminded her they were having dinner together again this evening. How nice it would be if they could dine in the hotel. They could even relax afterwards in the drawing room, before slipping upstairs to the comfort of her room. It sounded blissful; almost like an old movie.

However, she brought herself down to earth with a bump when she realized that dining in the hotel was out of the question. Harrison could be there and the last thing they wanted was for him to see them together.

Inside her room, she glanced at the note which had been slipped under her door. It was to inform the guests about the race meetings at Gosforth Park this week. She couldn't recall ever having gone there before. Truthfully, she wasn't really a horse-racing fan, but there were a few other things going on this week. She could blend in with the crowds of people and it would give her the chance to forget all about 'the man in black'.

She smiled to herself. *How strange I should still call him 'the man in black', even though I now know him as 'Richard Harrison'.*

She set the notice down on the dressing table. It would be something to go to another day – a day when it wasn't raining.

She called Ben and, after asking him to pick her up in the next fifteen minutes or so, she pulled a raincoat from the wardrobe and set off downstairs.

Ben dropped her off at the police station. She told him to wait, as her visit wouldn't take long. As it turned out, she was back in the cab after only a few minutes. The DCI and his sergeant were in a meeting, so she left the cutlery with another detective, telling her why she thought it might help them with the case.

She would like to have seen Alan again, if only for a few minutes, but she didn't want to keep Ben waiting too long. He would be losing money, as he had probably turned off the meter the moment he pulled up outside.

Shortly afterwards, Agnes arrived at the Eldon Square shopping centre. Ben told her to give him a call when she'd had enough and wanted to go back to the hotel.

"Had enough?" Agnes queried. "I adore shopping. You'll have to drag me away."

He laughed and gave her a wave as he drove away.

* * *

Agnes enjoyed her day at the shopping mall. She bought two dresses and a trouser suit. It had been some years since she had last worn trousers, but she loved the suit the moment she laid eyes on it.

She had lunch in a rather nice restaurant, before wandering around a few more shops in the mall. It was around four in the afternoon when she suddenly realised she was beginning to feel tired. Maybe it was time to go back to the hotel and put her feet up and relax for a while before Alan called to take her to dinner.

* * *

DCI Johnson's day wasn't going well. Harrison and the woman he was with had hung around the Baltic Art Gallery for quite some time. Either they were really interested in the arts, or they had picked up on the fact that Morris was following them and they were taking great pleasure in giving him the runaround.

The young detective had rung in at one point, but only to say that the couple had left the gallery and he was still on their trail. However, it turned out they had only gone from one building to another, as the next call from Morris was to inform the DCI that they were all now in the Sage.

Furthermore, there was still no information on the identity of their victim. Surely someone out there must have realised he was missing – unless, of course, he had been a visitor to England; either a tourist or on a business trip.

"Now, as if things aren't bad enough, Superintendent Blake has requested the pleasure of my company immediately after lunch," Alan told his sergeant, after putting down the phone.

Both he and Andrews had been mulling over the case when the phone rang.

"Requested the pleasure of your company?" Andrews raised his eyebrows.

"Well, he didn't use those words, but it means the same thing." Alan pulled a face. "He probably wants to know how the case is going and I can't tell him a damn thing." He paused to look at his watch. "Come on, get your coat."

"Where're we going?" Andrews leapt to his feet and grabbed his jacket.

"To the pub, I could do with a pint."

Chapter Twenty

During breakfast the following morning, Agnes pondered over the previous evening. She and Alan had dined together at a restaurant in the city. The restaurant had been pleasant enough, though it lacked the intimacy of the one they had used the night before. Or, might it simply have seemed that way due to Alan's frustration at the lack of evidence in his ongoing murder inquiry?

She couldn't really blame him. She would feel much the same if she were in his shoes. Come to think of it, she did feel the same and she wasn't even involved in the case – well, not officially, anyway.

At one point during the evening, Alan had mentioned being called to appear in front of the new superintendent earlier that day. From what he had told her, she gathered the interview hadn't gone well.

"At first, I tried to stay calm," Alan had told her. "I explained how even the stab wounds had been made by different knives, which means we weren't looking for one knife in particular, but several."

Apparently, the interview had droned on until Alan had stormed out of the office, slamming the door shut behind him. "I lost it," he had said.

Superintendent Blake! Agnes thought. *All you do is sit around your office fiddling with a pen and hope one of your officers is going to come up with the answers so you'll look good.*

Agnes picked up her cup and took a sip of tea. Maybe she was being a little hard on the superintendent. He must have been a constable at some time in his life; surely he knew what it was like, trying to find evidence when there was none to be found?

But then another thought popped into her head. If he had been through it all, the wretched man should empathize with his officers. Roll up his sleeves and help his men, rather than shift blame.

Pushing the thoughts from her mind, she looked around the dining room. Though she had arrived late, there had been quite a number of people still having breakfast when she walked in. But now there were only four left. If Harrison and Morris had breakfasted here, they must have left before she arrived. There was no point in her trying to catch up on their whereabouts. They could be anywhere by now.

She glanced out of the window, wondering what she was going to do with herself today. At least it was dry and the sun was making an effort to penetrate through the clouds rolling above the River Tyne.

She could go for a walk, or she could call Ben and ask him to take her to Low Fell, an area in Gateshead where she had been born. She had gone there on her last visit to Tyneside but hadn't managed to see everything.

Her mind almost made up, she recalled the leaflet lying on her dressing table. Hadn't it said something about an event at Gosforth Park Racecourse? It was only a week-long event, so perhaps she should go there today. Low Fell would still be there another day.

That decided, she went up to her room, phoned Ben and sorted out what she should wear. She would definitely need something warm.

* * *

Once Ben had dropped her off at the racecourse, Agnes made her way into the grounds. She had expected it to be busy, but not quite as hectic as this. With the schools on holiday, there were lots of young children chasing each other around, while others enjoyed the various fun rides.

As she carried on walking towards the racecourse, she made up her mind to have a flutter on one of the races, even though she knew nothing about how to go about it. She joined a queue at the stand of one of the turf accountants. There were several with shorter queues, but, after glancing down the course, the face of the man taking bets at this one looked kinder than some of the others. He might be more under-standing and explain everything more slowly.

Even so, she still hoped no one would join the queue behind her too quickly, as they might become impatient.

It seemed to take ages for the queue to move along. But at long last, she could see a light at the end of the tunnel; there were only three people in front of her. It shouldn't be long now and, thankfully, there was still no one behind her. The man at the head of the queue had finished placing his bet and was about to move away.

Only two more to go, Agnes thought, as she inched closer to her goal.

But then, as the man moved out of the queue, he swung his head around and she saw it was none other than 'the man in black', Richard Harrison himself.

How could she have missed that coat? The very coat which had given him away only a couple of days ago!

She quickly lowered her head, desperately hoping he hadn't spotted her standing there in full view. However, it appeared she needn't have worried; his attention seemed to be drawn elsewhere.

"Excuse me, are you in the queue?"

Agnes was startled at the sudden sound of the voice from behind. She had been so engrossed in keeping an eye on the suspect, she hadn't noticed the queue had moved up one, or that someone had appeared behind her. She swung around to find a woman clutching a twenty-pound note in her hand.

"Yes, no, I'm sorry. Yes, I was. But I see my friend has already placed our bet over there." Agnes waved her hand in the general direction of another bookmaker further down the course and swiftly slipped out of the queue.

Despite the interruption, she hadn't lost sight of Harrison. He was heading in the direction of the grandstand. There were a great number of people over there. She needed to start moving or else she might lose sight of him in the crowd.

She had only taken a couple of steps when someone stumbled into her. The jolt was so hard that she toppled, causing her lose her grip on her handbag. It fell to the ground; its contents spilling out onto the damp turf.

Chapter Twenty-One

"Are you sure about that, Morris?"

The DCI had just heard that Agnes Lockwood was watching their suspect at the Gosforth Race Course.

"I mean, couldn't you be mistaking this person for her?"

Alan glanced at his sergeant and shrugged. "He could be wrong," he whispered.

The phone was on speaker. Therefore Andrews could hear what Morris was saying.

"No, it's definitely Mrs Lockwood. I saw her while having breakfast at the hotel yesterday morning."

Still looking at Andrews, Alan raised his eyes towards the ceiling.

"What's she doing now?" Alan asked, looking back down at the phone.

"Nothing… She's still watching Harrison." He paused. "No, wait! He's going off somewhere and I think she is about to follow him."

"Stop her!" Alan yelled.

"But I was told I shouldn't make contact with Mrs Lockwood. It could blow my cover."

"I don't care what you were told, Morris. I'm giving you a direct order. Do whatever it takes to stop her from following Harrison." Alan ran his fingers through his hair in frustration. "Do you understand?"

"Sir…" Andrews tried to intervene.

However, the DCI held up his hand, preventing him from saying anything further.

"Do you understand, Morris?" DCI Johnson repeated.

"Yes, sir," the detective replied, before hanging up.

"Damn!" Morris muttered. "The first chance I get to go undercover and I have to blow it after a couple of days."

He was still watching Mrs Lockwood. She had only started to make a move and seemed to be fumbling around with her handbag. Was there a way he could stop her without actually having to give himself away?

Morris set off walking towards her. However, as he drew closer, he placed his phone to his ear.

"Hello," he said into the phone. He spoke loudly, so that anyone in close proximity would think he had just received a call from someone in the crowd. "Yes, I'm at Gosforth Park now. Where are you?"

By now, he was close to Mrs Lockwood. He swung around, as though he was looking for the person on the other end of the phone. But, at the same time, he took the opportunity to bump sharply into Mrs Lockwood and knock her handbag to the ground.

"I'm terribly sorry, madam," he said, making a big thing of bending down to pick up her bag.

He looked up at her so that she would recognize him.

"I was talking on the phone and didn't see you standing there."

"It's quite alright," Agnes replied, recognizing the undercover detective in an instant. "It's rather busy here today, isn't it?"

She bent down to help him gather up the things, which had scattered from her handbag.

"Yes, it is," Morris replied. He lowered his tone. "The DCI doesn't want you to follow Harrison."

"How does he know I'm here?" She closed her eyes for a second and shook her head. "There's no need to answer that, detective. I get it, you told him."

Morris nodded. "I was already on the phone to him when you popped into view."

All the while they were talking, Morris's eyes were fixed on the suspect.

Fortunately, Harrison hadn't looked around; he seemed focused on something ahead of him.

"I'd best get after him," Morris added. "I suggest you contact the DCI and reassure him you're okay."

He raised his voice, for the benefit of anyone passing by, to apologize again before moving away.

Agnes was about to call Alan when her phone began to ring. Alan's name appeared on the screen.

"Yes, Alan, I'm okay," she said before he could say a word. "I was just about to call you."

"Thank goodness for that. Is Morris there?"

Agnes couldn't fail to detect the note of relief in Alan's voice.

"No. He's tailing Richard Harrison."

She quickly explained what had happened. "No doubt Morris will be in touch with you at some point."

"So, what are you going to do now?"

"First, I'm going to put a bet on a horse, which is what I was going to do before I spotted Harrison," Agnes replied, slowly. "Then, I'm going to find the bar and have a stiff gin and tonic!"

"Agnes, get away from there. You could be in danger," Alan pleaded.

"For goodness' sake, Alan, there are so many people around, I doubt I will even see Harrison again today. By the way, were you able to get any prints from the cutlery I dropped off yesterday?" Agnes added changing the subject.

"They're still with the forensic team at the moment. But stop trying to change…"

Agnes didn't hear any more. She had already closed her phone and was heading back towards the friendly-faced turf accountant.

* * *

Sergeant Andrews was grinning when the DCI put down his phone.

"I guess Mrs Lockwood isn't about to leave the racecourse anytime soon."

"No." Alan looked back down at his phone in disbelief. "She's just hung up on me," he grumbled. "I'm only trying to look out for her. Yet she hung up on me. She seems to think I'm always telling her what she should do."

"Well, in a way, I suppose you are and…" Andrews paused, wondering whether to go on.

"And?" Alan prompted.

The sergeant lifted one shoulder. "And women don't like to be told what to do."

"I suppose you know all about women, Sergeant!"

"No, not everything. But I've sure as hell learned they don't like being told what to do."

Alan didn't reply. He merely waited for Andrews to continue.

The sergeant fumbled for a long moment with the paperwork on his desk.

"Okay, we both know that I've messed up in the past," he said at last. "Yes, I tried to be the 'one that knew it all' when I became a detective." He made quotation marks in the air as he spoke. "But I think I'm past that now."

He screwed up his face.

"Hang on a minute, sir," he added, wagging his finger at his DCI. "Wasn't it you who advised me to stop trying to be top dog by telling my girlfriends what they should and shouldn't do?"

"Well, it worked, didn't it? I understand you and Sandra are getting on really well." There was a twinkle in the DCI's eye as he spoke.

"Yes, it did, and we are," Andrews agreed.

A glazed expression spread over the sergeant's face as he thought of Sandra. She was the most wonderful woman he had ever met. He loved her so much. He had already bought the ring and was planning to pop the question very soon.

"Are you alright, Michael?"

The sound of the DCI's voice hauled Andrews back into the office and reason for this conversation.

"Yes, sorry, sir." Andrews coughed. "All I was trying to say is, aren't you behaving the same way with Mrs Lockwood? If you had your way, she wouldn't leave the hotel."

"I'm not as bad as that!" Alan replied, slowly. "Am I?

He looked at his sergeant. "It's just that I can't help worrying about her." He paused. "Wherever she goes, she seems to find trouble."

"Yes." Andrews nodded thoughtfully. "I can't argue with that."

Chapter Twenty-Two

Agnes was feeling rather pleased with herself. Her horse had come in second, so now she had some money coming her way. The kind-faced man, wearing a heavy overcoat, a thick scarf and a rather well-worn trilby hat, had patiently explained the procedure; suggesting that, as she was new to horse-racing, she should back the horse both ways.

She tilted her head to one side as she looked through the list of horses running in the next race. 'Studying the form', the man had called it. "You need to check how the horses and riders did on previous days."

Still befuddled by the information given on the racing card, she decided to choose a horse simply by its name; whether it sounded fun, appealing, or even cuddly. It seemed to work as, a short while later, she headed back to the bookmaker again to collect more of her winnings.

"Are you sure you're new to this?" He winked, before delving around in a bag to bring out a handful of notes.

"Yes, absolutely," she replied.

"Well, please don't tell anyone the secret of your success. It could cost me a fortune." He counted out two hundred pounds and placed it in her hand.

"Thank you. I've had so much fun today," she said, tucking the money carefully into her bag. "I think I'll find the bar and have a drink, before calling a cab."

Agnes was enjoying a large gin and tonic when she felt a tap on her shoulder. For a brief instant, she thought Alan had popped up to the racecourse to surprise her and there was a huge grin on her face when she swung around to greet him. However, the grin swiftly faded when her eyes fell on Richard Harrison. She was so taken aback, it took her a few moments to realise he wasn't alone. There was a woman standing next to him.

"Are they vacant?" Harrison pointed towards to the two seats on the other side of the table.

"Er, yes," she replied, trying to pull herself together. "Help yourself. I'll be off shortly, anyway."

While the couple were making themselves comfortable, Agnes took the opportunity to glance around the room. She had expected to find most of the seats taken. However, she was surprised to find there were several empty tables. She also hoped to see Morris, but there was no sign of him.

"Didn't I see you at the hotel yesterday morning?" Harrison enquired, once he and his friend were settled in their seats.

"Did you?" Agnes replied, raising her eyebrows. She had learned from an old friend that, if you were ever in doubt about someone, you should answer their question with a further question and watch their reaction.

It seemed to work, as there was a pause before Harrison replied

"Yes," he said, at last. "At least, I think it was you," he added.

Agnes shrugged.

He glanced towards the woman sitting next to him almost as though he was hoping she would help him out. However, she remained silent.

He shifted uneasily in his chair.

While all this shuffling was going on, Agnes took the opportunity to make a mental note of them both. Though she had seen Harrison at breakfast the day before, she had thought it best not to look at him to too closely at that time.

However, today was different. He had approached her and was now trying to start a conversation. Therefore, why not use it to her advantage?

Looking across the table, she surmised he was around her age or maybe a little younger. It was hard to put an exact age on him. Nevertheless, whatever his age, he was a rather attractive man; or he would be, if it wasn't for his piercing eyes. Even when he wasn't looking in her direction, she could sense those eyes probing her every move.

She hastily turned her attention to the woman.

Before the couple had sat down, Agnes had already noted that the woman was slightly taller than Harrison. Now, on closer inspection, she could see that her brown eyes matched the colour of her hair. Her makeup was immaculate; perhaps she had arrived at the racecourse immediately after a visit to her local beauty parlour.

Though the woman appeared to be carrying a little extra weight, her elegant blue dress hid it well. Draped around her shoulders was an expensive coat and her large, elegant handbag was certainly not the sort that you would find in a chain store. To top it off, the hint of a luxurious perfume wafted across the table.

Yet, despite all the pizazz, there was something about this woman that troubled Agnes. Though, at this stage, she couldn't put her finger on what it was.

"Perhaps I should introduce you to Joanne," Harrison said. "Joanne isn't staying at the hotel. She's my sister-in-law and lives in the area."

"I see. And you are?" Agnes asked. Even though she knew the name he had given at the hotel, she was playing the innocent.

"My name is Harrison – Richard Harrison. Pleased to meet you." He held out his hand across the table. "At last," he added, as he took her hand.

She wanted to ask what he meant by that statement, but decided to stick with her earlier plan; answer a question, with another question.

"At last?" Agnes queried.

"Doesn't my name mean anything to you?" Harrison asked.

By now, Agnes was beginning to feel uneasy. Harrison was her maiden name, but her father was an only child. She didn't have any relatives on his side of the family.

But then, out of the corner of her eye, she suddenly spotted Morris sitting at a table behind Harrison and felt a little better. If necessary, he would call in some help.

Composing herself, Agnes lifted one shoulder. "Should it?"

"What's your name?" Harrison asked.

"Why do you want to know?"

"Because I think we are related."

"If you think we're related, then you must already know my name," Agnes retorted.

"I just want to be sure."

Agnes stood up and picked up her handbag. "My name is Agnes Lockwood. Now, if you don't mind, I'm leaving."

"But what was your name before you were married?" Harrison said. He rose to his feet and grabbed her arm. "Damn it, woman! What was your maiden name?"

Caught off guard, she hesitated for one brief moment. But then she glimpsed Morris. "Morrison!" she lied. "My name was Agnes Morrison. Now take your hands off me."

Harrison glanced around at the people in the bar. Seeing that some were staring in their direction, he released her arm and sank back into his chair.

By now Morris was on his feet. However, he sat down again when Agnes indicated with a slight shake of her head that he should not intervene.

"Mrs Lockwood, sit down for a minute," Joanne said, pointing towards the chair. It was the first time the woman had spoken. She had a low, husky voice and Agnes wondered if she was a heavy smoker.

"Why should I?" Agnes said. "Give me one good reason why I shouldn't call the police right now?"

"Because Richard believes you are his sister. Or perhaps I should say his half-sister," Joanne replied.

"Very well," Agnes said, lowering herself back into her seat.

Now she was ready to listen. Harrison was getting to the point of why he was following her. But she needed to be on her guard.

"However, be aware that at the first sign of any provocation from Mr Harrison, I'm calling the police." Agnes pulled out her phone and placed it on the table in front of her to emphasize her point.

"Agreed," Joanne said.

Richard Harrison was still slumped in his chair. He hadn't uttered a word since Agnes had given him a false name.

Agnes took a deep breath. "Now, what's this all about?" she asked.

She looked at Joanne. "Sister-in-law… that would mean your name is Harrison, too."

"No." Joanne replied. "It's Lyman."

"I'm sorry, I don't understand." Agnes looked puzzled.

"I'm Richard's half sister-in-law, if there is such a term," Joanne began to explain. "I'm married to his half-brother, Joe. Richard was born after his mother had a brief fling with a man who turned out to be married. When the man heard about the baby, he refused to leave his wife. I understand he never ever saw his son. However, he must have felt guilty, as he sent money regularly to support him."

Joanne glanced at Richard. Though he appeared to be listening to the conversation, he made no attempt to join in.

"Later, Richard's mother met another man, who she married and they had two children," Joanne continued. "The three children got on well together, but Richard was different from the other two. He was more studious. His head was always stuck in a book."

Joanne paused. "Anyway, to cut a long story short, one day Richard's mother told him that her husband wasn't his biological father and since that day, he's been trying to find out who his real father was. Obviously, his mother helped him as much as she could, but she had no idea what had happened to his father. Once he said he didn't want to know his son, she never heard from him again."

"But where did the money come from?" Agnes asked. "I mean, if he was sending money, surely Richard's mother could have picked up something from the envelope?"

"Richard's father had set up a bank account in his name. Money was deposited in the account every month and his mother collected it. The bank informed her of the arrangement, but they wouldn't tell her exactly where it came from." Joanne shrugged. "We all – by that, I mean the family – believed it was part of the deal he had with the bank."

Agnes looked thoughtful as she sat back in her seat and stared at Richard.

"So where do I fit into all this? What led you to me? Why would you even think I am your half-sister?"

Agnes looked from one to the other as she waited for a reply to her questions. When Joanne first began telling her why Richard had been keen to meet up with her, Agnes hadn't been too interested. Yet, as the story unfolded, she had become curious. But now she was angry. How on earth could Harrison believe her wonderful father had been involved in some cheap, sordid love affair with his mother? Her father had been a loving, caring man.

When her question remained unanswered, Agnes tried again.

"Look, I can understand you trying to find out more about your past. Heck, I came back here to Tyneside last year to catch up with mine."

"Not quite the same thing, though – is it?" Richard said.

"No, I suppose not." She paused. "What was your father's name?" Agnes asked, trying to show a little interest.

"Derek," Richard replied. "Derek Harrison. Does that mean anything to you?"

For split second, Agnes was taken aback. Derek Harrison was her father's name.

"No," she said hastily. "You have the wrong person."

Agnes glanced over towards the door. Now would be a good time to leave. She had denied everything. But by now, her curiosity was nagging at her.

She turned back to face Richard. Over his shoulder, she could see Morris sitting at the table behind. He wasn't near enough to hear every word, but she would only need to raise her voice a little if there was any trouble.

"However, before I go, I would still like know how you thought I was your half-sister. I mean, you didn't know my name, or my father's Christian name."

"It was purely by chance. My brother happened to see your picture in a newspaper last year and he thought there was a resemblance to my father. He emailed me a copy of the photo so that I could check it out."

Agnes was about to interrupt, but he held up his hand.

"You're wondering how I know what my father looks like. Well, I have an old photograph of him. My mother took it without his knowledge when she realised he was leaving her stranded. She wanted it for me."

"But he didn't leave her stranded, did he?" Agnes said, quietly.

"No, but she didn't know that at the time."

"Have you got the photo with you?" Agnes asked.

"Yes." Richard reached into his pocket and pulled out a photograph.

Agnes swallowed hard as she watched him slide the picture across the table towards her. This was the moment when she could honestly deny that the man Harrison had referred to was really her father. Slowly, she stretched across the table and picked it up.

The black and white picture showed a man standing by a car. He was wearing a dark jacket with light coloured trousers. Peering closer, she saw that the man was smiling broadly at the camera with one arm resting on the roof of the car.

Agnes couldn't make out where the photo had been taken. She certainly didn't recognize the scenery in the background. Nevertheless, there was no mistaking the fact that the face of the man in the photograph was that of her father.

Until the moment she saw her father's face staring back at her from the picture, Agnes had stayed composed. Now, she felt sick. Yet, there was no way she was going let Harrison know he was right; not until she had more proof.

"Your father was a very handsome man," she said, placing the photograph back down on the table.

All Agnes wanted to do now was to get back to the hotel and think this through. Yet, to suddenly stand up and leave would indicate that she had lied about the photo.

Though she looked calm, by now Agnes's mind was racing. There had to be another explanation as to why Richard's mother had told him the man in the picture was his father. Maybe she had taken a photo of the first person she saw on the street one day, simply so her son could show his friends at school.

"What are you going to do if you find your father?" Agnes asked.

"I don't know. I would just like him to know that I did well on my own."

"Yes, I understand."

Agnes picked up her phone and placed it back in her handbag. "If you don't mind, I'm going now," she said, as she rose to her feet.

Richard stood up and held out his hand. "I'm sorry about earlier – you know, when I grabbed your arm."

"Apology accepted." Agnes smiled and shook his hand.

Looking over Richard's shoulder, she saw Morris had moved to another table a little further away.

Outside the bar, Agnes took out her phone and called Ben. She asked him to pick her up at the same spot he had dropped her off earlier that day.

There were still some children on the roundabouts and swings as Agnes made her way to the entrance. However, she didn't really notice them. All she wanted to do was get back to her room and burst into tears. Her world had fallen apart when Jim died and though it had started to pick up again recently, this afternoon it had been shattered all over again.

* * *

Back in the bar at the racecourse, Morris waited until Harrison had ordered another drink before he took out his phone to call the DCI.

Alan set the phone to the speaker so his sergeant could listen to the call.

Morris quickly explained how he had followed the suspect and a woman into the bar only to find Mrs Lockwood sitting in there.

"Even though there were plenty of tables free, Harrison and the woman made a beeline for her table."

He went on to tell the DCI how he was unable to hear all that was said. "However, it got a little nasty at one point, when voices were raised. I really thought I was going to have to intervene when Harrison grabbed her arm. She told him to leave her alone, which he did, but only after she gave him her maiden name. 'Morrison', she told him firmly."

There was silence at the other end of the line.

"Are you still there?" Morris asked.

"Yes," Alan replied. "What's Harrison doing now?"

"He's still here in the bar. He ordered another drink for himself and the woman he's with."

"Good work, Morris. Stick with him. Don't let him out of your sight."

* * *

DCI Johnson was thoughtful as he switched off the speaker.

"How strange that Harrison should want to know Mrs Lockwood's maiden name," said Andrews.

"Yes, it is," he said slowly. "Very strange." Alan looked at his sergeant. "We really need to know more about this man. Have we had anything back on the fingerprints taken from the cutlery?"

Andrews told him there hadn't been any report so far. "I'll go downstairs and see whether I can hurry them along."

Once Andrews had left the office, Alan continued to dwell on something Morris had reported – 'she told him her maiden name was Morrison'.

Yet, Alan knew for a fact her maiden was Harrison. They were at school together, after all! However, since they had met up again several months ago, he had always thought of her as Agnes Lockwood. Therefore, until a few minutes ago, it hadn't occurred to him that she had the same name as their suspect.

* * *

"That could have gone better," Joanne said.

"Yes." Richard Harrison picked up his glass of whisky and studied it for a long moment before taking a large drink. "Perhaps this wasn't the best place to bring up the subject. I'll try again at the hotel. I'm sure I'll 'bump' into her at some point."

"Truthfully, I thought she would have been easy pickings. You know what I mean… a woman on her own."

"Yes, I agree," Richard replied. "However, I'm sure we've set her thinking and, like I said, I'll catch up with her at the hotel. In the meantime, we've got someone else to speak to, haven't we?"

"Yes," said Joanne. She pulled a notebook out of her handbag and opened it at the appropriate page. "I hope this guy works out a little better for us."

"We've done well so far." Richard raised his glass. "To us!" he said. "We're a good team."

Chapter Twenty-Three

Ben picked up Agnes at the entrance to the racecourse. During the ride back to the hotel, he asked her how she had got on at the races.

"I did quite well, considering I don't know anything about horseracing," she replied. "However, one of the men…" She paused. "I think they call them turf accountants?"

"Yes," Ben replied, his eyes still glued on the road ahead.

"Well, he very kindly explained it to me," she continued. "But even then, I didn't have a clue."

She forced a laugh, her mind still focused on the couple she had left in the bar at the racecourse. Between them, they had totally ruined the lovely memories she held of her father.

Ben laughed. "Yet you did okay. You must have got something right today. Good for you."

"Yes," Agnes said, thoughtfully, though she wasn't really replying to his comment. She was still thinking of Richard Harrison and the wretched woman with him.

"So you'll be going back again for another flutter on the horses?" Ben's voice broke into her thoughts.

"I don't know… Sometimes it's a good thing to give up while you're ahead. Isn't that how the saying goes?"

By now, Ben was pulling up outside the hotel.

"Don't bother to look at the meter." Agnes delved into her bag and pulled out the money she had won earlier that day and thrust it towards Ben.

"I can't take all that!" he said.

"Yes, you can," Agnes replied. "I really enjoyed my day. It was fun. I put a couple of pounds on the right horse and it went on from there. I'm sure you will put it to good use, Ben," she said, pushing the money into his hand. "I don't need it and I would like you to have it."

It was true; she didn't really need the money. Her parents had left her a thriving business and Jim had made sure she and the children would be well taken care of if anything were to happen to him.

Ben was still staring at the money she had given him when she opened the car door and stepped out.

Upstairs in her room, Agnes pushed the chain bolt into place before throwing herself onto the bed and bursting into tears. No! It wasn't possible. Her lovely father would never have had an affair with another woman. She couldn't believe it.

Memories of her father and mother floated through her mind. She recalled how they had been so happy together. Her mother had never had any reason to believe her husband had been unfaithful. From what Agnes could remember, her father had worshipped her mother. Yet the photograph in Richard Harrison's possession clearly showed her father standing by the roadside with his arm resting on a car. He had looked so proud. But then, who wouldn't have been proud to own a car back then? Not many people's budgets would stretch to owning a car. Even her parents hadn't owned one until...

Hang on a minute! Agnes sat up quickly and wiped away the tears. Why hadn't she thought of it before? Her father didn't have a car. Not until the family had come back from abroad and even then, it wasn't the model he was leaning against in the picture.

Therefore, why would he be lounging against that car as though it belonged to him? It didn't make sense. Or was she clutching at straws, still not willing to believe her father could possibly have had an affair, let alone father a child and then want nothing to do with it?

Agnes cradled her head in her hands. It was aching due to her mind racing around trying to find answers. Yet, all she was coming up with were more questions.

* * *

Back at the police station, Sergeant Andrews returned to the office to find the DCI staring out of the window

"Has there been any further news?"

The DCI often stared out of the window when he had just received some information on a case they were working on. Other times, he would pace up and down the office as he thought it through.

"No," Alan replied, without turning around. "What about you?"

"It seems there were three sets of fingerprints on the cutlery – at least, only three sets of prints forensics could pick up. They're running them through the database, but so far they don't have a match. However, they also found some DNA on the prongs of the fork. They're going to try to match it to the clothes they took from our victim." He paused. "You never know, our killer might have left a drop of saliva or sweat."

"Let's hope they find something," said Alan, still staring out of the window. "And if they do, it'll be down to Mrs Lockwood having the notion to pick up the cutlery in the first place."

He turned around to face his sergeant. "I've been thinking about something Morris said."

Andrews waited patiently as Alan strode over back to his desk and sat down before he continued.

"Morris told us Mrs Lockwood gave our suspect her maiden name."

"Yes. I remember – Morrison, wasn't it?" Andrews said.

Alan nodded. "Yes, that's the name she gave. But her maiden name wasn't Morrison."

"So?" Andrews queried. He was unable to see what the problem was.

"She probably wanted to fool him," Andrews continued. "I wouldn't want to give some complete stranger my life's history, either."

"You don't understand what I'm getting at, Andrews," Alan replied. "You see, I know Mrs Lockwood's maiden name is Harrison." He shook his head. "Why the hell didn't I pick that up earlier?"

Andrews took a deep breath and leaned back in his chair. "I'm surprised it hadn't crossed her mind. But I suppose Harrison is a common enough name."

He thought for a moment. "So now you believe he has some ulterior motive for following Mrs Lockwood?"

The DCI didn't reply. Instead, he looked at his watch. "I think Mrs Lockwood should be back at the hotel by now. I'm going to pop over there. If you should hear anything from forensics, let me know."

"Yes, sir," Andrews replied. "You'll be the first to know."

Alan stopped in the doorway and winked. "Nice thought, sergeant, but I'll be the second to know. You'll be the first."

Chapter Twenty-Four

Agnes was still pondering over her meeting with Richard Harrison that afternoon when she heard a tap on the door of her room. At first, she didn't respond, believing Harrison might have found out her room number. It wouldn't be difficult; such an attractive man could probably talk any of the receptionists into giving away such information.

It was only when she heard Alan's voice that she hurried over to the door and unbolted the chain to let him in. However, before she closed the door behind him, she took the precaution of looking out into the corridor to make sure Harrison wasn't lurking around.

"I heard from Morris," Alan said, the moment he was inside. "He brought me up to speed on what had happened."

As there was no reply, he swung around to find Agnes sliding the chain bolt into place. While he was pleased to see she was heeding his warnings about keeping her door locked, he couldn't help being concerned that it had come to this.

"That man is crazy," Agnes said, as she sat down on one of the chairs by the table.

"Who, Morris?" Alan raised his eyebrows.

"No. I don't mean Morris. I was thankful he was there. I'm talking about the man calling himself Harrison."

She reached out and pulled a tissue from a box on the table by the bed and wiped her eyes.

"He was claiming that my father was also his father. But I soon put him straight on that point!"

"I know. You told him your maiden name was Morrison."

"Yes, I did." Agnes forced a laugh. "I just wanted to get him off my back. I wasn't sure what name to give until my eyes rested on Morris. The name Morrison suddenly sprang to mind. But then Richard produced a photo and claimed the man in the picture was his father. He said it had been taken by his mother."

"Well, that will have settled it. You should have no need to concern yourself further."

"That's what I thought," Agnes, said, wiping away more tears, "until he placed that damn picture in front of me!"

Alan placed his arm around her shoulders.

"You mean…"

"Yes! The photo showed my father standing next to a car." She shook her head. "I don't know how I kept my composure. All I wanted to do was to get out of there."

Alan was at a loss for words. All he could do was to pull Agnes closer to him and hug her tightly.

"But there's more, Alan," Agnes said, once she had calmed down a little. "When I got back here, I suddenly remembered that my father didn't have a car at the time he was talking about."

She pulled herself away from Alan and began to pace up and down the room.

"Unless…" Agnes halted sharply and turned around to face Alan. "But no! I won't believe that! It's not possible," she added, after a moment's thought.

"What's not possible?" Alan asked.

"For a split second, it crossed my mind that my father might have had a car tucked away somewhere without my mother's knowledge," Agnes replied. "But I'm sure Dad wouldn't have done that. Harrison is trying to twist my mind into believing that my father was unfaithful to my mother. He's a liar and a cheat," she muttered, punching her clenched fist into the palm of her other hand. "And I'm not about to let him get away with it."

"What do you mean about him being a cheat?"

"Richard Harrison said the hunt for his real father wasn't about money," she said. "He told me he'd worked his way up the ladder without any help from his father and had formed a company of his own. But..."

"But?" Alan prompted.

Agnes shrugged. "But I don't believe him. I think this is all about money." She stared at him. "Isn't that where you and Sergeant Andrews come in? Don't you guys check out this kind of thing?"

"What kind of thing, Agnes?" Alan replied softly, in an effort to lighten the mood. "Where he's a cheat or a liar?"

"Both!" Agnes sighed. "For heaven's sake, this man could be lying to countless people and cheating them out of money."

"Agnes! You don't have any proof of that."

"Then I am going to find proof!" Agnes retorted. "So far, this man thinks I've bought his story. Therefore, I'll play that option. If I see him in the hotel, I'll let him think I've forgiven him for grabbing my arm and that we're now on friendly terms. But all the while, I will be watching him – along with Detective Morris."

Just as Alan was about to protest, she smiled sweetly and swiftly changed the subject. "Now, about this evening... where are we having dinner?"

* * *

Alan had been reluctant to leave. But once it had been decided they would go back to the restaurant they had used a couple of nights ago, Agnes had insisted, telling him they could discuss it all later. "Besides, don't you have a day job?" she had added pointedly.

After he left, Agnes sat down at the table by the window to think it all through once again. She was angry. But more than being angry at the wretched man, she was furious with herself for having had doubts about her lovely father.

It's all down to that awful man, she thought, as she gazed down at the Millennium Bridge beneath her window.

Perhaps Detective Smithers had got it right after all. Maybe there had been a note of hesitation in Harrison's voice when he gave his name to the receptionist. If this man was pulling some sort of confidence trick, it could be that he had many names up his sleeve and, for a split second, he forgot who he was supposed to be that day.

Agnes realised that sitting here alone wasn't doing her any good. She needed to get out, even if it was only to her favourite café on the quayside.

* * *

"Have you heard from forensics?"

Alan had arrived back at the station to find his sergeant poring over a file on his desk.

"No, I'm afraid not," Andrews replied. "This has just arrived from the station in Gateshead. It seems that the chief inspector has let their man go – not enough evidence…"

"Not enough evidence!" Alan sneered. "There wasn't *any* evidence. He had absolutely nothing to go on and pulled a man off the street to make himself look good."

"Anyway," Andrews jumped in, when the DCI paused for breath, "he's sent a copy of their file on the murders. He thinks we might find it useful as the killer seems to have moved across the Tyne."

"It's about the only sensible thing he's done since he took over," Alan said, grudgingly.

"Is Mrs Lockwood okay?" Andrews changed the subject.

"No – not really," Alan replied after a brief pause. "Harrison is claiming – or perhaps I should say, *was* claiming – that her father was also his father."

Alan went on to explain how he had even produced an old photograph of Derek Harrison, saying it had been taken by his mother many years ago.

"Yes, I can imagine how angry she must be," Andrews said, when the DCI had finished speaking. "But these things happen. Perhaps her father did mess up."

"I wouldn't like to be in your shoes if she overhears you saying that." Alan chortled.

"Yes, maybe I'd best leave it alone." Andrews swallowed hard. He hadn't forgotten the run-in he'd had with her a few months ago.

"Getting back to our case, what on earth are forensics doing down there? Surely it doesn't take this long?" Alan held his hand out for the file.

"I asked the same thing when I tried to get more info." Andrews grinned as he passed the file to the DCI.

"And what was the excuse?

"The lady calmly reminded me that we were not *NCIS* and her name wasn't Abby Sciuto!"

Chapter Twenty-Five

When Agnes stepped outside the hotel, she changed her mind about going to the café. She suddenly had the idea of walking along the quayside towards Bessie Surtees House. Why not? It was still quite pleasant and she had plenty of time before she needed to shower and dress for her date with Alan. He wouldn't be picking her up for another three hours yet.

Besides, she had promised herself another visit to the house and now was as good a time as any. The stroll might even help to clear away the thoughts of what had happened earlier that day. It seemed to be working as, shortly after she set off, she began to feel much better.

However, Agnes should have known it would be too good to last. She had almost reached the bottom of The Side, with Bessie Surtees House just around the corner, when she spotted Richard Harrison lurking in a doorway. She quickly turned away and walked over to gaze across the River Tyne.

She felt sure he hadn't seen her. His gaze seemed to be fixed on something or someone further ahead. Though she knew she should turn around and walk back towards the hotel, her curiosity was telling her to stay where she was and try to find out what Harrison was so interested in.

Agnes quickly pulled her mirror and lipstick out of her bag. Holding the mirror in a position where she could see Harrison, she poised the lipstick close to her lips, hoping to give the impression to any passerby that she was fixing her make-up. She angled the mirror into a position where she was able to follow the direction of Harrison's gaze and a few yards away, she saw Joanne, his so-called sister-in-law, talking to a man.

Agnes was too far away to make out the features of the man. The best she could do was to note that he was wearing what looked like a tweed overcoat. But, as Newcastle wasn't too far away from Scotland, tweed was popular in this area. Therefore, she dismissed it as being insignificant.

Still watching Joanne's reflection as best she could through the small mirror, Agnes noted that she glanced towards Harrison before taking the man's arm and apparently encouraging him to come with her. However, the man shook his head and snatched his arm away from Joanne's grasp. Then, without another word, he turned and walked away.

Agnes wondered whether Joanne might be tempted to follow him. However, after a glance towards Harrison, Joanne began walking back towards him.

What are they up to now? Agnes wondered, turning the mirror to catch the reflection of Joanne and Harrison walking off together. They were heading in the direction of the hotel and appeared to be in a deep discussion about something.

Agnes placed her mirror and lipstick back into her handbag. She had half a mind to follow the couple, but decided to keep away. If they were to spot her, it might give them cause to wonder whether she had seen Joanne's interaction with the man in the tweed coat. Perhaps it would be best if she were to stay on the right side of them – at least for the time being. That way, she might learn more about what they were up to.

Agnes continued on her walk towards Sandhill. Bessie Surtees House was only a few minutes away. Nevertheless, those fleeting moments gave her time to meditate on what she had witnessed.

Could Richard and Joanne have been trying to pull the same stunt they had tried on her earlier that day? But then Agnes dismissed that idea. Surely they had more sense than to attempt to con someone into believing they were related out here in the open. But, on reflection, was the bar on a racecourse a good place to pull a stunt like that?

She had almost reached Bessie Surtees House when another thought struck her. Maybe the couple had already conned this man; drawn him into their web with their lies and he had handed over some money. It could be that they had tried to get even more, but he had refused!

By now, Agnes had reached the museum. She looked in the window for a few minutes to calm herself down before stepping inside.

"Good afternoon." The voice came from a man sitting at a desk on the other side of the counter. He stood up and walked towards her. "Can I help you?"

"Do you know whether there is a ghost in the house?" Agnes asked. The man looked stunned.

Agnes hadn't meant it to come out like that. She had already decided that she would mention the ghost thing, but only after they'd had time to chat for a while. But it was too late now.

"A ghost?" he said at last. "Whatever makes you think we might have a ghost?"

Agnes smiled. "I'm probably being silly, but I thought I saw one a few months ago when a friend and I were walking back to the hotel from a restaurant across the road. It was the night the body was found outside on the pavement."

"I recall that night," the man said thoughtfully. "The police kept coming here for days afterwards. But you're mistaken about a ghost. There aren't any ghosts here."

Though he sounded positive, Agnes couldn't help noticing that he glanced swiftly over his shoulder as he spoke – almost as though he was expecting to see someone garbed in white looming up behind him.

"Yes, I expect you're right," Agnes laughed. "It was very late and, what with the body lying there on the pavement, maybe my imagination ran away with me. But I thought I would mention it as I was passing."

"Yes, of course," the man said. "However, now that you're here, would you like to take a walk around the house?"

Agnes had looked at the rooms upstairs during her last visit to Tyneside, but why not have another look? She had time to spare. Besides, she had enjoyed seeing it the last time; the experience had swept her back to a bygone age.

"Yes, thank you. I would."

Upstairs, Agnes found a few other people wandering through the rooms. They were obviously taking advantage of the quiet season. She wandered across towards the window where, all those years ago, Bessy Surtees had climbed out to elope with her young man.

This was the very window Agnes could have sworn she had seen being closed the night she and Alan had found the body. Had she imagined it, or might she be the only person who had been fortunate enough to have laid eyes on the ghost?

She was gazing out of the window, still absentmindedly pondering on the question of a ghost in the house, when she suddenly saw Richard Harrison standing on the corner of the road. He was alone. Yet he appeared to be looking for someone, as he kept glancing up and down the street. Could he be looking for Joanne? The last time she had seen them together, they had been going in the opposite direction to Bessie Surtees House.

Agnes took a step back from the window, not wanting to be seen. But, at the same time, she wanted to be in a position where she could see who Harrison was waiting for.

"Are you okay up here?"

Agnes jumped at the sudden sound of the voice behind her. She had been concentrating so hard on Harrison that she hadn't heard anyone come up the stairs and enter the room. She swung around and found the man she had spoken to earlier.

"Yes, I'm fine, thank you. I was just wondering how Bessie Surtees managed to get out of this window," Agnes lied.

The last thing she wanted to do now was to move away from the window.

"It's quite small, especially for a lady wearing a crinoline dress," she added.

She turned back towards the window and made a few gestures with her hands, as though she was trying to figure out how it might have been possible. However, her eyes were focused on the corner of Sandhill. Thankfully Harrison was still waiting there.

"I agree," the man said, enthusiastically. He moved closer to the window. "But not only that, she had to carefully place her feet onto a ladder and climb down to the street below." He paused. "Most admirable, wouldn't you say?"

"Yes," Agnes nodded. "Most admirable. Not many women back then would have dared to defy their father, let alone leave the house through a window some distance from the ground."

"We close in about fifteen minutes," the man said, walking back towards the stairs. "But there's no need to rush. I have some paperwork to finish so I'll be here for a little while yet."

"Thank you," Agnes called out. "I won't be much longer."

At least, I hope not, she thought.

She didn't want to be turned out onto the street while Richard Harrison was still hovering around. But what else could she do if he didn't move on?

Ten minutes ticked by, then another five and Harrison was still kicking his heels on the corner of Sandhill. Agnes was beginning to get desperate. What could she do if he continued to stand there?

Should she call Ben and ask him to park on the pavement while she ducked into the back of the cab? If he was seen and fined, she would be happy to pay his fine. But he could lose his taxi driver's license or whatever the hell they called it, and then he would be out of work.

Another option would be to call an ambulance and declare that she couldn't walk and needed to be carried out of the building on a trolley. However, Agnes quickly dismissed that idea. By calling an ambulance, she could be taking the crew away from a real emergency. No! She couldn't bring herself to do that.

The only other thing she was left with was to call Alan. With head-lights blazing and sirens blasting, Harrison might get the impression they were looking for him and run away. Yet, that would be called wasting police time. She was still trying to think of something else she could do to get out of the building without being recognised, when she suddenly saw Joanne appear.

Agnes heaved a sigh of relief as she watched Joanne walking to-wards Harrison. Now, with a bit of luck, they would both move on and she would be able to leave the museum without being seen. She was still gazing down at the pair through the window when Joanne reached into her pocket and gleefully waved something in the air. Whatever it was, it seemed to lift Harrison's spirits. He raised his arm and did a high five.

Unfortunately, Agnes was too far away to see what it was that had so delighted Harrison. Nevertheless, after her earlier thoughts that day, she felt sure it would have something to do with money.

She blew out a breath. How did she keep getting herself mixed up in such things? First, she had discovered a body in the park; then yes-terday, she was informed by Harrison that they had the same father. It was only a matter of time before he got around to telling her what he was really after. Maybe she should pack her bags and go back to living a quiet life in her small village in Essex before anything else happened.

She cast her mind back to the genteel afternoon teas in the village hall; the cricket and football matches held on the grounds skirting the village, and the various other refined clubs which had sprung up over the years, many of which she had been involved in. For a brief moment, it sounded very appealing.

Yet, who was she fooling? Was that really how she wanted to live out the rest of her life? No! She didn't want to watch the world go by from a cosy armchair; she wanted to be a part of it. Agnes screwed up her eyes. Besides, this was personal. Harrison had involved *her* father this time and she wasn't about to let him get away with it.

By now, Harrison had placed whatever Joanne had given him in his pocket and they were already heading back around the corner towards the quayside. Agnes breathed a sigh of relief. At least she could leave before the man downstairs had to throw her out. She took out her phone and called Ben to pick her up.

She could very easily have walked back to the hotel. It still looked rather pleasant outside. However, using the taxi would give her an alibi if Richard and Joanne were near the hotel when she arrived. Hopefully, they would believe she had gone on somewhere else after she had left the racecourse and couldn't possibly have seen them accosting the man in the tweed coat on the quayside.

"Good timing," the man on the desk said cheerfully, as she descended the stairs. He went on to ask her if she had enjoyed her visit.

She told him it had been most informative.

"Does that mean you saw 'the ghost'?" he asked, making quotation marks in the air.

She flashed him a grin. "No, I didn't. I guess I made a mistake about seeing a ghost."

Out of the corner of her eye, she saw Ben pulling up outside.

"Well, I best be off and let you finish. Thank you for allowing me to stay on."

* * *

Back at the police station, the DCI paced back and forth in his office as he stared down at the forensics report.

"No match," Alan said, after a long moment.

Not all the DNA found on the man's coat had come from the victim. Therefore he had hoped they would find a match from the cutlery. However, that was not the case.

"That means Harrison isn't our man after all." Sergeant Andrews picked up his phone. "I suppose we should call Morris and tell him to come back to the station."

Alan stopped pacing and swung around. "No! Put the phone down," he said. His voice was sharper than he had meant it to be.

The sergeant replaced the phone as Alan strode across to his desk and hurled himself into his chair.

"Not yet." His tone was a little softer. "Harrison's not off the hook yet. He could still be a con-man and don't forget he's still staying at the same hotel as Mrs Lockwood. He might try getting at her again."

"But if the superintendent gets to hear that Harrison isn't the killer, he'll want to know why we haven't called Morris back. We're supposed to be on a tight budget."

"Yes, I know all that, Andrews." The DCI sounded impatient. "But just keep it quiet for the moment. If the superintendent starts complaining, I'll speak to him – I'll even offer to pay for Morris's room."

Sergeant Andrews lifted one shoulder. "If you say so."

Alan nodded. "Right, so that's sorted." He rubbed the side of his nose. "So, if Harrison *is* out of the frame for murder, we're back to square one," he continued. "And why the hell hasn't anyone reported our victim missing? Surely someone must have noticed he wasn't around by now. You'd think that once the newspapers and television started reporting the case, relatives and friends of any missing person would have flocked to police stations all over the northeast."

Unsure whether he was meant to say anything or not, Andrews decided to remain silent. Sometimes it was best to let the DCI do all the talking when he was in this kind of mood.

"Then there's the tie pin and cufflink we found." Alan added. "We still haven't had any luck with finding out where they were purchased." He shook his head. "We just seem to be going around in circles."

Chapter Twenty-Six

Alan picked up Agnes at the hotel, using the same ruse as the night before. He still wasn't sure whether Harrison was aware he was a detective. Yet it was better to be safe than sorry.

It didn't take long to reach the restaurant and they were given a warm welcome as they walked in. Both the waiter and the wine waiter remembered them from a couple of nights ago.

"So nice to see you both again," the waiter said, as he led them to their table.

"Thank you," Agnes said, as she sat down.

Once they had ordered their meal and a bottle of wine, Agnes placed her elbows on the table and leaned across the table.

"How is the case going? Please tell me that you found something from the cutlery I dropped off at the station."

Alan pulled a face.

"Does that face mean you didn't find anything or that you did, but don't want to tell me?"

Agnes sat back in her chair when the wine waiter appeared with the bottle of wine they had chosen. He opened the bottle in front of them and was about to pour a sample when Alan intervened.

"We had the same wine the other night. I'm sure it will be fine."

"Thank you." The waiter tipped his head slightly and moved away.

Alan poured the wine and raised his glass. "Cheers," he said.

"Cheers," Agnes echoed, as she took a sip from her glass.

"I'm afraid the results of the tests taken from the cutlery didn't reveal anything," Alan said, replacing his glass on the table.

Agnes was about to speak, but Alan held up his hand.

"What I mean is," he continued, "the fingerprints didn't match anyone in our database." He went on to tell her that forensics had even tried to match DNA on the fork to that taken from the clothes from the victim.

"Again, there was nothing – at least, there was no match to Harrison."

"I see," Agnes said, thoughtfully. "So he's off the hook."

Alan nodded. "Yes, for the murder. However, after your meeting with him today, I still think he could be a bit of a dodgy character and we should keep an eye on him. Therefore I have decided not to pull Morris from the hotel."

Agnes gave a quiet sigh of relief. "Thank you, Alan. Now I'll tell you what I saw today."

She quickly told him how she had seen Joanne and Harrison on the quayside and then again on the corner of Sandhill.

"I have no idea what they wanted with the man on the quayside, but he wasn't having any of it. Maybe if I had been a little closer…"

"No!" Alan interrupted. He held up his hand. "If you had been any closer, then it's possible they might have seen you. You need to stay well away from both of them. It sounds to me like they are pulling some sort of stunt."

"Alan, I could bump into him anytime in the hotel," said Agnes.

"Bumping into him in the hotel is one thing, but if he keeps seeing you outside, he might think you're following him and turn really nasty."

He glanced up as the waiter approached carrying two plates.

"Now, let's forget about Harrison for a little while and enjoy our evening."

* * *

They had almost finished their meal when Alan's phone rang.

"It's Andrews," he said, as he flipped it open and looked at the screen.

"What is it, Andrews?" he said into the phone.

Agnes watched Alan's jaw drop as he listened to what his sergeant had to say. This didn't look good.

Alan asked Andrews to send a car to the restaurant. "I'm sorry Agnes, I'll have to go," he apologized. "Another body has been found. They're sending a car. I can drop you at the hotel…"

"No, Alan. I'll call Ben. He'll be expecting a call from us, anyway. You go as soon as the car arrives." She paused. "Where was the body found?"

"The park," Alan said, before beckoning the waiter to ask for the bill. "I gather it's rather like the last one."

"Mutilated? Oh, my goodness!" Agnes clasped her hand to her mouth.

"I don't like leaving you like this. The least I can do is see you safely back to the hotel."

"I'll be fine, Alan. Ben will see me back to the hotel." She raised her eyebrows. "Unless you'd like me to come with you…"

"No! Definitely not, Agnes."

There wasn't time to say anything further as a police car pulled up outside the restaurant. Though the sirens weren't blaring, the blue lights were flashing, causing the diners sitting near the window to gaze out to see whether there was something going on outside.

Alan quickly stood up and stepped around the table. He handed Agnes some money. "I'll leave you to pay the bill. Let me know if it's any more."

He bent down and gave her a brief kiss before grabbing his coat. He stopped and looked back at her, before disappearing through the door.

* * *

By the time Alan had arrived at the scene, temporary lights had been set up and he was able to see the body quite clearly.

"Who found the body? And what the hell was he or she doing here at this time of night?" he asked, as he looked down at the victim lying at his feet.

Andrews gestured across towards a young couple sitting in a police car. Transferring his gaze towards the car, Alan didn't recognize either of them.

"Okay, I don't need to know the last part," Alan winked as he turned back to face his sergeant. "Have you interviewed them?"

"Yes, but they can't tell us much. It seems they stumbled across the body a few minutes after they entered the park."

Alan looked towards the entrance, which was only a short distance away. "Sounds feasible," he said.

"Yes, I agree," Andrews replied with a grin. "Anyway, the young man, whose name is Peter Hammond, phoned the police and an officer was dispatched to verify what he'd said. Once they knew it wasn't a hoax call, I was informed."

There was a slight pause before he continued. "I have to say Hammond doesn't seem to be fazed at finding a mutilated body."

"And the woman?" Alan asked.

"Ah now, she is totally different. Anne Jones hasn't said a word. Truthfully, she hasn't stopped shaking since I arrived."

"Has anyone taken their statements?" Alan asked

"Yes," Andrews replied.

"Right, get an officer to take them home," Alan replied. "There's no point in keeping them here any longer."

Just then, Doctor Nichols arrived on the scene. "Sorry, I'm a bit late. I was enjoying an evening out."

"Join the club," Alan replied.

Chapter Twenty-Seven

At the restaurant, Agnes was lost in thought as she waited for Ben. He had told her that he was already on his way to pick up another fare, but he would be with her as soon as possible. She wondered how Alan was getting on at the park. At least when she had found a mutilated body, it had been during the daylight hours. Whoever discovered this one must have received a terrible fright.

She was still thinking about it when the restaurant door opened and Ben walked in. When he saw Agnes sitting alone, he glanced around as though he was expecting the DCI to be somewhere close by.

Agnes rose to her feet and pulled on her coat. "I'm on my own, Ben. I'm afraid Alan was called away on a case. Another body has been found in the park."

"I guessed something must be going on somewhere as I've seen several police cars chasing about the city centre."

"Back to the hotel?" Ben asked, once they were inside the taxi.

"Yes, I suppose so," she replied.

However, after a moment's hesitation, she changed her mind.

"Do you think we could maybe swing around by the park?"

Ben turned around to face her. "I don't think that's a good idea. The DCI won't be very happy if you turn up in the middle of a crime scene, especially at this time of night."

"The DCI needn't know. I won't get out of the taxi." She grinned. "Come on, Ben, just drive slowly past the park and then you can take me back to the hotel."

"Okay," said Ben. He turned back and started the engine. "But if he sees you, then you can do the talking!"

"It's a deal," Agnes said, settling back in the seat.

It wasn't long before they reached the park entrance. There were a couple of police cars parked on the road and, as they drew closer, Agnes could see two policemen standing by the entrance. Stark beams from the temporary lights set up by the police could be seen shining through the trees.

"Oh, I wish I was with them in the park," Agnes said. "I'm sure I could be of some help."

"Yes, I'm sure you could," Ben said, not taking his eyes off the road. "However, it's more than my job's worth to let you get out here."

"But you would have to let me out if I lived here," Agnes argued.

"But I happen to know that you don't live here. Therefore I am not stopping the car."

"Okay," Agnes replied sullenly, knowing she was defeated. "But when you get to the top of the road, turn around and come back down. Then you can take me back to the hotel."

However, on the ride back down, Agnes was convinced that she saw someone in the trees a little way from the entrance. Obviously, the two police officers hadn't seen anything.

"Slow down, Ben," she called out. "I thought I saw someone lurking around."

She leaned forward in her seat to get a better view of the trees, but it was too late; they had already passed the point where Agnes had seen the mystery figure.

"It's no good," she said, flopping back down into her seat. "You'll have to drive back up here again."

"You're having me on, aren't you?" Ben said.

"Please, Ben. I'm sure I saw someone."

"Okay, but then we're going back to the hotel – right?"

"Right! But only after you turn around at the top and drive back down again."

Ben shook his head as he turned the car around and drove back up Claremont Road. He slowed down as he approached the park entrance.

"Now, keep your eyes peeled," he said.

But Agnes was already sitting up in the back seat, staring out of the window.

"There!" she squealed, as she saw a figure peering through the trees into the park. "Quick, quick! Turn around somewhere and go back."

Ben drove a little further up the road and turned around. "This is the last time, so watch carefully," he said.

Ben slowed down as they approached the park gates.

"It's somewhere a little way past the gate... *There*!" Agnes said triumphantly. "I can see someone and they appear to be very interested in what the police are doing. If only they would turn around for a second – however, it's so dark I doubt if I would be able to see their face."

At that point, Ben flicked on the main beam, causing the person in the trees to swing around. The light was so bright that the person quickly covered their eyes, but not before Agnes saw the face.

"Can we go now?" Ben asked.

"Yes, Ben. Head for the hotel."

"Did you see who the person in the trees was?"

"Yes, thanks to your quick thinking with the headlights," Agnes replied. She sank back into the seat, with a satisfied smile on her face.

"What I mean is, did you see them clearly enough to be able to describe them to the police?" Ben asked, his eyes still glued to the road ahead.

"Yes, Ben, I saw the person very clearly indeed – and I know exactly who it was."

All she had to do now was to figure out how she was going to tell Alan who she had seen, without him going berserk about her going up to the park in the first place.

She was still thinking about it when Ben pulled up outside the hotel. She paid the fare and stepped out of the taxi.

"Thank you, Ben. You are a star."

She felt sure that no other taxi driver would have whirled her back and forth and up and down the road near the park, purely to satisfy her whim.

Ben grinned. "Thank you."

At the top of the steps by the entrance, Agnes turned around and saw Ben still by the kerb. She had only paused for a second to look at the lights on both the Millennium and Tyne Bridges. They always looked so amazing. However, she guessed Ben was waiting to see her safely inside before he moved away, so she gave him a wave and opened the door. She was right; it was only when she had closed the door behind her that, through the glass, she saw Ben driving away.

As she approached the reception desk, the security officer on duty asked whether she had enjoyed her evening.

"Yes, thank you. Very much so," she replied.

Out of the corner of her eye, she saw someone leaving the bar. She glanced across to see who it was and found it to be Richard Harrison. He was carrying a large glass of what she thought was whisky and, from the way he was weaving around, it appeared it wasn't his first drink of the evening.

"Ah, Mrs Lockwood," Harrison said. "I had hoped to catch up with you this evening."

He staggered towards her, the glass wobbling perilously in his hand.

"Careful! Watch what you're doing!" The voice came from the security officer.

"Oops! Sorry," Harrison said. He pulled a face and giggled. "Maybe I should sit down for a moment."

He slowly made his way across to a sofa.

"I suggest you go up to your room and sleep it off," the security man said.

"What do you think, Mrs Lockwood?" Harrison asked. "The night is still young." He patted the seat next to him. "Maybe you and I could have a drink together. I really would like to talk to you."

Until now, Agnes had remained silent, hoping he would take the security officer's advice and disappear upstairs. However, it seemed that wasn't going to happen.

"I'll pass, if you don't mind," she said. "I'm feeling rather tired and I would like to go to my room."

But Harrison wasn't about to be put off. "That's a good idea!" His voice was slurred. "We could have a drink in your room."

He made as if to stand up, but the sofa was quite low and, in his inebriated state, he couldn't quite make it. He sank back down onto the sofa, spilling some whisky in the process.

"Goodnight, Mr Harrison," Agnes said firmly, as she turned and walked across towards the lift.

She hoped he wouldn't try to follow her. The last thing she wanted was for him to learn which room she was in. However, she saw his reflection in one of the large mirrors. He was still seated where she had left him and the security man was walking towards him.

The lift door swung open as she approached and Larry, the lift attendant, stepped out. "Going off duty?" she asked.

"I was, but I can hang on a few minutes to see you safely upstairs."

"Thank you, Larry."

"Bit of trouble, was there?" he asked.

Agnes realized he must have noticed the tone of relief in her voice.

"Yes, you could say that," she replied. "One of the guests has had a little too much to drink."

Just as the lift doors began to close, she caught a glimpse of Morris. He was standing in the doorway leading into the bar. She was thankful that he was still watching Harrison.

Larry was about to press the button for her floor when she intervened.

"Take me to level five," she said. "I'll take the stairs down from there."

He nodded. "You're catching on."

"Thank you," Agnes said, as the door opened on the fifth floor. "I hope you don't get caught up with him when you go back down."

"Um, good thinking. I think I'll take the back stairs – just in case," Larry replied.

He stepped out of the lift, then leaned back inside to press the button which would close the doors and take the lift back to the ground floor. "Goodnight," he said, as he hurried towards a door bearing the sign, *Staff Only* at the other end of the corridor.

Once Agnes reached her room, she unlocked the door and went inside. She made sure the chain was securely in place before throwing her bag onto the bed and removing her coat. She yawned. The bed looked so inviting and, come to think of it, it had been a long day.

Climbing into bed, Agnes realised she still hadn't figured out the best way of telling Alan who she had seen hanging around outside of the park. Whichever way she worded it, there was no getting away from the fact that she had been at the park when he had told her to go straight back to the hotel.

But she could think about all that tomorrow. Maybe the right moment would present itself.

* * *

In another corner of the hotel, Richard Harrison threw himself on top of the bed. He hadn't meant to drink so much. But one glass had led to another and then another. He had been hoping to catch up with Agnes Lockwood in the bar or the drawing room. Maybe she would have been more pliable in the luxurious surroundings of the hotel. Confronting her in the bar at the racecourse had been a bad idea.

She had said her maiden name was Morrison. But he was sure it was Harrison; he and his friend had done their homework. So far, they hadn't got it wrong once. He would try again tomorrow or the day after. There was no point in rushing it. There was too much at stake.

Chapter Twenty-Eight

Detective Inspector Johnson looked at his watch. He and his sergeant were still at the crime scene. Though it was only a little over an hour since he had left Agnes at the restaurant, he felt he had been here half the night. He had been enjoying the evening until receiving the call from Andrews.

He rubbed his hands together and stamped his feet. It was so cold. Shielding his eyes from the lights set up by his colleagues, he could see the moon shining down from the cloudless sky. Little wonder it was so damn cold.

"That's it. We're done."

Alan had been so lost in thought that he had failed to notice Dr Nichols walking towards him.

"Is there anything you can tell me, Keith?" Alan asked.

The pathologist cocked his head to one side. "What do you think?" He gestured towards the body being wheeled towards his van. "You'll have to wait until I get him back to the morgue."

He paused "All I can say at the moment is that judging by the way the body has been mutilated, I would hazard a guess that he was murdered by the killer you're already looking for."

"Thank you, Doctor," said Alan, blandly. "I'd already figured that out for myself."

Nichols shrugged. "Not much help, I know." He smiled. "But, you never know, I might find something in the post-mortem, or one of the forensic guys could pick up a clue out here. Meanwhile, I have to go."

He turned as though to leave, but then swung back to face Alan.

"Have you seen anything more of that lovely lady I met here a few days ago?"

"Yes, I have. Actually, I was enjoying dinner with her this evening, when I was called away," Alan replied.

"Ah well, lucky you." The pathologist winked as he turned away and headed off towards his van.

"We're finishing up here as there's nothing more we can do tonight," Andrews said, as he stepped alongside the DCI. "We haven't found anything so far, but we've cordoned off the area. We'll take another look first thing in the morning. You never know, there could be something we've missed."

Alan looked across to where the forensics officers were packing their bags. "Okay. Like you say, we'll take another look around tomorrow."

Andrews went back to speak to his colleagues, leaving Alan staring down at the spot where the body had been found.

This was the second body to be found in this park in a matter of days. In each case, it seemed the victim hadn't actually been targeted and murdered here. Even though it was dark and the police had had to use temporary lights to enable them to check the scene, it was evident there wasn't enough blood around the body to show that the murder had taken place here. The park was merely being used as a place to dispose of the bodies. It was dark and it was quiet and there were lots of large bushes to hide a body without being seen.

Alan was about to walk away when something occurred to him and he looked back at where the body had lain when he first arrived. It had been half hidden by the bush. The rest of the man's body was lying across the pathway. Why was that?

When Agnes had found the first body a few days ago, it had been well hidden behind a bush, even though it hadn't been far from the pathway. It might have lain there for much longer if her attention hadn't been drawn to the birds hovering around.

Therefore, had the two people who had found the body, moved it before calling the police? But why would they have done that? Yes, the young man was a bit of a cheeky rascal, but the girl was totally shocked at finding the body. Surely he would have had to comfort her; not ask her to help him pull the mutilated victim out of the bushes for him to pore over.

No, the most likely answer to his question was that the killer was still carrying the body to wherever they wanted to leave it, when he saw or heard the couple coming towards them.

They were most likely chatting or giggling, in high spirits after a night out together, when the killer spotted them. The murderer probably panicked, dumped the body and hurried away without realizing it wasn't completely hidden. If the killer was still skulking around when the couple found it, he must have been horrified at his mistake.

If only the couple had been a few minutes earlier, they might have seen the killer and been able to give a description to the first officers on the scene. But, Alan quickly realized, if that had been the case, they might both be dead now. This was a killer without mercy.

"Sir, we're leaving," Andrews called out. As there was no response, he called out again, this time a little louder. "*Sir!*"

Alan looked up sharply. Andrews was staring at him, though his finger was pointing towards the team who were already on their way out of the park.

"We're leaving," the sergeant repeated.

"Sorry." Alan walked across to Andrews. "I was just thinking through a few things."

"Anything you want to share?"

Alan shrugged. "I haven't much to share. Like I said, I was just thinking about where the body was found. If you give me a lift, I'll tell you about it in the car."

"Not a problem," Andrews replied.

* * *

Alan was the first to arrive at the station the next morning. He hadn't been able to sleep for thinking about the latest murder. Tossing and turning all night, he had churned the events over and over in his mind. He couldn't stop feeling guilty about having thought it would have been helpful if the young couple had arrived in time to see the killer! If that had been the case, they could both be lying dead in the morgue by now. Even now, the killer might try to track them down, fearing they may have seen something.

Then, his troubled mind had shifted back in time to the day Agnes had found a body. What if she had arrived in the park just in time to see the killer dumping the victim? She could be dead right now and he, as the SIO, might be heading the inquiry into her murder.

It had been that terrible thought which had made him leap out of bed in a cold sweat. He was desperate to catch this murderer before he killed Agnes, the young couple, or indeed, anyone else. This meant he would have to put every man at his disposal on the case.

He toyed with the idea of bringing Morris back to the station. Maybe his sergeant was right. With Harrison out of the equation for the murder of the first victim, there was no real need for Morris to stay undercover when he could be more useful working on this case.

But the more Alan thought about it, the more uneasy he felt about removing Morris from the hotel. Harrison was still a con-man. He could still try working on Agnes to get whatever it was he was after.

With these thoughts still tumbling through his mind, he had showered, dressed and headed for the police station.

* * *

"You're an early bird," Andrews said, as he entered the office.

"I couldn't sleep," Alan replied. "I thought I might as well be here as anywhere else."

"What are you reading?" Andrews asked. "Is there something new?"

The DCI looked up. "No, there's nothing new. I was just going back over what we already had. I had an idea we might have missed something."

"Did you find something?"

Alan slammed the file shut in disgust. "Some chance! There's not a damn thing. As far as I can see, we've covered everything."

"Would you like me to go through it?" Andrews asked. "A new pair of eyes might see something."

"Why not?" Alan picked up the file and thrust it towards his sergeant. "Though you've been through the case file several times already." He sighed. "Maybe we should start again from the beginning and look at *why* these murders are taking place, instead of trying to find out who is committing them."

"I thought we had already included the 'why' in our investigations," Andrews said, opening the file.

"Yes, we did," Alan replied. "But maybe we didn't dig deep enough."

Chapter Twenty-Nine

Agnes awoke to the sound of rain pounding against the window. For a moment, she thought of snuggling back down in her warm bed for another half hour, but, changing her mind, she threw back the covers.

Pulling back the curtains, she peered down towards the quayside below. However, it was difficult to see anything clearly due to the rain streaming down the glass panes.

Usually, at this time of the morning, there were quite a number of people bustling around the quayside as they made their way to work. But, from what she could see, there were notably fewer this morning. Evidently many had opted to take the bus today.

Those who were braving the deluge by attempting to walk to work, were struggling with their umbrellas against the strong wind. Even the river, which usually flowed gently towards the sea, was crashing against the sides of the quay, causing huge waves to splash over the pavement.

This was the first time she had ever seen the river so turbulent and, for a few moments, she felt anxious about staying in a hotel so close to the swirling waters. Should the weather worsen, the hotel could even be flooded. You read about this sort of thing all the time.

Agnes shook her head and stepped away from the window. She was letting her imagination run away with her. The hotel was set well back from the river. Besides, storms such as this must be a regular occurrence at this time of the year.

Unplugging her phone, which had been charging overnight, she switched it on. She wondered whether Alan might have sent her a text message before leaving for the office. However, the phone remained silent. *No doubt he'll be in touch later in the day,* she thought as she went to take a shower before heading down for breakfast.

Downstairs in reception, Agnes bought a newspaper in the hotel shop to read over breakfast. It wouldn't take very long to read the newspaper. The news was always the same these days and she had read most of it before. All she was interested in was whether there was anything new about the body found last night.

Though the rain had eased a little, it was still very wet outside; not the sort of day to go strolling around the quayside. Agnes still hadn't heard from Alan; obviously he was too busy. She hoped the forensic team had managed to collect any evidence from the scene before the rain started. If it had been left until this morning, it would have been washed away. She doubted even those tents the police used would have been much good in this weather.

Harrison was still having breakfast when Agnes walked into the dining room. She was surprised to see him here so early, especially after his drinking session the previous evening. She had thought he might have felt the need to sleep it off this morning.

He lifted his head feebly and gave her a thin smile as she walked past his table. He was nibbling dry toast; his knife and fork lay at the side of his plate, unused. Obviously, he was giving his usual cooked breakfast a miss this morning. Perhaps he was a little worse for wear after all. She replied by giving him a slight nod.

Shifting her eyes across the room, she saw Morris sitting a couple of tables away from Harrison. A newspaper, propped up by some condiment bottles, was spread out in front of him

Agnes had just given her order to the waiter when a man appeared in the doorway of the dining room. She wouldn't have taken any notice of him if he hadn't looked so uncomfortable standing there as he gazed into the room.

He was fairly tall and looked rather bulky; maybe not the sort to get into an argument with. Nevertheless, he looked smart in his navy-blue jacket and dark grey trousers. A newspaper was tucked under one arm, which suddenly fell to the floor when he raised his hands to fix his tie.

Agnes hid a smile when he bent over and gathered up his paper. Glancing around the room again, the man appeared to be relieved when his eyes fell on Harrison.

As he walked further into the room, Agnes had a feeling she had seen this man somewhere before but, for the moment, was unable to think where. Though, if he was staying at the hotel, it could be that she had seen him wandering around. Realizing she was staring, she turned her attention back to her newspaper.

The man took a seat opposite Harrison and, after peering at the menu, he called the waiter and ordered breakfast. Once the waiter moved away, the two men began talking to each other. Their conversation appeared to be very intense. However, their voices were so low, Agnes couldn't hear a word. She glanced towards Morris, wondering whether he would be able to hear anything from his position. However, despite him being on the other side of Harrison, he was too far away.

Allowing her mind to drift a little, she wondered whether Morris, in his capacity as an undercover detective, might have something plugged into his ear; the sort of thing that picked up various sounds and enhanced them. Perhaps there was someone in the control room back at the police station listening in to every word. She was forced to give up on this line of thinking, as the waiter appeared with her breakfast.

Agnes was draining the last drop of coffee from her cup when Harrison and his companion suddenly rose to their feet and left the dining room. Due to the angle of the mirrors, she was able to watch them as they strode across the reception area in the direction of the lift. The lift doors had barely closed behind them before Morris leapt to his feet and headed towards the stairs.

Once she was back in her room, Agnes wondered what to do that day. She had hoped the rain would stop, but, though it *had* eased slightly, it was still pretty miserable outside. Just then her phone rang; it was Alan at last.

He began by apologizing for having to leave her in the restaurant the previous evening.

"It wasn't your fault," she replied. "I feel so sorry for the person you found in the park." She paused. "Was the body in the same condition as the one I found?"

"Sadly, yes," Alan said.

"So we are looking at the same killer?"

"Yes." Alan picked up on the word 'we' in her reply, but chose not to mention it. He knew by now that it wasn't worth arguing about.

"I don't suppose the killer got careless this time and left a couple of clues?"

"If only," Alan replied. "It's getting ridiculous. All this technology at our fingertips and we still can't find a single clue. I sent a couple of men back there this morning to take another look, but it's a waste of time. Anything we missed last night will have been lost with all this rain."

Agnes looked across to the window; outside, the rain was still pouring down and the sky looked grey. "I agree, but you feel you have to do something."

"Look, Agnes, I'll have to go. I just wanted to say hello while I had the chance. Superintendent Blake has reared his head again. The wretched man has called a meeting this morning. I'm not sure what he thinks his get-togethers achieve; he's the only one who gets a kick out of them. I just wish we had something to tell him. At least it would get him off our backs."

"Alan, I think I might have something…" Agnes began, suddenly seeing the opportunity to tell him about who she saw lingering around the park the previous evening. However, she got no further.

"Sorry, Agnes, I've got to go. Blake is on his way. I'll get back to you later."

"Alan! *Alan*…" Agnes called out. But it was no use, he had gone.

* * *

The DCI replaced the receiver. He felt bad about cutting Agnes off like that, but he wanted to be in the incident room before the superintendent arrived. Blake seemed to take delight in making anyone who arrived after him feel like a schoolboy late for class.

Picking up a couple of files from his desk, he made his way out into the corridor. He wondered what Agnes wanted to tell him, though he doubted she could have any new information regarding the case. It had been late last night when he was called away and it was only mid-morning now. Nevertheless, he made a mental note to get back to her the moment Blake finished his rallying speech to the men.

When Alan entered the incident room, he found his men were grouped around the board, which showed the photographs of the two bodies found in the park. There were also a few close-ups of some of the knife wounds. Alan had already pinned up photographs of the tiepin, cufflink and the piece of material he and his sergeant had found at the scene after the first body was found. However, apart from that, the board was conspicuously bare.

There was none of the usual information, such as the names of the victims or their addresses. No names of parents, relatives, close friends or even their place of work – anything which normally gave the detectives working on the case somewhere to start.

A few minutes later, the superintendent marched through the door. He glanced around the room before striding towards the notice board. Throwing the folder he had been carrying onto a desk, he gazed at the photographs, his hands clasped behind his back.

The DCI raised his eyebrows knowingly at his sergeant. This didn't look good.

"Is this it?" Superintendent Blake asked. He unclasped his hands and swung around. "Is this all you have – a few photos taken at the scene?" He tapped his knuckles sharply on the board. "And you call yourselves detectives! You should…"

"But…" The voice came from somewhere behind him

"I don't want to hear your excuses," Blake turned to look at the man who had dared to interrupt him. "I want to hear something positive. Surely that isn't too much to ask?"

The superintendent prattled on about how things should be done… what he expected of his men.

However, DCI Johnson had stopped listening a while back. He was angry. No, more than that, he was seething. He didn't like this man. He had never liked him. From the moment Blake had first taken up the post earlier that year, Alan had taken an immediate dislike to him. He hadn't been sure why. There had just been something about his manner which had rung warning bells and the superintendent hadn't done anything over the last couple of months to appease him.

All Blake ever seemed to be interested in was taking credit when a case was closed. Then, he could be found sitting in his club drinking champagne with his chums, or in the press room giving an interview on how he had solved the case.

Alan had been sorry when Superintendent Slatten had been forced to retire due to ill-health. He had been a good officer and a good man. He listened to his men and took everything into account before saying a word. Not at all like the man standing before them now.

Yes, Blake was his superior. However, Alan was not going to stand by and watch this man run down his detectives.

"With all due respect, Superintendent," Alan took a step forward. His voice was quiet, yet a steely determination was evident. "Perhaps you're unaware that there were no clues left at the crime scenes. Or that there wasn't anything found on the bodies at the post-mortems, apart from the multiple stab wounds, all made from several knives. Even the victims' teeth had been smashed. All of which left Doctor Nichols with very little to tell us." Alan paused.

"Dr Nichols is the pathologist, by the way, just in case you haven't yet come across him due to your busy schedule. However, now you have been informed of the facts, maybe you will appreciate that we are all doing everything we can with absolutely nothing to go on. *Sir!*"

That last word hung in the air. Normally, it was a sign of respect for a senior officer. However, the way Alan had used it a moment ago, it sounded more like a sneer. A deathly hush followed, as the superintendent stared at the DCI as though he was unable to believe he had been spoken to in such a way, especially by a subordinate.

Alan glowered back, determined not to be the first to look away. Why the hell should he? The words were out and he had meant every one of them. Besides, to apologize now would only be a sign of weakness.

Still staring at his superintendent, Alan wondered where on earth that last thought had come from. But then he remembered. It was on the TV show called *NCIS*.

As it turned out, it was Superintendent Blake who looked away first. He glanced around the room looking for a show of support. But there was none. It seemed the detectives had taken the side of the DCI.

Suddenly feeling awkward, Blake picked up his folder and headed towards the door. "You haven't heard the last of this!" he roared as he left the room.

"He'll go to the Chief Superintendent," Andrews murmured, as the superintendent stormed off down the corridor.

"I know," Alan replied. "But I'll be ready when I'm called into the office."

Chapter Thirty

Once the telephone conversation with Alan had ended, Agnes decided to go downstairs to the drawing room to finish reading her newspaper. As much as she loved her room with its wonderful views up and down the River Tyne, she didn't feel she could sit there all day. Besides, the domestic staff would be coming in shortly to tidy around and she would only be in the way.

She had thought about sending Alan a text about who she had seen outside the park, but decided against it. She would rather tell him on the phone, or face to face. That way, she would witness his reaction to hearing how she had gone up to the park after he had told her to go straight back to the hotel! Anyway, it wasn't as though she had seen the killer; it was probably only someone as inquisitive as herself.

Agnes found that quite a number of seats were already occupied when she arrived in the drawing room. It seemed several other guests had had the same idea. Nevertheless, she was still able to find a comfy sofa furnished with large, plump cushions. It was close to the electric fire; the sort that displayed lifelike flames dancing in a grate of real coal. She was a little surprised that this sofa was still vacant. Unless someone had just left before she walked in.

Just the thing for such a stormy day, Agnes thought, glancing out of the window. The rain was pouring down from the thunderous-looking clouds rolling across the sky.

Making herself comfortable, Agnes opened her newspaper. She had already read the front page headlines, which screamed out about the body found in the park the previous evening. The story continued over four pages of the paper. She was surprised that the murder had been picked up so quickly. This must be a second edition.

As she read through each of the reports, Agnes realised they were all the same. Yes, they were written by different reporters, but they told the same story. At the end of the day, none of them told the readers anything new. How could they? Even the police didn't know anything. They had nothing to go on.

Lowering the newspaper, she cast her mind back to the previous evening, when she had seen the person loitering amongst the trees. She knew she should have called Alan immediately and given him the heads-up, but this might have given him the idea that she had ignored his instructions. Though, on reflection, she had *totally* ignored him!

Nevertheless, she knew she should have made him listen to her earlier this morning. It might have helped him at his meeting.

Feeling a little guilty, she changed her approach to the situation. Might she be letting her imagination run away with her? After all, she didn't for a moment believe she had spotted the killer lurking in the trees. Nonetheless, they might have seen who disposed of the body.

But then she had another thought; if that was the case, why hadn't that person already gone to the police? Maybe they already had…

Agnes folded her newspaper and tossed it to one side. All this thinking wasn't doing her any good at all. She glanced towards the window and wished the weather would clear up. She needed to get outside and walk around. It would help to clear her head.

"Do you mind if I join you?"

Agnes looked up to the unwelcome sight of Richard Harrison standing in front of her. Without waiting for a reply, he sat down on the sofa beside her. She inched away from him, not wanting to be too close.

"I would like to apologize for my behaviour last night. I think I had a little too much to drink."

"You *think*!" Agnes said coldly.

He grinned. "It happens sometimes. Don't tell me you haven't ever had one too many?"

"Yes, maybe," Agnes replied. "But I don't think I ever upset anyone with suggestive remarks."

"Okay, I'll say it again. I am *very* sorry about last night." He smiled. "Now that's out of the way, shall I order coffee for two?"

Agnes's first thought was to say, 'no thank you' and then tell him to park himself somewhere else. But she was curious about him and his sister-in-law, Joanne. What were they really up to? The only way she would learn anything from him would be to let him think he had fooled her.

Out of the corner of her eye, she saw Morris settling himself on a seat near the door and she immediately felt more at ease. At least he would be there if things got out of hand.

"Coffee would be very nice," she said, forcing a smile.

"Great," Richard said. He raised his hand to gain the attention of a waiter serving coffee to some guests nearby. "Coffee and scones for two, please, when you're ready."

Once that was done, he settled back in the sofa and stretched out his long legs.

"It's rather a disappointing morning, weather-wise." He nodded towards the window. "Did you have any plans for today?"

"No, not really. I tend to wait until I see what the weather is like, then I decide what I would like to do."

"Good idea. Weather can be so changeable at this time of the year. It's very difficult to plan ahead."

The waiter arrived with the coffee and scones and Richard paid the bill. She watched carefully as Richard poured out the coffee, to make sure that he didn't slip something into one of the cups.

Once he had finished, he set down the coffee pot and slid a cup towards her. Everything looked above board. Nevertheless, just to be on the safe side, she decided not to take even a sip until he had taken a drink from his cup.

Maybe she was being paranoid, but the last time she had accepted a drink from one of the guests, it had been laced with a drug. She'd had to be helped upstairs to her room before she fell into a sort of coma. She had awoken to find herself locked in the storeroom at the top of the hotel. There was no way she was going to allow that to happen again.

Richard offered her a scone, but she held up her hand.

"Thank you, but it isn't long since I finished breakfast."

"Me too," he said, taking one for himself. "But the ones they bake here are too delicious to pass up."

There was a brief silence while he munched his scone. He wiped some crumbs off his mouth, then asked, "have you visited many places in the world?"

"Yes, quite a few." Agnes mentioned some of the countries she and her husband had been to over the years.

She had actually been to many more places with her parents, due to her father's work in the Foreign Office. However, under the circumstances, she was determined to leave her father out of the conversation. Perhaps that was what this sweet talk was all about. Harrison might be trying to make her bring up the subject of her father.

"Very interesting," Richard said.

He went on to talk about some of the places he had visited in the past and then followed up by telling her where he would like his next port of call to be.

"Australia," he said, throwing his hands into the air with a flourish. "That's where I plan to go next. It's big, bold and beautiful."

"And in the meantime, you're here in Newcastle-upon-Tyne. What made you decide to come here?" There was brusqueness in her tone.

By now, she was fed up with all this chat and wished Richard would get to the point. She felt sure that the coffee, the scones, and the comfy tête-à-tête in front of the fire in the drawing room were all an effort to gain her confidence after he and Joanne failed so miserably the previous day.

Agnes had guessed he would try again, especially as he was staying at the same hotel. Wasn't that why he was staying here in the first place? Maybe that was why he had hung around the bar last night – to ply her with drink and lead her into believing he was her stepbrother. Let him try as many times as he liked. There was no way her father had had a sordid affair with his mother.

She was still reeling from the fact that she had even considered his accusation might be true when he had caught up with her at the racecourse. Harrison was a con-man and he was good at it. Even she had to admit that he researched his victims well; making sure it would be worth his while. She wondered how many people he had fleeced in the past. Now, it appeared it was her turn and he probably knew exactly what she was worth. Not only was he after her money, but she guessed he also had his eye on a share of the business her parents had left her.

* * *

Alan had been expecting a call from Chief Superintendent Lewis demanding he should report to his office immediately. Yet so far, it hadn't happened.

It had been well over an hour since Superintendent Blake stormed out of the incident room. He had sounded so angry when he left, Alan felt sure he would head straight to the chief superintendent's office to report him.

In the meantime, the DCI and his sergeant were mulling over the case for the umpteenth time. They had both been through the files several times already. Yet, once again, nothing stuck out at them.

"I'm going to call Agnes," Alan said, throwing down the file. It had suddenly occurred to him he had promised himself he would phone her once he was free. But instead, he had got caught up reviewing the case. "She seemed keen to tell me something."

However, just as Alan took out his mobile phone, it began to ring.

"It's Morris," he said, flipping it open.

"Sir, I don't have anything to report. Harrison didn't leave the hotel this morning. At the moment, he's sitting in the drawing room talking to Mrs Lockwood."

"Does everything look alright?" Alan asked. He placed his hand on the back of his head as he spoke. "I mean, does she give the impression that she's in any trouble?"

"She looks fine," he paused. "Though, from her expression, maybe she is getting a little bored with his company. He's been with her for some time now."

Alan didn't like the sound of it at all. However, there wasn't anything he could do, but at least Morris was there. He was relieved that he had decided to leave the undercover detective at the hotel.

"Okay, but stay with him. Don't let him out of your sight and get back to me if anything doesn't look right."

"Yes, sir," Morris replied.

Alan would have liked a few minutes to think it all through, but the phone on his desk rang. The call was from Detective Jones.

"Sir, I think we might have a lead on the cufflinks and tiepin," Jones said. "I suddenly remembered hearing about a fairly new jewellery shop on Pink Lane and wondered whether they might know something. Anyway, I decided to find the shop and show them a photo of the items. The owner, a Mr Anderson, told me he ordered the set for a customer shortly after he opened the shop."

"Are you still there now?" Alan asked, excitedly. This was the first break they'd had and he wanted to follow up on it immediately.

"Yes."

"Stay there, we'll be with you in a few minutes."

"Grab your coat, Andrews," Alan said, slamming down the phone. He hurried across to the coat stand. "Jones has found the shop that ordered the cufflinks we found in the park."

Just as they were leaving the office, the phone on Alan's desk began to ring.

"Shouldn't you get that?" Andrews asked, looking back towards the desk. "It could be the chief superintendent."

"Leave it," Alan said. By now, he was half-way down the corridor. "If it's the chief superintendent asking me to pop in for a chat, he'll have to wait. This is more important."

Andrews smiled and shook his head. Would he ever have the nerve to be so flippant?

Chapter Thirty-One

Agnes was still sitting in the drawing room with Richard Harrison. He was droning on about something. Though, truthfully, she didn't know what; she had lost interest a while back. Instead, she was thinking about Alan and where they might go this evening.

Glancing towards the windows, she was thankful she didn't have to venture out today. It was raining heavily now, with the wind howling like a lone wolf as it blasted between the tall buildings on the quayside. She shivered at the thought of being out in such weather.

She closed her eyes and continued to plan their evening together. If only they could have dinner here at the hotel. Alan could spend the night...

"Tell me about our father. Was he good to *you*? He certainly could have done more for me."

Agnes snapped her eyes open wide and glanced around the room, wondering whether anyone had overheard Richard's remark. However, she found that many of the guests had left and those remaining seemed to have dozed off. Even Morris seemed to have disappeared. Where had he gone?

How had she failed to notice the drawing room was thinning out as the morning wore on? She looked at her watch. It was almost lunchtime. Maybe she had dozed off with boredom.

"What are you talking about? I thought I'd already told you that the man in photo wasn't my father," Agnes said, defiantly.

She was in two minds whether or not to tell Harrison she'd had enough and walk out. However, she remained seated. She needed to get this over and done with; only then would he stop pestering her.

Her eyes were now fixed on the door. She could see a few people hovering around in the reception area. None of them were wearing coats, which meant they weren't going out. She hoped one or two of them might decide to make their way into the drawing room.

Thankfully, two couples walked in and settled themselves down onto the sofas. They looked quite young and, more importantly, wide awake and ready to chat to their companions.

"But it *was* your father. Why deny it?" Harrison shrugged. "He gave you a good life, while he gave me nothing."

"He was *not* your father. I would stake my life on that." Agnes paused. Out of the corner of her eye, she saw Morris walking back into the room.

"What are you hoping to achieve by all this nonsense?" she added.

"It isn't nonsense. I want what should have been mine!" Harrison almost spat out the words.

"And what would that be?" Agnes tried to keep her voice calm, though she was almost shaking with anger. But, for the moment, she wanted to keep him talking. Maybe he would slip up.

"You know what that is," he retorted. "The money, the business and..."

"And what about me?" Agnes retorted. "If your claims were to be true, wouldn't I have been entitled to a share?"

"You didn't need it," Richard snapped back at her. "You did okay. You married well and I understand your husband left you a great deal of money."

"How would you know what my husband left me?" Agnes responded, quickly. "That has absolutely nothing to do with you." She paused for a moment. "Or have you been prying into my husband's business as well?"

Harrison didn't answer. For a moment, he looked rather taken aback. But, pulling himself together, he reached into his pocket and drew out the photo he had shown her at the racecourse.

"This is your father – don't deny it!" he snapped, thrusting the picture into her hand.

Reluctantly, Agnes took it from him. She had hoped she would never set eyes on it again. Nevertheless, now that she was holding the picture in her hand, she took a swift glance at it. But then something struck her and she took a closer look. Yes, it certainly looked like her father, yet there was something about the whole image that didn't ring true.

"Where did you say you got this?" Agnes asked, still peering at the photo.

"I've already told you. My mother took it many years ago."

He reached out to take the photograph back, but she was too quick for him and swiftly pulled her hand away.

"May I hang onto it for a while?"

"Why? Surely you already have lots of pictures of our father. Why do you want this one?"

"Don't worry, I'll give it back to you," Agnes said.

She avoided answering his question. It was her intention to show the photo to Alan; he would be able to find out if it had been tampered with.

Harrison looked at her for a long moment. "Okay," he said, with a shrug. "Why not take a copy and add it to your family album? You've got everything else." He raised his voice as he uttered those last few words.

The buzz of conversation coming from the people who had entered the drawing room a little earlier, suddenly stopped and the room fell silent. Agnes didn't look up from the photo, yet she could feel their eyes piercing her.

She had to admit, this man was good. He knew how to work a crowd. Though there wasn't exactly a crowd here, he had certainly caught the attention of the few.

His casual demeanour about lending the only photograph he had of his father to a half-sister who wanted nothing to do with him, had given the impression that he was the good guy. Agnes knew there was nothing she could say or do at this stage which would help her situation. She would just have to continue to look like the bad guy until she could prove, once and for all, that Harrison was a con-man.

"Thank you," she said, with a smile that didn't quite reach her eyes. "I might just do that."

While Agnes was reaching down to place the photograph in her handbag, she saw him shift uneasily on the sofa. Perhaps he wasn't quite as blasé about her borrowing the picture as he had made out. Maybe he had hoped his cutting remark would have made her throw it back at him. If that was the case, it hadn't worked. Once it was safely tucked inside her bag, she pulled the zip closed, fearing he might try to retrieve it when she wasn't looking.

Just as she sat up, her mobile phone rang. Pulling it out of her pocket, she saw that the call was coming from Alan.

"Hello, so lovely to hear from you," she said. "I do hope your meeting went well this morning…"

Chapter Thirty-Two

It took longer for DCI Johnson and Sergeant Andrews to reach the jewellery shop on Pink Lane than they had first thought. With the weather being so bad, more people had decided to drive to their place of work, rather than walk or stand in bus queues.

More than once, Alan had been tempted to switch on the blue flashing lights fitted to his car for emergencies, but he kept telling himself that this wasn't an emergency. Or was it?

The person who had ordered the cufflinks and tiepin from the shop could already be trying to flee the area. Worse still, he could already be out of the country. The police hadn't allowed the information about the items found to reach the press or the television news broadcasts, fearing it would alert the killer. Yet, if they did belong to the murderer, would he hang around once he noticed they were missing?

Finally, Alan reached Pink Lane. Now, they would need to keep their eyes peeled to find the jewellery shop. The area was known more for its restaurants, bars and nightclubs, though, in the past, jewellery-cum-silver gift stores had also been in the zone.

"Jones said the shop is quite small and is tucked between two coffee shops," Alan told his sergeant.

"There!" Andrews pointed across to where Smithers was waving at them. He laughed. "I should have guessed Smithers would be here, too."

Alan flashed his headlights, indicating they had seen him and a moment later Smithers had disappeared from view. Who could blame him, in this weather?

When the DCI and Andrews walked into the shop, they found it a great deal larger than they thought it would be. Judging from the narrowness of the shop front, they had believed it would be quite tiny inside. However, it seemed the new proprietor had put a great deal of thought into his purchase to make maximum use of the space.

Outdated cupboards and anything else believed to be redundant in this day and age, had been torn down and replaced with more up-to-date shelving to display the merchandise. On the counter lay what appeared to be a large catalogue. Presumably, it showed items not normally held in stock, but which could be ordered for customers wanting something a little bit different. Towards the back of the store, Jones and Smithers were sitting in comfortable chairs near a large, ornamental fire.

Alan shook his head slowly as he looked around. He had seen all this before. Yes, the shop was warm and felt very comfortable, but he was sure it wasn't due to the imitation fire. That was only meant to entice customers inside during the cold weather. No doubt the heat was being blasted out from unseen radiators.

Seated next to the detectives was another man. He was wearing a smart business suit and a bow tie. Alan took him to be the owner of the establishment.

"Mr Anderson?" Alan queried.

"Yes, that's me, Charles Anderson."

"I'm DCI Johnson and this is Sergeant Andrews."

"Please take a seat," said Anderson. "Would you like some tea or coffee?"

"No, thank you, I'm fine," Alan said, pulling up a chair. He was anxious to get straight to the point. "Mr Anderson…"

"Charles, please,"

Alan nodded. "Charles, I understand from my officers that you recall ordering a tiepin and cufflinks matching the ones we found at a crime scene. Do you keep records of the people who place orders?"

"Indeed I do," Charles replied, with a broad smile. He held up a large folder stuffed with orders. "Even though I haven't been on these premises very long, I've had quite a number of people through the doors. Word seems to have got around that I am in a position to order items from all over the world. I have contacts everywhere."

"Does that mean you have the name and address of the man who ordered the cufflinks and tiepin?" Alan asked hopefully. It would be good to have luck on their side for a change.

"No, I'm afraid not," Charles replied. He opened the folder and pulled a sheet of paper from the top of the pile and handed it to the Chief Inspector. "I found the order in question shortly before you arrived. You'll see that the items were ordered by a woman – Mrs Elizabeth Small. I understand they were to be a special anniversary gift for her husband."

"But didn't she leave an address?" Alan sounded frustrated that his hope for a stroke of luck was about to collapse. "How were you supposed to get in touch with her when the items arrived?"

"You'll see that she left her mobile phone number," Charles replied, pointing his finger towards the order sheet, which Alan was still holding. "Apparently, she and her husband were staying at one of the hotels in the city but were being forced to check out the following day. It was all to do with a mix-up of dates at the time of booking. She was going to call into another hotel once she left the shop."

"Didn't you think that was odd?" Alan queried. "I mean, weren't you surprised that she and her husband had left it until almost the last minute before starting to look for somewhere else to stay?"

Charles shrugged. "I didn't think about it at all. It wasn't any of my business."

Alan shook his head in despair, before trying again. "But, looking at it from a different angle – which, I hasten to add, is *your business* – weren't you even a little concerned they might not find accommodation to their taste? If that were the case, Mr and Mrs Small would have no choice but to vacate the area, leaving you to bear the cost of the items."

Charles Anderson grinned and tapped his nose, knowingly. "Chief Inspector, clearly you are not a businessman, whereas I am. You see, the moment Mrs Small mentioned the uncertainty of her whereabouts when the goods were due to arrive, I suggested she paid up-front. I told her I was quite prepared to take a cheque, though I would need to wait for it to be cashed before I ordered the goods. She didn't quibble. She simply opened her handbag and paid the full amount – in cash."

"She paid in cash?" Alan gasped. He glanced again at the sheet of paper in his hand, thinking he must have misread it the first time. But there it was; the bill showed the cost at almost a thousand pounds.

Alan recalled Morris telling him the tiepin and cufflinks were expensive when he first saw the photographs in the incident room. Nevertheless, he had never even imagined that a mere set of cufflinks and a tiepin could cost so much. 'Expensive' to him would have been about one hundred pounds – at the most.

"Didn't you wonder," Alan continued, "why anyone would be wandering around the city with that amount of cash in their…" He broke off,

held up his hand and shook his head. "No, don't bother to answer that. I know… it was none of your business."

"Exactly, you've got it!" Charles said, clapping his hands together. "Why should I ask any questions? I had the money. For me, it was a win, win situation." He smiled. "I see you catch on quickly, Chief Inspector. I'll make a businessman of you yet!"

"Okay," Alan said, pulling himself together. "You called her and she came to collect the items. Did she say where she was staying? Did she mention how difficult it had been to find another hotel?"

"No, she didn't say anything much at all, actually. She looked at the tiepin and cufflinks and remarked on how her husband would love them. We shook hands and then she left."

"So, we've wasted our time here today." Alan slumped further down in the chair. "You can't really tell us anything new."

"That's because you didn't ask the right question," Charles said, excitedly. "You didn't ask whether I might be able to give you a description of Mrs Small."

"And can you?" Alan said doubtfully. By now, he'd had enough disappointments for one day. "Are you able to describe the woman?"

"I can do better than that," Charles said, leaping to his feet. He hurried over to his desk. "I have a photograph of her."

"Why on earth didn't you tell me that earlier?" Alan said, suddenly sitting bolt upright in his chair.

"You didn't ask!"

* * *

Back in the car, Sergeant Andrews tried to keep a straight face as the DCI mumbled on about the attitude of Charles Anderson.

"Can you believe it?" Alan raged. "The man seemed to be treating the inquiry into two murders as a sort of game." He paused. "*I see you catch on quickly*," he mimicked. "I hope I get the chance to show him exactly how quickly I can catch on."

Andrews and the other two detectives had remained silent while DCI Johnson questioned the shop owner. At the time, Andrews had wondered why Jones and Smithers hadn't already acquired the information regarding the CCTV camera and the photo from Charles Anderson, before they arrived. However, now, with hindsight, the shop owner probably ran rings around them, too.

"I agree," Andrews said. "He was a little over the top."

By now, they were back at the station. Once they were inside, Alan handed the photo to Andrews and told him to get copies made and handed out to all the detectives.

"Should I get on to the press?" Andrews queried. "We could get a lead if her picture is blasted on the front page of the newspapers."

Alan placed one hand on the back of his head and paced up and down the office for a long moment. He needed to think this through.

His sergeant was right. Newspaper headlines had certainly helped the police on more than one occasion. However, at this point in the investigation, he felt loath to broadcast the fact that they were looking for a woman who might be in a position help with their inquiries; well, not yet, anyway.

So far, they had got away with concealing the fact they had found the evidence at the scene, fearing the person would see the headlines and flee the area. Now, if it were known they were looking for a woman who could help with their inquiries regarding the said items, the whole episode would have to come out and both persons might leave on the next available flight out of Newcastle.

"No."

His mind made up, Alan stopped pacing and swung around to face his sergeant.

"Not yet. Give a copy to every police officer in the station. Tell them to study it and keep it with them. They need to look out for this woman. Inform the detectives to show the photograph at every hotel, restaurant, café and coffee shop in the city." He paused. "If Elizabeth Small gets wind that we're looking for her, she is likely to disappear – assuming, of course, that she is still in the area."

"I understand, sir. I'll shoot off to the lab and have them scan the photo and check the database. You never know, this woman might have popped up somewhere before. I'll distribute the copies as soon as I get them."

Alan nodded and the sergeant hurried out of the office and down the corridor.

Now that he was on his own, Alan realised he still hadn't telephoned Agnes. He walked across his office and closed the door. It usually stood open; he liked his detectives to think he was available at all times and, yes, he was. There wasn't anything he wouldn't do for them.

But right at the moment, he wanted a quiet moment with the woman he had loved since his childhood.

Chapter Thirty-Three

"Hello there. I am so happy to hear from you." Agnes said, when she answered her phone. She was so relieved to hear a friendly voice, having been stuck with Richard Harrison all morning.

"Are you okay?" Alan asked. "I heard from Morris. He told me Harrison had planted himself next to you this morning." He paused briefly. "Is he still there?"

"Yes," Agnes replied. She looked towards the window to make Richard believe she was talking about the weather. "Yes, it's still pretty miserable here."

Alan felt annoyed there wasn't anything he could do to stop Harrison from pestering Agnes. But unless she made a formal complaint to the police, his hands were tied. Maybe he would suggest that to her when they met up.

"On a brighter note, will you have dinner with me again this evening?" he asked. "Though, if this weather doesn't clear up, I'm not sure where we'll go. It's pretty miserable to drag you too far from the hotel and..."

"I'll call you back," Agnes interrupted and ended the call.

She had just thought of the most wonderful idea. Now, the last thing she wanted was for Harrison, who no doubt was hanging onto to her every word, to know her plans.

"Sorry, Richard," Agnes said. She leaned down and picked up her handbag. "This is a private call and I would rather take it somewhere else." She stood up and left the room.

* * *

Alan closed his phone, slowly. What was that all about? Had he heard her correctly? Agnes had interrupted him so suddenly and spoken so quickly, he might have misunderstood. She may have been in trouble. She may even have been asking for help.

Someone, presumably Harrison, could have snatched the phone away from her before she could say any more. In his agitated state, he began to call Morris, but then replaced the receiver. If Agnes *was* in trouble, Morris would already be trying to sort it out. To call him now and draw him away from his duty would be foolish. He needed to be patient. But, as most of his detectives knew, being patient was not one of his strongest features.

* * *

Upstairs in her room, Agnes called Alan back. From the way he spoke earlier, she got the impression he was alone and she hoped that was still the case.

"It's me," Agnes said, even though she knew he would have known who it was the moment his phone rang.

"I'm sorry about cutting you off earlier," she continued. "But I had a wonderful idea for dinner this evening and I didn't want Richard Harrison to know about it – nor any of the others who might have been interested in our conversation," she added, casting her mind back to the people sitting in the drawing room.

"Fine," Alan said. "Whatever it is, I'll go along with it."

"Then why don't we have dinner here?" Agnes continued. "By that, I mean *here*, in my room." She glanced around her room. "It's dry and warm, I have a TV, a radio, a table with two chairs and a sofa... in fact, I have all mod-cons."

Her eyes drifted towards the bed and, for one brief moment, she was tempted to suggest he stay the night, but held back. Let the evening take its own course.

"Anyway, what do you think?"

"Agnes, what can I say?"

Alan's first thought had been that she was about to put off their evening out due to the extremely inclement weather. Until now, they had tried to keep their relationship secret from Richard Harrison by going to restaurants away from the quayside; fearing he might see them together. However, luckily for them, the weather had been on their side – until today.

"You could say yes," she replied, coyly.

"Yes. Thank you, that would be wonderful."

"Great, I'll organize room service. Now, have you any news about the case?"

Alan told her about the photograph they had acquired that morning. "It's the first real lead we've had. Andrews is checking the database. He's also printing off some copies. I'll have one with me this evening. You can take a look, though I doubt you'll have come across her." He paused. "What were you so anxious to tell me about this morning?"

She was about to mention who she had seen outside the park the night the second body was found, but she didn't get the chance as there was a sudden commotion in Alan's office. Alan told her to hold on for a moment, while he listened to what one of his detectives had to say. Though Agnes couldn't hear every word of the conversation, she did grasp that a person had been reported missing. This could be another lead.

"I'm sorry, but I'll have to go," Alan spoke back into the phone. "Something's happened…"

"Yes, I heard," Agnes interrupted. "You must go. We'll speak again later."

Alan said goodbye and followed his detective down the corridor towards the incident room. Sergeant Andrews was handing out copies of the photograph they had received that morning. One was already pinned to the notice board.

"Nothing in the database so far," Andrews said, when he saw the DCI stride into the room. "But I left before the search was complete, so we could still hear something."

"I doubt it," Alan replied, shaking his head. "I think our best bet is to get out there with these photographs. Show them to everyone we can and hope that someone recognizes her." He paused. "Now, about this missing person… Who is it and who's reported him missing?"

It turned out that the call had come from the police station in Whitley Bay, a seaside town situated on the east coast of Newcastle. Sergeant Andrews read out the report, which had been handed to him by the desk sergeant.

"Mr and Mrs Patterson, the parents of a young man named John, had been abroad on business for a few weeks. They had left him in charge of the family business while they were away. However –" Andrews broke off and looked up at the DCI. "Do you want to read this out?"

Alan shook his head and gestured for his sergeant to carry on.

Andrews nodded and looked back down at the report. "They arrived home to find their son missing. It seems he was due to pick them up from Newcastle Airport, but he didn't turn up. Assuming he was either still at the office or caught up in traffic, they rang his mobile to let him know they would make their own way home, but there was no reply.

"Once they reached home, they immediately set about looking for their son. They called into the office and contacted his friends, but no one had seen him for several days. They all thought he had decided to 'take off' for few days. But his parents said he would never go off without a word to anyone. That was when they decided to contact the police station in Whitley Bay. A photograph and further details of the missing man were emailed here. However, Doctor Nichols believes they could fit a number of people."

Andrews looked up from the report. "The parents are on their way here right now. I instructed Jones to pick them up from their home."

Alan nodded his approval, before focusing his attention on the photographs pinned on the board, especially the two showing the murder victims.

Behind him, Andrews instructed the detectives to start making enquiries at hotels, restaurants and anywhere else they thought the woman in the photo might have been seen. "Be sure they all take a good look at the photograph. It is imperative that we find this woman," he told them.

Once the detectives had left, Andrews stepped alongside the DCI.

"I know what you're thinking," he said. "Those people are going to get a terrible shock when they see the bodies. If only there was some other way."

"We're told we should always try to prepare relatives, before they enter the morgue." Alan sighed, as he gestured towards the photos of the mutilated bodies. "But how can you prepare anyone for something like that?"

Turning away from the board, he paced up and down the floor, his hands clasped firmly behind his back.

"We must ask the parents whether their son has any distinguishing marks on his body," Alan continued. "You know the sort of thing I mean. Something they would recognize – a mole, a birthmark, or even a tattoo. I know it's a long shot. Doctor Nichols didn't find anything special on the bodies. However, there isn't anyone who knows a son better than his mother and, if there was something, Nichols could check it out. It could save the parents having to look at the bodies."

Andrews didn't say anything; there was no need, as the expression on his face said it all.

Alan took a deep breath. "Okay, I'm clutching at straws, but let's give it a try, anyway."

There wasn't time to say any more, as Jones walked into the incident room with the news that he had left the parents in the DCI's office.

"WPC Marriot organized some tea and she's with them now." He lowered his eyes for a moment. "They're in a bad way."

Alan glanced at his sergeant, before looking back at the detective. "Thank you, Jones. Leave it with us."

"*Us?*" Andrews enquired, once Jones had left.

"Yes, us," Alan replied, walking towards the door.

"Sir, are you saying that you want me to be there with you in your office when you talk to the parents?" Andrews questioned.

He hadn't thought he would be involved in the painful interview with the bereaved relatives. He had done this kind of thing before, but not when the bodies had been left in such an appalling state. Usually, the senior officer took over.

"Don't you think that will be a little intimidating for them?" Andrews said, as he followed his DCI out of the incident room. "Er, I mean, aren't they already going through a bad time?"

"Yes, they are. But it'll be good for them to see that we're putting everything into catching the killer of their son – if one of them turns out to be their son. Besides, it'll be good practice for you when you get to be a DI."

Alan swung around to face his sergeant. "Of course, if you aren't up for it…"

Sergeant Andrews took a deep breath.

"I'm up for it," he said as he followed his DCI down the corridor.

Chapter Thirty-Four

It was just after eight when Alan arrived at the hotel. They normally met up at around seven or seven-thirty. However, today had been exceptionally busy at the Newcastle Police Station.

First, there was the photograph of a woman said to have ordered the set of cufflinks and tiepin found at the crime scene. Then a couple had come forward and, after having seen both victims, they identified one of them as their son.

During the initial interview with Mr and Mrs Patterson, they stated that John had no birthmarks or tattoos. Therefore, it had been necessary to warn the parents that they might need to view two bodies; something Alan had hoped to avoid.

The two victims had been lying side by side in the morgue when Elaine and William Patterson stepped inside.

Doctor Nichols uncovered one of the bodies and, though both parents had been shocked at the sight, they shook their heads, indicating that it wasn't their son.

However, they had both recoiled in horror when they viewed the next victim.

"It's John – our lovely son. No! No! This isn't happening!" Elaine Patterson had screamed. Her voice had echoed around the walls of the morgue and she had clung to her husband for support, as the white sheet was hastily drawn back over the body of what had once been their young and vibrant son.

"I'll never forget the look on their faces until I find this killer and put him behind bars," Alan said grimly, as he paced up and down Agnes's room. "I have got to make this man pay for his terrible crimes."

He hadn't intended to start talking about his day; not in such depth, anyway. But he had looked so drained when he arrived that Agnes had guessed immediately that something had happened.

"What can I do to help?" she asked quietly, when he had finished speaking. "And don't tell me to stay out of it. From what you've told me, I gather it was me who found the body of their son."

Alan stopped pacing and hurried over to Agnes.

"Okay, that's true," he said. "Nevertheless, it doesn't mean you need to get any further involved."

"But I do," Agnes insisted. "I want to help catch this... murderer."

Alan fumbled around in the pockets of his jacket as he suddenly remembered the photograph he had acquired from the jewellery shop that morning.

"Why don't you take a look at this? Have you seen this woman before?" Alan held out the photograph.

He hoped that showing her a picture of someone she had probably never seen in her life would persuade Agnes to believe she had done her best... that from now on, she would leave the police to get on with solving the crime.

Agnes took the photo from Alan's hand. She looked at it for a moment before sinking into a chair by the table.

"You've seen this woman?" Alan asked. He sat down next to her and took her hand.

"Seen this woman? Yes, I have," Agnes replied, still staring at the photo. "But more than that, I've actually met her."

Alan was astounded. "You've met Elizabeth Small?"

However, before any more could be said, there was a knock on the door, followed by a voice calling out, "Room service."

It was only after the waiter had delivered their meal and left the room that they were able to continue their conversation.

"No, I haven't met Elizabeth Small," Agnes said, tapping the photograph. "But," she said, shifting her focus to Alan, "I *have* met Joanne Lyman."

"You mean this is the same woman Richard Harrison introduced you to?"

"Yes, and it was she who was hustling the man on the quayside that same day. But there's more, Alan. I saw this woman again the night the second body was found."

"You mean you saw her at the hotel?"

"No. It wasn't at the hotel." Agnes hesitated. She had been dreading having to tell Alan what she had got up to the night he had been called away.

"I saw her standing outside the park. She was watching the police while you were all at the crime scene."

"Agnes! What the hell were you doing there?" He stood up and began to pace up and down the floor again, one hand placed firmly on the back of his neck. "You could have got yourself killed!"

"Don't worry, I wasn't alone. Ben was with me and I didn't get out of his taxi. And, before you get all grouchy at him, it was all my idea. I insisted he drove past the park before bringing me back to the hotel. He agreed, albeit reluctantly, though he told me he wouldn't stop the car." She heaved a sigh. "Anyway, Alan, do you want to hear about it or not?"

Alan stopped pacing and went to sit beside her. "Of course I do." He took her hand. "I'm sorry I got angry, it's just that I worry about you all the time."

"I know you do, Alan, and I really appreciate it. But you must try to understand that I have always been my own person. I can't change now."

She glanced at the trolley; their food was being kept warm inside. Even so, it wouldn't stay hot forever. "Look, why don't we have our meal while we talk?" she added.

Alan nodded and pulled the trolley closer to the table. He opened the doors and, donning the oven gloves left by the waiter, he pulled out the plates and several serving dishes.

"This looks wonderful, Agnes," he said, as he uncovered each of the dishes. "But there is so much food here. Are you expecting anyone else for dinner?"

"I forgot to ask you what you'd like for dinner this evening, so I ordered a few things from the menu. I thought we could mix and match."

Once they had helped themselves to the food and were comfortably seated, Agnes told Alan about how she had seen Joanne Lyman at the park the night the second body was found.

"Like I said, I saw someone hanging around in the trees, but I couldn't make out who it was, so I asked Ben to turn the car around and drive past the park again."

She went on to explain how, only after a great deal of perseverance on Ben's part, she had been able to see the face of Joanne Lyman.

"I have to admit it's very strange her being there," Alan said, thoughtfully. "However, I'm not sure she's the killer. For one thing, I can't imagine a woman doing such a horrific thing as mutilating a body like that, let alone being able to carry it into the park. Both men were large and, while not particularly overweight, they were heavy."

"I agree," Agnes replied.

"You do?" Alan sounded surprised.

"Yes, well, about the weight of the bodies, anyway," said Agnes. She shrugged. "I'm not sure about the other thing, though."

"Maybe Harrison is still in the frame after all," Alan said, deciding not to delve any further into whether a woman was capable of carrying out such a heinous crime. He picked up the bottle of wine and refilled their glasses. "Perhaps he did the deadly deed and his woman friend went out there to make sure he hadn't left anything behind which might incriminate him. But before she got there, the body had been found."

"You're forgetting something."

"I am?"

"Yes," said Agnes. She took a sip of wine before continuing. "You're forgetting that Detective Morris has been tailing Harrison for the last few days."

Alan slapped his forehead. "Of course he is! What am I thinking?"

"Besides," Agnes continued, "when I finally arrived back at the hotel that night, Harrison was staggering out of the bar. He was well and truly drunk. It looked as though he had been there all evening." She grinned.

"He didn't look too bright at breakfast the following morning, either, though he cheered up a little when a friend joined him for breakfast," she added thoughtfully.

"Male or female?"

"Male," Agnes replied. She thought back to the morning in question. "The thing is, I had a strange feeling I'd seen him before." She shrugged. "But I couldn't think where."

She held up her glass. "Any more wine in that bottle?"

"We should have ordered two," Alan said, as he refilled her glass, "though maybe I shouldn't have any more."

"I did order two," Agnes replied, pointing to another bottle standing on the dressing table. She tipped her head to one side. "Why can't you have another drink? You're not driving, are you?"

"No, I took a taxi."

"Then for goodness' sake have another drink, Alan. Let your hair down!"

Alan ran his fingers through his hair, ruffling it a little. "What do you think?"

"It suits you."

Alan swung around in his seat to take a look in a mirror. "You think?" he said, touching the top of his head.

Agnes clenched her lips together, trying hard not to laugh. But the style was so out of keeping with his normal well-groomed look, she couldn't hold back for long and burst out laughing.

Alan took another look in the mirror and pulled a face. "I look like one of those pop singers – well, perhaps an older model"

"Shall we see what they've sent for dessert?" she said when she finally stopped laughing. "There were so many wonderful things on the menu, I found it difficult to choose. Therefore I told them to include whatever was at the top of their list of specialities."

"Agnes!" Alan gasped when he saw the superb selection the kitchen had prepared. "They all look so delicious. It will be hard to choose."

At the end of their meal, they moved away from the table and settled themselves on the sofa.

"What are we going to do about this woman, Joanne Lyman? Or is it Elizabeth Small?" Agnes thought for a moment. "I wonder how many other names she is known by?"

"I need to think about it," Alan replied. "But, if you should happen to meet her again, don't say anything about the photo, or that the police know about her other name. We don't want her running off somewhere."

There was silence for a long moment before Alan spoke again.

"Morris told me you were having a rough time with Harrison this morning."

"Yes, he was trying to get his hands on my business."

"Your business?"

"Yes, my business."

Agnes slid around on the sofa and looked at him squarely. "I should have told you all this before, but the topic never came up. When my father stopped working for the government, he decided to set up his own business. He opened a small shop in north London selling men's suits, shirts and ties at very reasonable costs. You might recall that even then, not everyone was able to afford High Street prices."

She paused for a moment, reflecting on the shop in Tottenham.

"Once the word got around, the business took off," she continued. "My mother suggested he should buy larger premises and include women's clothes and accessories in his stock. She told him she would be willing to look after the women's department.

"Anyway, to cut a long story short, while my father was still thinking it through, the shop next door suddenly went up for sale and he decided to buy it. They cut an arch through the wall, making it into one store. True to her word, my mother took on the women's clothing side of the business and between them, they did well. In fact, they started selling other items in the shop and in the end they had to expand even further."

"They bought another shop?"

"Yes, but not in Tottenham. Though the original store is still there to this day. The staff had been so loyal, my parents couldn't bear to let it go. They even appointed one of their most faithful employees as manager." Agnes smiled. "Actually, that man's son is in charge now."

"So where did they decide to open their new shop?" Alan asked.

"Guess!" she said.

He slapped his forehead as he suddenly recalled the name of a large store in London.

"Surely you don't mean Harrison's – *the* Harrison's? The department store in London?"

Agnes nodded. "Yes, I do. Okay, I know it sounds unbelievable, but it's true and I inherited it when my parents died. I kept their name above the door and I have someone who runs the business for me – someone I really trust. Believe me, if I didn't trust him, he would be out on his ear."

Alan smiled. He could believe that. He doubted anyone would pull the wool over her eyes.

"There are a few shareholders, but not many," Agnes continued. "I still hold the majority of the shares – by more than fifty-one percent. I make it my business to go to any key meetings, no matter where I am. Also, the final decision on anything important in the running of the company is mine. In other words, the company is mine and will be until…" She swallowed hard, "until my boys need to take over from me."

"It's unbelievable," Alan gasped. "I didn't have a clue you were *that* Harrison."

"Why would you? I'd never mentioned it and I don't suppose it ever occurred to you to look into my background."

She shrugged, still trying to puzzle it out in her head.

"For instance, how did Harrison know my name in the first place? As I recall, he saw me for the first time the day you caught up with me in the park. And you didn't mention my name – certainly not my surname."

Alan stood up and began to pace up and down, as he pondered over what Agnes had said. Suddenly, he stopped pacing and turned back to face her.

"It's possible Richard Harrison first heard of you when you made the headlines last year."

"But they would only have known me by my married name," Agnes pointed out.

"That's true." Alan scratched his head for moment while he gave it more thought. "However sometimes, when a newspaper wants to get one up on another, they do a little extra research. I seem to recall it was mentioned that you were visiting your hometown, when you were suddenly plummeted into a murder inquiry. Maybe one of the researchers came up with your maiden name. They might also have found out that your father had worked for the government. All this new information could have been mentioned at some time. If Harrison saw it, then…"

"You're saying that Richard Harrison started tracing my past from that moment?" Agnes interrupted.

"I'm speculating, Agnes. "I could be wrong. I'm just thinking aloud."

"Sorry." Agnes gestured for him to carry on.

"However, if I'm right and Harrison did start researching your past last year, he could have put two and two together and come up with the right answer. But by then, you had left the area."

Alan sat back down on the sofa and took Agnes's hand.

"He might have put the whole thing down to a waste of time. However, seeing you in the park the day after the murder, he quickly decided to pick up where he'd left off."

Agnes shook her head slowly. "It sounds so plausible. I believe you could be right." She sighed. "But I only went to the park to pick up on my past."

"I know. It was just a stroke of bad luck that Harrison happened to be there at the same time."

"And a stroke of good luck that you were there, too," Agnes quickly replied. "Now, can we change the subject?"

"It's stopped raining," Alan said, glancing towards the window.

"Is that the best you can come up with?" Agnes laughed.

"That depends. What do you suggest?"

"I thought you'd never ask!"

Chapter Thirty-Five

When Alan arrived at the station the following morning, he headed straight for the laboratory.

"Can you tell me whether this picture has been tampered with?" Alan said to the first technician he met. He held up the photograph Agnes had given him the previous evening.

The technician, a woman wearing a white coat, took the photograph from him and peered at it through her heavily-rimmed glasses.

"I'll need to look at it in detail, Chief Inspector," she said, still staring at the photo. "But what I *can* tell you right away is that this photographic paper is not what they would have used back when the picture was originally taken."

She glanced up at Alan and smiled. "This is more modern, the type of photo-paper many people use today to print out copies of photos from their albums." She paused and looked down at the picture again. "But that doesn't mean it's been Photoshopped. Someone might have reprinted it to keep the original from being ruined altogether."

"That's true," Alan replied. "Nevertheless, I'd be grateful if you'd examine it as soon as you can and let me know if you find anything that doesn't seem quite right."

"Will do," she said. "I'll start right away and get back to you later."

In the incident room, Alan informed his team of what he had learned the previous evening.

"I have been informed that the woman," he said, stabbing a fore-finger at the photograph pinned to the notice board, "who we first believed to be Elizabeth Small, is also known as Joanne Lyman. For all we know, she might be using a stream of other names. Bear that in mind when you're out there today showing the picture to the shops and restaurants in the city."

There was the usual hum of voices after the DCI had given his instructions. However, Alan hadn't finished. He held up his hand to halt the buzz of conversation.

He went on to inform them that the woman in question had been seen hanging around the trees at the edge of the park the night the second body was found; though he held back from naming Agnes as the person who had seen her.

"I'm sure you'll agree it is imperative that this information is not leaked to the press. This woman," Alan stabbed his finger at the photograph again, "must not learn we're looking for her. I don't want her to suddenly up sticks and leave the area before I have the chance to question her." He glanced around the room. "Does anyone have any questions?"

Once it was clear no one had anything to say, Alan wished them all good luck as they left the room.

"I assume it was Mrs Lockwood who gave you the other name for the woman we know as Elizabeth Small," Andrews said, as he and the DCI walked back down the corridor.

"I certainly can't fool you, Sergeant." Alan grinned as he pushed open the door to his office. "The woman was introduced to Mrs Lockwood by Harrison when he caught up with her at the racecourse."

"She's actually met this woman?" Andrews uttered.

"Yes," the DCI replied. He allowed the door to swing shut once they were both inside the room. "And, though it would probably help our case enormously if she did," he continued, as he strode across to his desk, "I hope she never comes into contact with the woman again."

Andrews nodded, thoughtfully.

"What else is on your mind, Sergeant?" Alan asked.

He lifted his elbows onto the desk and made a steeple with his fingers.

"I'm trying to figure out who told you that Elizabeth Small – or is it Joanne Lyman? – was hanging around the park when we were investigating the murder."

Alan didn't say a word. He simply tipped his head to one side and continued to watch as his sergeant mulled it over.

"Of course!" Andrews slapped the side of his head. "It was Mrs Lockwood." He narrowed his eyes. "But what the hell was she doing there?"

"Don't bother to go down that road. I asked the same question, Andrews."

"And?"

Alan removed his elbows from the table. "It's a long story, Sergeant. However, you can be sure that I didn't take her there. Mrs Lockwood is a law unto herself."

"Amen to that," Andrews replied.

* * *

Agnes wasn't sure whether to go downstairs for breakfast and risk running into Richard Harrison in the restaurant, or have it served in her room. It was his piercing eyes that she couldn't stand. They seemed to bore a hole right through her whenever he looked in her direction.

If Alan hadn't had to leave so early, she would have ordered breakfast upstairs for the two of them and the problem would have been solved. Besides, having breakfast together would have been the perfect end to the blissful night they had spent in each other's arms.

However, when he told her that it was important that he should pass on the information she had given him regarding Elizabeth Small to his team, she had fully understood. After all, Alan was working on a pretty gruesome murder inquiry. He had also said he would speak to the lab about the photograph and promised to get it back to her later that day.

After a great deal of deliberation, she decided to go downstairs for breakfast, realizing that she couldn't stay hidden in her room forever. When she stepped out of the lift, there wasn't any sign of Harrison hanging around the reception area. She breathed a huge sigh of relief when she found he wasn't in the dining room, either.

Over breakfast, Agnes wondered how to spend her day. The weather was much better than it had been the day before, though there were a few dark clouds hovering overhead. After some deliberation, she finally decided to visit the shopping centre. If it did rain, she wouldn't even know about it until she left. But, more importantly, she would be so involved with what the shops had to offer, she could forget all about Richard Harrison.

* * *

Shortly after Alan had ended his briefing in the incident room, he received a call from the laboratory.

"The photograph you left with me has been Photoshopped."

"I'm on my way," Alan said. He replaced the phone and leapt to his feet. "I'm just going downstairs," he told Andrews, as he hurried towards the door. "I'll tell you about it when I get back."

Downstairs in the laboratory, the woman Alan had spoken to earlier was waiting for him when he strode into an office used by most of the technicians. Several desks were crammed into the small space and she was standing by one of them.

She looked very different without the white coat she had been wearing earlier. It was only due to her distinctive glasses, and the auburn hair which now fell loosely around her shoulders, that he recognised her. When they had met earlier, her hair had been tied in a tight knot at the back of her head. The style had made her look much older.

"You have some news for me, Ms Swinton," Alan said, looking at the name badge pinned on her sweater.

"Yes, like I said on the phone, this picture has been Photoshopped," she replied. "I have to admit that whoever worked on it was very clever and knew what they were doing. Anyone simply being shown the picture would assume it was the real deal – and most of it is. Nevertheless, after careful scrutiny, I can assure you that it has been tampered with."

She pointed at the man in the photograph. "This is not the face of the person who was in the original shot. The head has been replaced by the one we see now. You can see what I mean here on the screen."

She gestured toward a laptop where the photo had been greatly enlarged.

"There is a hint of a join here." She indicated to where the head and neck met. "Obviously, the new head didn't quite fit the body and whoever Photoshopped the picture did the best they could by emphasizing the shirt collar. There are a couple of other things, but that is the most obvious." She shrugged. "Perhaps if they had worked on it a little longer, it wouldn't have shown up. But maybe they were pressed for time."

"I think that's the answer," Alan said thoughtfully, still staring at the screen. "It was a rush job. Though quite honestly, even if I had scanned the photo into my computer and enlarged it, I doubt I would have noticed the join."

"That's what they pay us for, Chief Inspector!" She laughed.

"Probably not enough," Alan replied.

"That's true. Nevertheless, I enjoy what I do and helping to bring criminals to account more than makes up for the lack of money."

Alan had a huge smile on his face when he stepped back from the laptop.

"You look very pleased with yourself," she remarked.

"Indeed I am, Ms Swinton. Your findings have set me on the path to catching a fraudster."

"Then, like I said, I'm delighted to have been able to help."

* * *

On his way back upstairs, Alan called Agnes and told her the good news.

"We have him," he said, the moment she answered. "I had the photo checked out in the lab and they tell me it's been Photoshopped."

"That's brilliant news, Alan. You can't believe how relieved I am to hear that."

"What's all that noise in the background? I can hardly hear you."

"I'm in the Eldon Square Shopping Mall." She raised her voice, to make herself heard above the racket going on around her. "I thought I needed to get away from the hotel for a while and what could be better than a few hours shopping?"

Alan had never understood what women loved about shopping. When he wanted something new, he went to one of the few shops he frequented, chose what he wanted, paid and left. They all knew him and made sure they always had the items he needed in stock. He had never gone from store to store looking for an item, only to end up back at the first one and purchase it there.

"If you say so, Agnes," he chuckled.

Yet, despite his frivolity, he was reassured to know that she was in a crowd, rather than tucked away in the corner of the hotel at the mercy of Harrison and Joanne Lyman, or whatever the wretched woman was calling herself today.

"If I get the chance, I'll meet up with you for a quick lunch."

Alan had almost reached his office by the time his call with Agnes ended. He stopped for a moment and stuffed the phone into his pocket before opening the door.

Andrews looked up as the DCI walked in. "Anything to go on?" he asked.

"Yes, but not with the murder case," Alan replied. "It seems that the man we know as Harrison really is a fraudster."

He went on to tell his sergeant about the photograph Agnes had been concerned about.

"It's a fake!" he declared. He handed the photo to his sergeant. "I took it to the lab and had it checked out. The technician assures me it has been Photoshopped… Agnes's father's head grafted onto someone else's body."

"It looks real enough," Andrews said, staring down at the picture.

"I agree, but take a look at this." Alan held out an enlarged photo. "She showed me this on a laptop and I asked her to print out a copy."

Andrews whistled through his teeth. "I would never have spotted that."

"No. I didn't see it, either."

By now, Alan was pacing up and down the floor of the office. "However," he continued, "now that we know what he's up to, we've got to put a stop to his game. How many people has he fooled into parting with their hard-earned money, simply by changing the face on a photo?"

"But," Andrews took a deep breath, "where does the woman, Elizabeth Small, also known to Mrs Lockwood as Joanne Lyman, fit into this puzzle? Are we looking into her for fraud or murder?"

"That's a good question, Andrews."

Alan stopped pacing and walked over to look out of the window. "And I've got to find the answer ASAP."

"Do you mean before Mrs Lockwood does?" Andrews grinned.

"Exactly." Alan winked.

Chapter Thirty-Six

Agnes was enjoying her shopping trip. She had bought a few things and had now decided to stop off in a coffee shop for a few minutes to rest her legs. She hadn't wanted to go to a restaurant, as Alan had said he would try to join her later. Despite knowing he was working on a murder case, she hoped he might find time to grab a sandwich with her.

Sipping her coffee, Agnes relaxed into the comfortable leather chair and looked around the café. Most of the other customers seemed intent on their laptops, only pausing now and again to take a sip of coffee.

However, one man in particular caught her eye. He wasn't using a laptop. Instead, he was focused on the newspaper spread out in front of him. He looked very like the man who had joined Richard Harrison in the dining room for breakfast the other morning.

She looked away, not wanting to draw attention to herself, though she doubted if he would have recognised her even if she had been sitting opposite him. On the morning in question, he hadn't appeared to pay much attention to her or anyone else having breakfast, as both he and Harrison had been deep in conversation about something.

Nevertheless, she couldn't afford to take the risk. He might end up tailing her for the rest of the day. She did consider taking a photo of him, but changed her mind. If the flash went off, everyone would turn to look in her direction.

Agnes kept her face turned away from him until she had finished her coffee and swiftly left the café. Outside in the mall, she hung around for a few moments to see whether he followed her out. When there was no sign of him, she breathed a sigh of relief.

Shortly afterwards, she had a call from Alan.

* * *

"What was it about the photo that made you realise it was a fake?" Alan asked, once they had been seated in a restaurant on the corner of John Dobson Street.

He placed the photograph on the table in front of Agnes. "I left this picture with a technician in the laboratory and she later told me it had been Photoshopped. She showed me exactly where the original face had been replaced with this one."

He pulled the enlarged copy from his pocket and placed them side by side. "I didn't spot the join. Did you?"

"No," Agnes said, peering at the photos more closely. "I didn't see that at all."

"Then what was it in the picture that set you thinking about its authenticity?"

Agnes pointed at the left arm of the man in the picture. His elbow was slung over the top of the car while his forearm hung over the side. "This man is not wearing a watch. My father never went *anywhere* without his watch."

Tears welled in her eyes and Alan reached across the table to take her hand.

"One day, I asked him why he wore it all the time," Agnes continued. "He explained that it meant a great deal to him. He told me his parents had never been wealthy, yet they had saved a little money every week for several years to buy him something special for his coming of age, as it was called back then."

Alan nodded.

"Dad told me it was one of the best watches on the market at the time. He had seen them advertised in the newspapers and longed to own one, though he never thought he would. He learned later that the jeweller had ordered it from somewhere in London, though he

214

demanded a large deposit up front before agreeing to even place the order."

She looked at Alan. "I don't know why I'm telling you all this. All I really meant to say was that my father was so emotional about how his parents had strived to give him such a wonderful present, he vowed he would wear it forever."

She smiled and nodded through her tears. "And he did. My father wore it all the time. It never once let him down. It was almost as though that watch knew what it meant to him." She paused. "Now I suppose you think I'm being silly."

Alan shook his head. "Not at all, Agnes."

He fingered the watch on his own wrist. His parents had done much the same for him.

"Anyway," Agnes added, "getting back to your question. That's the reason I knew the man in the picture wasn't my father. But I needed further proof. No one would take my word alone that the picture was a fake. They would have argued that he had left his watch at home that day."

"Our lab technician proved you were right," Alan said.

"Yes. But only because *you* asked them to check it out," Agnes quickly replied. "Think about it, Alan. If I had walked into any police station in Newcastle and asked the officer on the desk to have this photo checked over, would he have taken any action?"

Alan didn't quite know how to reply to her question. With all the recent cuts in the police budget, she could well have been told to wait and see whether she was bothered again before taking further action. Fortunately, he was let off the hook and didn't need to say anything, as the waiter suddenly appeared, carrying their lunch.

They had only just finished eating when Alan received a call from his sergeant. "I'm on my way."

"Sorry, Agnes," he said, once the call had ended. "I'm going to have to go." He pulled out his wallet. "A woman has just reported her husband missing."

"It's okay." Agnes rested her hand on his arm. "You go. I'll get this."

"Thank you. Hopefully, we can have dinner together this evening. I'll call you later."

"That would be lovely, Alan. But, if you find yourself stuck for time, we could always have room service again."

"Only if I can bring a clean shirt with me this time." Alan laughed. He picked up the shopping bags Agnes had acquired that morning. "I'll put these in my car, to save you carrying them around."

"Great," she called out as he hurried towards the door. "Now I can buy a whole load more stuff!"

Chapter Thirty-Seven

Sergeant Andrews was pacing the floor when the DCI walked into his office.

"Looks like my habits are rubbing off on you." Alan threw his coat over a hook on the stand by the door. "I take it the lady hasn't arrived yet?"

"No," Andrews replied. "Mrs Ann Western is on her way down from Bamburgh." He looked at his watch. "She might be a little while yet."

Bamburgh is a small coastal town in North Northumberland, well known for the twelfth-century castle poised high above the town.

"Is there anything you can tell me before she arrives?"

"Mrs Western's husband, who runs his own business, had taken time off to go on some sort of safari. He had told her he would call when he could. By that, he meant when he had a signal, which was why she wasn't unduly worried until the day before yesterday. That's when he was due home. I understand she called his phone, but when it kept going to voicemail, she tried ringing the airport. However, there was no record of him even being on a flight to or from Africa. That's when she started to panic and called the police. I understand her niece is driving her down here."

Alan nodded thoughtfully.

The couple, who identified the first victim as their son, had told the police he was looking after the family business while they were away. Now, it appeared the second victim was also a man with his own business. If that was the case, there was a pattern forming.

Alan narrowed his eyes. "Harrison," he mumbled.

"Sorry, did you say something?" Andrews asked.

"I was thinking aloud," the DCI replied. "It suddenly came to me that Harrison might fit into this somewhere." He paused. "You recall me telling you how he had tried to con Mrs Lockwood out of money?"

Andrews nodded.

"Well, I had a notion he could be our murderer," Alan continued. "But then I suddenly remembered that the night the second body was found, he had spent the evening in the bar at the hotel. Mrs Lockwood told me she saw him staggering around the reception when she arrived later that evening." He shrugged. "Besides, Morris has been tailing him for a while. He would have seen anything suspicious and reported in for back-up."

The sergeant glanced down at the paperwork on his desk for a moment. But then he quickly looked back up at the DCI. "Have you heard from Morris lately?"

"No." Alan frowned. It wasn't like Morris to stay silent for so long. "Try giving him a call."

Andrews punched in the number of Morris's mobile phone. It rang for some time before going to voicemail. He looked across at his DCI. "No reply."

"Try again," Alan said. His voice was sharp, with the urgent tone that no one in the team dared ignore.

Andrews stabbed the number into his phone for the second time. Yet again there was no reply. He looked at the DCI and shook his head.

"Give it a few minutes and try again."

Alan was growing concerned. Against his better judgement, he had allowed himself to be talked into allowing the young detective to go undercover at the hotel. Morris hadn't been with the Newcastle Police Force for very long and had never done undercover work before. What was worse, Alan knew he should have pulled him out once Harrison was out of the frame for murder. Yet he had insisted Morris stay in the post; mainly because he needed to know someone was watching out for Agnes. But now, the young detective hadn't checked in, nor was he answering his phone.

"Still no reply," Andrews said, as he put down his phone. "I'll try again in about ten minutes. It could be that he simply doesn't have a signal at the moment."

Alan nodded.

Nevertheless, it was obvious to Andrews that the DCI wasn't convinced.

"I'll give Mrs Lockwood a ring and ask her to let us know if she sees any sign of Morris when she gets back to the hotel."

"When will that be?"

"I have no idea, Sergeant. She's out there on a mission."

"What mission, sir? Where is she?"

"The Eldon Square Shopping Centre," Alan replied.

"Oh well, yes, I see." Andrews swung away to hide his grin.

* * *

Agnes went back to the shopping centre after she left the restaurant. Maybe it would have been better if Alan hadn't relieved her of the things she had already purchased. That way, she might have called a taxi straight after lunch and gone back to the hotel. However, unhindered by her packages, she had followed her shopping urge and headed back to the mall. Now, the problem was that she could see Richard Harrison heading towards her.

She would have liked to turn around and slink off into one of the shops in the mall and pretend she hadn't seen him. However, that wasn't possible. He quickened his pace and called out to her.

"Hello, Agnes. My lovely sister."

"I am *not* your sister," she said as he drew close, "and it's Mrs Lockwood to you."

Agnes looked at the flood of people rushing around behind Harrison, hoping to catch a glimpse of Detective Morris. But she couldn't see any sign of him. Hopefully, he would be hovering around in the background.

"Oh dear, Agnes, is that any way to treat your brother?"

"How many times do I have to tell you that you are *not* my brother?" Agnes spoke firmly.

"But what about the photo I showed you? That proves we had the same father. Therefore I am your half-brother."

"The man in that picture is not my father and you know it!"

Agnes reached into her handbag and pulled out the photograph and threw it at him. "Take it away and stop pestering me."

Harrison grabbed the photo before it fell to the floor. For a moment, he looked angry. But, realizing that a few people had stopped to see the commotion and were now staring at them after her outburst, he quickly pulled himself together.

"What are you talking about, Agnes? Of course it's our dad." He looked at the photo.

Agnes made a move to leave, but he looked up quickly and grabbed her arm.

"Where do you think you're going?" Harrison hissed.

"Back to the hotel," she retorted. She looked down at her arm. "And take your hand off me or I'll scream for help!"

By now, Agnes felt afraid, yet she managed to inject a tone of confidence into her words. She glanced around the mall again. Where the hell was Morris?

Reluctantly, Harrison released his grip on her arm. "Perhaps we could share a cab and go somewhere to discuss our parentage in a quieter and more private setting."

"There is nothing to discuss." Agnes looked him straight in the eye. "That picture is a fake. For a start, the man isn't wearing a watch. My father never went anywhere without his watch."

Harrison looked down at the photo.

"You can see for yourself that the man is not wearing a watch," she continued. "Secondly, I know the picture has been tampered with because I've had it checked out. You probably found a photo of him in some old newspaper and decided to use it to your advantage. Well it didn't work."

Agnes took a deep breath. "Now, will you get out of my way or do I have to call the police?"

Harrison's jaw dropped as he watched her storm off towards an exit leading out onto Northumberland Street.

The moment Agnes was sure she was out of his line of sight, she slipped into a shop and pulled out her phone.

Chapter Thirty-Eight

Both Mrs Ann Western and her niece, Janice, were distraught when they identified the body in the morgue as that of John Western.

"Why? Why? Why?" Vera Western had wailed, when Doctor Nichols peeled back the sheet covering the face and upper part of the victim. She would have fallen to the floor if Alan and the pathologist hadn't caught her in time.

"I don't mean to upset you any further, Mrs Western, but how can you be so sure that this man is your husband?" Alan asked, once Mrs Western had recovered from her ordeal. By now, both she and her niece were seated in more relaxed surroundings at the police station.

"His hair," Ann Western replied. She glanced across at her niece and Janice nodded.

"You see, John never changed his hairstyle. Styles came and went, but John was a man who stuck with what he thought suited him." She wiped away the tears rolling down her cheeks.

"He was a good man and a good husband," she added. "He never did anyone any harm. He was a pillar of the community in Bamburgh and he worked hard at the business his mother had set up. She left it to him when she died."

The DCI shifted his gaze to his sergeant for a moment, before looking back Mrs Western. "What sort of business is it?"

"It's a shop on the main street. John's mother opened a small grocery shop many years ago. It was a time when people didn't have the transport to take them into larger towns. However, competition grew when larger stores began to appear and people had more money to buy their own vehicles. That was when she started to sell other goods... items tourists were interested in. It seemed to take off, so she made room for a small café."

She paused. "But now I'm rambling. John took it on when his mother died and he extended it even further. I gather some large concern is interested in becoming involved. John was so excited about it and..." she wiped her eyes, "... and now look what's happened."

She stared at the DCI. "Who could do something like that?"

"That's what we intend to find out." Alan assured her.

Shortly after the two women left the police station, the DCI's mobile rang.

"Alan, I have just had the most awful encounter with Harrison. Thankfully I was in the middle of the shopping mall, so he couldn't get too nasty, but..."

"Where are you now?" Alan interrupted.

There was a pause while Agnes tried to find the name of the shop she had rushed into. Unfortunately, she couldn't see the sign without going outside and she was reluctant to do that. "I don't know. I hurried away from him and dived into a shop once I was out of his line of sight. All I can tell you is that the shop is located near to the main entrance..."

Suddenly the connection was lost.

Alan didn't hesitate.

"Get your coat, Andrews. You're coming with me."

"Where are we going?"

"I'll tell you on the way."

* * *

Agnes was in the middle of her call to Alan when her phone was snatched out of her hand. She was slightly relieved when she turned to find herself staring into the face of a woman. She had expected to find Richard Harrison glaring at her.

"What do you think you're doing, Joanne? Give me back my phone."

Agnes reached out to take her mobile back, but Joanne quickly moved her hand out of the way.

"Who were you talking to just then?" Joanne asked.

"That's none of your business."

Joanne shrugged. "I'll make it my business."

She flicked through the phone until she came to the list of recent calls Agnes had made.

"So, who is Alan?" she asked. "You seem to call him a great deal."

"He's a friend – we see each other for dinner now and again." Agnes retorted. "Though, as I said, it is none of your business. Now, give me back my phone."

"I think you should come with me," Joanne said, as she placed the phone in Agnes's outstretched hand. "We need to talk."

"Talk about what?" Agnes snapped. "We have nothing to talk about. Just go away."

"Please. I know a quiet little café where we can talk without being interrupted."

"What is it with you and Harrison? Why do you want to get me on my own?"

Joanne nodded towards the other customers in the shop. "We just think that we can work this out in a more civilized way, without drawing attention to ourselves. I'll call a taxi and we could be there in no time at all."

"Listen to me…" Agnes spoke slowly emphasizing every word. "There is no way I am going anywhere in a taxi with you. Now, leave me alone."

"Hello, Agnes, how nice to bump into you."

Agnes was so relieved to hear Alan's voice behind her. "Hello," she said. "What are you doing here? Shopping isn't really your thing, is it?"

"I'm with a friend." Alan gestured towards his sergeant. "This is Michael. He's looking for some sportswear. I said I would drop him off, but then I thought I would grab a bite to eat before going back to the office."

The sergeant nodded at the two women.

Alan looked at the woman standing next to Agnes. "Is this a friend of yours?"

"Not really," Agnes replied. "This is Joanne. We met briefly at the racecourse and just happened to bump into each other again a few minutes ago. However, we've finished chatting now, so maybe I could join you for a coffee, if that's okay with you?"

"I would be delighted," Alan replied.

"Well, I'd better be off," Joanne said. "Hope to see you again sometime soon, Agnes."

"Not if I see you first," Agnes mumbled, as Joanne hurried off into the crowded shopping mall.

Alan instructed his sergeant to follow Joanne. "Don't let her out of your sight."

He turned back to Agnes. "Come on, we'll go and get that coffee, just in case anyone is watching us."

Over coffee, Agnes explained how she had bumped into Harrison and then, having only just managed to escape from him, had her phone snatched away from her by Joanne.

"What started out as a lovely day turned into a nightmare."

"Maybe you should allow me to book you into another hotel." Alan tried once again to make Agnes see reason. "At least while Harrison is still prowling around The Millennium. In the meantime, we're keeping a close eye on him. Once we have absolute proof he is conning people of their money, we'll pick him up."

But again Agnes refused to agree to his suggestion. "I won't be forced out of my hotel." She smiled. "I know you're worried about me, Alan. But I've never run away from anything before and I don't intend to start now. Besides, Morris is there. He'll watch out for me."

Alan stroked his chin, thoughtfully.

"Is there something you're not telling me?" Agnes frowned. "Have you pulled Morris away from the hotel and don't know how to tell me?"

"No, he's still tailing Harrison. The problem is that we haven't heard from him." He paused. "Did you see any sign of Morris when you were talking to Harrison?"

"No," she replied, recalling the scene when Harrison had confronted her. "I looked around, hoping to see him hovering somewhere in the background, but there was no sign of him. However, he may just have been keeping a low profile." She hesitated. "Do you think something's happened to him?"

"I don't know. I certainly hope not." Alan shrugged. "It could be that he wasn't in a position to answer his phone."

"Nevertheless, you're quite concerned about him?"

Alan nodded.

Agnes glanced around the café, unsure what to say next. If only she had seen him hiding in a shop doorway, it would have reassured Alan that the young detective was still out there alive and well. "If I see him when I get back to the hotel, I'll call you right away. In the meantime, I'd better get back to the hotel."

"I'll give you a lift. I'm parked right outside." Alan said.

"But I thought Northumberland Street was a no-car area."

"It is – unless there's an emergency and your call certainly sounded like an emergency to me." Alan pulled out his phone as he spoke. "I'd better let Andrews know what's happening."

Chapter Thirty-Nine

Back at the hotel, Agnes sorted out her shopping before deciding to go downstairs. The chatter coming from the drawing room when she passed the door earlier indicated there were a few people already seated in there. Even if Harrison were to drop in for one of his cosy chats, there would be witnesses should he suddenly turn nasty.

Agnes found a comfortable chair in the drawing room. It was near the door, which would be handy if she needed to make a quick getaway. She had brought a book to read. However, she couldn't concentrate and snapped it shut after a few minutes. Her mind kept mulling over the events of the afternoon.

On the way back to the hotel, Alan had told her that the second body had been identified. There hadn't been time to say much more just then. Though Alan had mentioned how the victim had owned a business in Bamburgh.

Agnes shook her head, sadly. Both victims had had so much to live for. Both were relatively young, had a loving family and a business to run. That last thought made Agnes sit bolt upright in her chair – they had both either owned a business, or were in line to inherit one. Then another thought crossed her mind. Had the victims that were found dead and mutilated in Gateshead, owned a business, too?

"Can I get you anything – tea or coffee?"

Agnes looked up quickly to see a waitress standing in front of her. She had been so deep in thought, she hadn't noticed anyone approaching.

"A large glass of red wine, please," she replied with a smile.

Though Agnes was still watching the waitress as she made her way out of the drawing room, her mind was already racing back to her last line of thought. Was that why those men had been killed? If that was the case, might she be next? Yet why would someone seek out someone and kill them, simply because they had a business?

Agnes felt a headache coming on. There were too many questions without answers; perhaps it was time to look at it from another angle. After all, she had a business, a damn lucrative business. Even the con-man, Harrison, had tried to get his hands on it by claiming he was her half-brother. Yet, she was still alive and kicking.

But then another thought crossed her mind. No matter where her thoughts took her, Richard Harrison seemed to be in there somewhere. Was it possible that he had tried the same con trick on all the victims, both here and in Gateshead? Had he murdered them all after getting what he wanted?

But then Agnes realised there was a flaw in her thinking. Harrison couldn't be the killer. The night the second body was found in the Exhibition Park, he was here in the hotel. Morris had been watching him all evening.

The waitress arrived with the wine Agnes had ordered and set it down on the coffee table.

"Is that any good?" she asked, nodding towards the book Agnes had discarded.

"I haven't really got into it yet," Agnes replied, while she rummaged around in her bag for her charge-card. "But I've enjoyed other novels by this author, so I'm sure this one will be good."

"I quite like Agatha Christie books myself," the waitress said, just before moving away.

"Me, too," Agnes said, more to herself than the waitress. "I wonder what Miss Marple would have made of this case?" she mumbled.

She glanced at the book lying on the arm of the chair. Maybe she should stop thinking about what Harrison was up to and get back to reading the novel. The thoughts running around in her head weren't really getting her anywhere. However, after reading the first paragraph three times, she heaved a sigh and gave up. It was no good. The book would have to wait until another day.

Meanwhile, she wanted to focus her attention on the murders and that meant getting back to the big question: if Harrison wasn't the killer, who else might have had such a grudge against the victims?

That line of thought didn't take her anywhere. For a start, she didn't know anything about the victims or their families. Therefore, how could she possibly even try to make a guess at what they did or who they saw in their daily lives? No one really knew whether they had even come into contact with Harrison.

Agnes shook her head. She was back to square one again.

Taking a sip of her wine, she sat back in her chair and recalled the night the second body had been found in the park. She had already gone over it several times in her mind. Yet she had never come up with anything other than seeing Joanne Lyman lurking in the trees near the scene where the body had been found.

Why was Joanne so interested in what the police were doing? Had she anything to do with the murder? Could she have left the body lying near the bush where the other one was found?

Agnes dismissed the last question instantly. A lone woman could not have lifted the dead man in and out of a car; Alan had already described the victim as being tall and rather well-built. Besides, the young couple who found the body had told the police they had neither seen nor heard a car in the park. Therefore the body must have been carried into the park from a car outside the gates. Joanne Lyman couldn't have done that. Certainly not on her own, anyway, and, if someone *had* helped her dispose of the body, why hadn't she disappeared into the night with her companion?

That left her with two questions.

One: why was Joanne so interested in what the police were doing? But, recalling how her own curiosity had taken her up to the park, Agnes hurriedly dismissed that one as well. Maybe she had heard police sirens and had gone to see what was going on.

Two: had Joanne some involvement in the actual murder? Yet, if that was the case, why would she be hovering around the park? Her part in the dirty deed would have been done – finished. She would have got away as fast as possible, in order to avoid suspicion.

Agnes shook her head. Yet again, she was back to where she had started.

"We meet again."

The unwelcome sound of Richard Harrison's voice broke into her thoughts.

"Would you like to join me over there?" He gestured towards a sofa at the far end of the room.

"I don't think so," Agnes replied, patting the arm of her chair. "I'm quite comfortable here. But you go ahead. I'm sure you'll find someone else to join you – someone much more vulnerable to your con tricks than I am."

Agnes bit her lip. She felt uncomfortable about suggesting that Harrison find himself another victim. Though she knew Alan had instructed his team to look into Harrison's background, he had informed her they would need more than her testimony alone to convict him of fraud. Therefore, it was imperative that someone else should come forward and claim he was a confidence trickster.

"I don't know what you're talking about," Harrison blustered.

"I think you do," Agnes said quietly. She had meant to leave it there, but, reflecting on her thoughts before Richard had arrived, she added a footnote. "By the way, where is Joanne?"

"Joanne?"

"Yes, Joanne," Agnes replied slowly. "You must remember Joanne –after all, she's your half sister-in-law."

Harrison coughed. "Yes, of course. I believe she's out shopping somewhere. I don't usually hear from her once she's in shopping mode." Regaining his composure, he smiled deviously. "But no doubt she'll be in touch very soon."

Agnes didn't reply. His last remark troubled her. It wasn't so much his remark, it was the way it came out. Trying to look unconcerned, she picked up her book and began to read the first paragraph for the umpteenth time.

She sensed Harrison's eyes staring down at her, but she didn't look up. After what seemed like an age, he started to move away, but he tripped over her handbag, which was on the floor by her feet.

"Sorry," he mumbled. He reached down and put it back into place, before slinking off to the sofa at the other end of the room.

Agnes kept her eyes focused on her book. With a bit of luck, Harrison would get fed up and disappear upstairs – hopefully, to pack his bag and leave the hotel forever.

However, a few minutes later, out of the corner of her eye, she saw a man hovering in the doorway. Without moving her head, she swept her eyes in his direction and breathed a sigh of relief when she saw Morris. Alan would be pleased to learn the detective was still active.

Lowering her book, she leaned over to pick up her wine from the coffee table. But before her fingers touched the glass, Morris suddenly lurched into view. His sudden appearance, and the chain of events that followed, left her totally immobilized for a long moment. It was almost as though she was watching a film in slow motion.

The detective, trying to regain his balance, stumbled into the coffee table in front of her. The sudden jolt on the table sent her glass of wine into a spin, before it slid perilously towards her. Agnes stretched her hand out further, hoping to catch it before it fell over. But she was too late. She could only watch as the glass fell and the wine spilled over onto her dress.

Suddenly feeling activated again, Agnes leapt to her feet and looked down at her dress.

"I do apologize. I think I slipped on something." Morris looked down at the floor behind him. "Please allow me buy you another."

"I need to change," Agnes replied, without looking up. She gathered her things together and headed towards the door.

"I really am sorry." The detective spoke loudly as he followed her out into the reception. "I don't know what else to say."

Once they were clear of the door, he quickened his pace and moved alongside Agnes.

"I think there's something you should know," he said, lowering his voice.

* * *

Earlier, after Alan had dropped Agnes off at the hotel, he headed straight back to the Eldon Square Shopping Mall. The last he had heard from his sergeant was when he had spoken to him before he and Agnes had left. At that point, Sergeant Andrews had assured him that he was still following the woman known to them under two names. He had added that there was nothing suspicious to report.

"Nevertheless, keep an eye on her until I get back," Alan had instructed. "Don't forget, half our men are looking for this woman and you have her in your sights. We can't afford to lose her now. I'll call in and have a couple of detectives over there ASAP."

Now, back inside the mall, Alan contacted his sergeant. "I'm near the Monument entrance. Where are you?"

Andrews explained he was in a large coffee shop not too far away. "Ms Lyman, or whoever she's calling herself today, stopped off here about ten minutes ago. Harrison joined her shortly afterwards." He paused briefly. "I haven't seen a sign of the detectives you sent over here. I guess they've blended in well."

"I know where you are, I'm on my way," Alan said, as he made his way through the mall to the location of the coffee shop. "However, I won't come in. I can't risk Joanne Lyman seeing me again. I'm supposed to be back at the office. But don't hang up," he added. "Keep your phone open."

A few minutes later, the DCI heard Andrews telling him to keep his eyes open if he was anywhere near the café. "Harrison is leaving."

Realizing he was only a short distance from the café, Alan turned away and peered into a shop window. By now, his phone was almost glued to his ear. "I'm close by. Tell me which direction Harrison takes once he steps outside the door."

There was a pause before Andrews replied. "Harrison has just left the café, sir. When he stepped out of the door, he turned right. Joanne Lyman is still here."

"Yes, I see him. I'll follow him," Alan replied. "Meanwhile, you stay with the woman, Sergeant. We need to know what she does next. However…" Alan broke off when, in the crowd, he saw two familiar faces. It took him a couple of seconds to realise who they were.

"Are you okay, sir?" Andrews sounded alarmed.

"Yes, I'm fine," Alan chortled. "I just spotted the undercover detectives I asked for earlier."

Chapter Forty

DCI Johnson managed to have a quick word with his detectives before he began to follow Harrison. He instructed them to take over from Andrews and follow Joanne Lyman when she left the cafe.

"The sergeant has been with her for some time," he told them. "She's going to twig if he continues to show up everywhere she goes. By the way," he added, before he set off to follow Harrison, "I love the disguise."

Alan followed Harrison through the mall. Thankfully, he didn't stop to look at anything, which made it easier for the DCI to stay with him at a safe distance. Following a suspect who broke off every few minutes to check a shop window or anything else that might take their eye, meant having to dodge in and out of doorways until the subject decided to move on.

Harrison carried on walking until he reached one of the exits. Once outside, he made his way to a taxi rank.

"Damn," Alan muttered to himself. He had left his car standing outside another entrance to the mall.

Figuring out how far away it was, he realised he didn't have time to get to it. Therefore, the only other option was to grab the next cab in the line and hope the driver would be able to keep up with Harrison, despite the traffic.

"Follow that cab," Alan said, flashing his badge. "But don't let him know he's being followed."

"Are you for real?" The taxi driver swung around to face the DCI.

"Yes, I'm for real. Now get a move on. I don't want to lose him."

The driver glanced at Alan's badge. "Okay, mate, hang on."

The only way out onto Percy Street was by going through the bus station on the far side. Though Alan had secured his seatbelt the moment he sat down, he was still thrown forward when the taxi swerved suddenly to avoid a bus that was in the process of reversing from its stand.

"That's him," the driver said as he slowed down.

"Right, now stay with him, but keep out of sight," Alan replied.

The driver nodded and continued to follow the taxi as it wound its way through the streets. It soon became obvious that Harrison was going back to the hotel.

Once Harrison stepped from the taxi and mounted the steps leading into the hotel, Alan's first instinct was to follow him inside. The urge to see Agnes again, even for a few minutes, was very tempting. However, she could be in one of the public rooms and Harrison might see them together; something they were both still trying to avoid.

Alan was so deep in thought, he didn't see the taxi pulling up close to the hotel a few moments after Harrison entered the building. It was only when he spotted Detective Morris alighting from the passenger seat that he really sat up and took notice.

He was relieved to see his detective was okay and still following Harrison. However, at the same time, he was irritated that Morris hadn't answered his phone when he and Andrews had tried to contact him. Realizing this wasn't the time or the place to lose his temper, he told his driver to take him to Grey's Monument where he could retrieve his car. This whole thing had turned out to be a bit of a wild goose chase.

He could only hope the detectives following Joanne Lyman were having more luck. No doubt he would hear about it when he got back to the station.

* * *

"What should I know?" Agnes asked as she approached the lift. "What else is there to know? You knocked over my glass..." She peered at him. "Have you been drinking?"

"We must keep walking," Morris replied. "Try to look as though you are still angry with me," he continued, ignoring her last question.

"That shouldn't be difficult. I *am* still angry with you!" Agnes retorted. But then the penny dropped; obviously there was more to what had happened in the drawing room than she had first thought. "Sorry, go on. Tell me what I should know."

He held his forefinger to his lips before he spoke. "I saw Harrison slip something into your glass," he whispered. "So when you reached out to pick up your wine, I knew I had to do something fast, without letting Harrison know I'd seen what he'd done. Knocking your glass off the table seemed to be the only option."

"Why are we whispering?" Agnes asked, keeping her voice low.

"I think he dropped something into your bag at the same time. It could be a small microphone."

"A bug?" Agnes's eyes widened at the thought.

By now they had reached the lift. Fortunately, it wasn't standing open on the ground floor, so they had a few moments to spare. Agnes glanced towards the drawing room door. There was no sign of Richard Harrison. He was probably still sitting inside, seething about the fact that his little plan hadn't worked on this occasion. She would need to be extra careful until he either moved on, or the police had enough evidence to charge him with fraud.

Nevertheless, she was aware that just because Harrison hadn't followed them out, it didn't mean he wasn't watching them. The strategically placed mirrors throughout the ground floor meant people could be seen from all angles. His eyes could be focused on them both at this very moment.

She frowned at Morris and thrust her hand down to the stain on her dress. To anyone watching, she was a very angry woman.

"I only hope this stain comes out. Have you any idea what this dress cost?" Speaking more quietly, she thanked the detective. "I'm just so relieved you were there to catch him in the act. Spilling my drink was quick thinking on your part. Harrison could have been trying to kill me."

"I'm terribly sorry, Madam. I didn't do it on purpose," Morris replied, keeping up the charade. He lowered his voice. "When you change, please put your dress into a plastic bag and pass it on to the DCI or one of his team as soon as possible. Forensics might be able to detect what Harrison dropped into your glass."

Agnes didn't have any time to reply as, just then, the lift doors swung open and two people stepped out. All she could do was wink at Morris and hope he understood.

"Going up?" Larry asked.

"Yes, please," Agnes replied. She pointed down to her dress and then towards Morris. "Can you believe it? He's just knocked my wine all over me."

Upstairs in her room, Agnes quickly changed out of her dress and dropped it into a bag she retrieved from the waste bin. That done, she tipped the contents of her bag onto the bed and searched through them. Sure enough, Morris was right; there was a tiny black object among her things that shouldn't be there. She picked it up to take a closer look. It looked harmless enough. However, if it was some sort of listening device, someone could be eavesdropping right now, hoping to pick up some snippet of information.

Putting it back down onto the bed, she picked up her phone and hurried across to the bathroom. Once inside, she closed the door and called Alan.

"It's me," she said, the moment he answered. "About ten minutes ago, Detective Morris saw Harrison drop something into my wine glass when I wasn't looking."

She went on to tell him how Morris had prevented her from taking a drink from the glass. "He followed me to the lift and told me to place my dress in a bag to pass on to forensics."

A cold shiver ran through Alan at the thought that Agnes could quite easily have been poisoned if Morris hadn't arrived in the nick of time.

"I'll get a female detective over there right away," he said. "She'll say she's your cousin and give her name as Sue Wilberforce."

"But that's not all," Agnes interrupted. "Morris saw Harrison drop something into my bag. I found it when I got upstairs. We think it might be a bug."

"Where is it now?" Alan asked.

"I left it lying on the bed. I'm making this call from the bathroom."

"Wrap it in a towel or something and give it to the detective when she calls for the dress. I'll see whether we can trace it."

"Okay, I'll sort that now," Agnes replied.

"Meanwhile," Alan continued, "don't let Harrison anywhere near you." He paused. "I wish you'd let me find you another hotel until we can nail this man. Won't you reconsider? I was already worried about you being in the same hotel, but now I'm almost frantic!"

"Stop worrying. I'll be okay," Agnes said.

"Tell me how to stop worrying." Alan sighed. Nothing she said would prevent him worrying about her. "I'll get the detective over to you and warn forensics I have something urgent on the way."

* * *

Once he had sent the detective to the hotel and informed forensics of the task ahead, Alan sank back in his chair and shook his head. He was so deep in thought that he didn't hear his sergeant enter the office.

"Bad news?" Andrews asked, as he hung up his coat.

"The worst," Alan replied. He looked up. "Harrison slipped something into Mrs Lockwood's drink when she wasn't looking."

"Is she okay?"

"Yes, thanks to Morris. He happened to catch Harrison in the act and knocked over her glass before she could drink it."

"Well done, Morris," said Andrews.

"Yes, indeed. But what would have happened if he hadn't been in the right place at the right time?"

"But look on the bright side for a change. He *was* in the right place and he did the right thing."

Alan sat up in his chair. His expression had changed from one of despair, to faith. "Yes, he was and, yes, I'm grateful for that. We'll make a damn good detective of him yet. Now, let me bring you up to speed on what else has been happening."

Chapter Forty-One

Shortly after she had spoken to Alan, Agnes received a call from reception telling her that her cousin, Sue Wilberforce, was asking for her.

"Send her up, please," Agnes replied.

Alan had said a detective would be with her shortly, but she was rather surprised she had arrived so quickly. Nevertheless, though Agnes was expecting the knock on her door, she took the precaution of looking through the peephole and asking who it was before she opened the door.

"Sue Wilberforce."

"I understand you have something for me to take back to the station," she said, as she entered the room.

"Yes." Agnes slowly walked across to where she had left the bag containing her stained dress.

She was puzzled. There was something slightly familiar about this woman. Yet she couldn't recall where she had seen her.

By now, Agnes's mind was racing; tracking every person she had seen with Alan. She remembered seeing a woman detective with him once before, but that was certainly not the person standing in front of her now.

She had been a brunette and slightly built. Whereas this woman's hair was honey-blonde and she was wearing glasses with large purple frames. Therefore, where had she seen this woman?

"Maybe you should stay here for a few minutes," Agnes said, turning back to face the woman. "After all, you *are* supposed to be my cousin. Surely one of my relatives wouldn't rush in and out again so quickly? The ladies on the desk in reception are quite observant."

"But this is important," the woman insisted. "I need to get your skirt back to the station as quickly as possible."

"Yes, of course. You're right," Agnes said, reaching down to pick up a bag from the floor. "Sorry about that. I guess I'm just looking for some company."

Agnes handed the bag over to the woman and showed her out of the door. "Hope your team is able to find something," she said.

The moment Agnes saw the woman enter the lift and the doors close, she went back into her room and slammed the door shut. As an extra precaution, she slid the safety chain into place. Once that was done, she picked up her mobile phone and called Alan.

"I have just had a woman here calling herself Sue Wilberforce," Agnes said, the moment he answered the phone. "She said she'd come to collect the bag. However, I don't believe she was the detective you sent. There was something about her..."

"That's impossible!" Alan intervened. "How could anyone have known about our conversation?"

"I have no idea," Agnes replied. "I left the little black thing on the bed and went into the bathroom when I called you." But then she had a sudden notion. "Is it possible it was so finely tuned, or whatever it is they call it these days, that it allowed voices to be picked up even when in an adjoining room? Anyway, whoever came to my room went off with my laundry."

* * *

Sergeant Andrews couldn't help noticing that the DCI had turned pale during his second conversation with Agnes. Once they had finished talking, Alan pocketed his phone and said, "I need to get over to the hotel. Someone planted a listening device in Agnes's handbag..."

"Yes, you told me that," Andrews interrupted. "She found it and –"

"And whoever was listening in was still able to hear her earlier call to me," Alan interrupted. "How else would they know a person by the name of Sue Wilberforce was going to pick up the stained dress?"

"But I gathered from what I picked up from your conversation that Mrs Lockwood didn't hand over the appropriate item to whoever was impersonating the detective," Andrews replied, grinning.

"No." Alan smiled back. "Mrs Lockwood is a cunning woman. The woman went off with her dirty washing. I guess they're in for a surprise. The real bag containing her stained dress and the listening device is on its way here now. Thank goodness our detective hadn't even reached the hotel when the impostor struck, otherwise who knows what would have happened to her."

He shook his head. "But, getting back to Mrs Lockwood, what the hell are they going to do when they find out she's fooled them? I really need to get her to move into another hotel, but she won't budge."

There was a pause while Alan pulled on his coat.

"Hang on a minute," Andrews said, suddenly remembering something. "Aren't you supposed to be seeing the Chief Superintendent shortly? You've put him off several times already."

"In that case, he'll be getting used to it by now. Agnes and Morris could be in real danger. I need to be there."

"I'm coming with you." Andrews jumped from his chair and grabbed his coat.

"But, this is my problem…" Alan began.

"No buts, sir, I'm coming with you."

Chapter Forty-Two

By the time the DCI and his sergeant had reached the hotel, they had worked out a plan. Entering separately, Alan would make his way up the stairs to Agnes's room, leaving Andrews to walk casually into the drawing room. Both had left their coats in the car some distance away, making it appear they were staying at the hotel and had merely popped outside for a cigarette.

Agnes peered through the peephole when she heard the knock on her door and was relieved when she saw Alan standing outside. She opened the door and quickly pulled him inside.

"Isn't this exciting?" she said.

"Exciting, Agnes? I was already worried sick about you and now I'm concerned about Morris." Alan sat down on the edge of the bed.

"Oh my goodness, I'd forgotten about Morris." She clasped her hand to her forehead as she thought through the recent events.

"If my voice could be heard while I was in the bathroom, it's likely they heard Morris talking to me in the reception area, even though we were whispering. They'll know he knocked my glass over on purpose." She sat down beside Alan. "If that's the case, they'll be onto him. You've got to get him away from this hotel. He isn't safe here anymore."

"My sergeant is downstairs looking for him right now," Alan replied. "But you must remember you aren't safe here either, Agnes. That's what I have been trying to tell you for the last few days. However, if you won't listen, what makes you think Morris will?"

"Because he's young and has his whole life ahead of him," she suggested.

"Yet, if he's as stubborn as you are, he'll opt to stay on," Alan retorted. "But doesn't the fact that you outrank him have anything to do with it?" Agnes replied quickly, not wanting to be outdone. "If you order him off his assignment, then he won't have any other option."

She frowned. All this arguing wasn't getting them anywhere.

"Isn't there something else we could be discussing? What happened after you sent your sergeant to follow Joanne Lyman?"

"Not a great deal, really." Alan shrugged. "I understand she visited several shops in the shopping mall, before going to a coffee shop. Harrison joined her shortly afterwards. It was then that I rang in and ordered a couple of detectives to take over from Andrews."

He laughed out loud. "I know I told them to try to blend in, but I had to look twice when I first laid eyes on Jones and Smithers. I couldn't believe my eyes. They were both dressed as women. They looked quite good, too."

He paused for a moment.

"I wonder whether they would be interested in this year's pantomime?" Alan mused. "We do a charity thing at Christmas," he explained, glancing at Agnes. "Anyway, getting back to the point, I left them to it while I followed Harrison. But when he came back here and I saw Morris arrive a few minutes later, I went back to the station."

He glanced at his watch. "That all happened some time ago, though and since then, I haven't heard back from either of them."

He looked at Agnes, but she was staring at the wall in front of her and, from her expression, he could tell she hadn't heard a word he had said. Alan had seen that look before. It was a look she gave when her mind was elsewhere, trying to pull together the many thoughts racing around in her head.

"Did you know that pancakes turn green when the batter is poured into the pan?" Alan asked.

"Yes," Agnes replied, automatically.

"Which, I understand, is why the moon turns green during the month of February," Alan added.

"Could be," she answered, her voice still in automatic mode.

"Okay, Agnes, I know that look. What're you thinking?"

Agnes held up her hand. "Give me a moment; I was thinking about something you said regarding your detectives."

Alan opened his mouth to reply, but his phone rang, interrupting whatever he was about to say.

"You'd better get that," Agnes said. "It could be important."

Alan reached into his pocket and pulled out his mobile phone. Looking at the name on the screen, he saw the incoming call was from Detective Smithers.

"Yes, I need to take this... What do you mean, you lost her?" Alan yelled into the phone. He stood up and began to pace the floor. "When did you lose her?"

There was no reply.

"For heaven's sake, man, when did you lose her?" Alan repeated.

"About thirty minutes ago... or maybe it was forty-five. Look, we were following her, but then she took a phone call and disappeared into one of the ladies' rooms. We both hung around outside, but she never came out."

"Why didn't one of you follow her in there?

"We didn't like to. Besides, we thought she would come out after a few minutes."

The DCI blew a sigh. "Okay, go back to the station and get changed. We'll talk about this later."

Once the call had ended, Alan punched his sergeant's number into his phone and passed on the news before looking at Agnes.

"I gather your detectives lost Joanne," she said.

Alan nodded. "It seems they were reluctant to follow her into the ladies' toilets. I can't say I blame them. Anyway, they waited outside for a long while, but she never reappeared."

"That's odd," Agnes said thoughtfully. "She can't have been in there all that time."

"Could there have been another door?" Alan queried, raising his eyebrows.

"There could have been, I suppose." Agnes shrugged. "It might have led out into another corridor in the shopping mall."

Just then, Alan's phone rang again. This time it was the laboratory at the station. He listened carefully to what they had to say. Once the call was over, he hung up and thought for a long moment before turning to face Agnes.

"That was Dr Nichols. I asked them to do a test on your dress ASAP. His initial findings show that there was definitely something added to your drink. It will be difficult to tell exactly what it was. However, he suspects it was something which would have knocked you out, rather than poison you."

"So that means they haven't finished with me – yet," Agnes replied. "Perhaps Harrison was trying another method to force me into signing over my family business."

Alan opened his mouth to say something, but she jumped in first.

"And, before you even suggest it, yet again, I am not moving out of this hotel." She paused. "Surely you can arrest Harrison now. Your own detective saw him drop something into my drink and he also saw him place a listening device in my handbag." She thrust her hand towards the bed where her bag was lying. "For goodness' sake, haven't you enough to charge him with something?"

"In the old days, yes," Alan replied. "But as the system is today, it is his word against Harrison's. We can't do anything until…"

"Until what," Agnes interrupted, "until the victim is found dead!" She broke off. "Oh Alan, I'm sorry, but things are not how they used to be. In the old days…" She gave an expressive shrug.

"I know," Alan said as he placed his arms around her. "If only there had been two witnesses when he contaminated your drink, then I could have arrested him. It would have been more difficult for him to deny the charge. Don't you see, Agnes, you really must leave this hotel. You need to get as far away from him as possible… even if it means you returning to Essex."

"What are you saying, Alan?" Agnes pulled herself away from him. "You can't mean that?"

"I'm only thinking about you. Of course I don't want you to go so far away. But I don't want you in danger, either and it strikes me that Harrison is out to get his hands on your money one way or another."

Agnes didn't reply straight away. She walked across to the window and peered down at the quayside as she thought about Alan's last remark.

"What if I were to agree to let Harrison have the business," she said slowly, without turning around. "Do you think he would leave me alone? Would he simply disappear to London to run the department store and let me carry on here in Newcastle as though nothing had happened?"

"Agnes, you aren't thinking of…"

"No, of course not." She swung around to face him. "I was simply running something past you. I want you to put yourself in his shoes for a moment."

Alan scratched his head for a moment before he replied.

"Okay, I'm not sure he would see it as easy as that," he said. "Harrison would always be wondering whether you might suddenly regret your decision. He could end up watching his back day and night, fearing you might go to the police and ask them to start an enquiry."

"Exactly! I totally agree."

"You do?"

"Yes," Agnes replied. "Except for one thing."

"And that would be?"

"I would go to the police and *demand* they start an enquiry," Agnes replied, with a wink. "But getting back to what you said – you're right. Harrison and his accomplice could never, ever be sure I wouldn't suddenly turn up and cause trouble. The only way they could possibly avoid that happening, would be if I was dead. Maybe he killed those two men you have in your mortuary once he had conned them out of their businesses."

"But you said yourself, Harrison couldn't have killed the last victim, the man in the tweed coat who the young couple found, as he was here at the hotel all evening."

"I know and that's what puzzles me."

Agnes looked up sharply suddenly picking up on something Alan had said. "Hang on a minute. Did you just say the second victim was wearing a tweed coat?"

"Yes, why?"

"Do you recall me telling you about how I saw Joanne harassing a man on the quayside one afternoon? He didn't seem to want anything to do with her."

"Yes, I remember. We were having dinner together before I was called away. But what has that got to do with anything?"

"The man I saw talking to Joanne that day was wearing a tweed coat."

"Are you sure about that?"

"Absolutely." Agnes frowned. "Yet we've virtually ruled Harrison out of the actual murders."

"He and Joanne might have another accomplice," Alan suggested. "One instructed to murder the victims once they have signed over their business."

"I suppose it's possible," Agnes admitted, reluctantly. She pulled a face. "Yet," she continued. "I still have this niggling feeling that there are only the two of them in this scam."

Alan didn't look convinced

"Think about it." Agnes began to explain the reasoning behind her thoughts. "The more people there are in a group of thieves, the less they get when the money is split. Plus, there's always the chance that one of them will get greedy and demand more money because they believe they're doing more than the rest of the gang – especially if that person happens to be the appointed killer. They have much more to lose."

Alan nodded his head in agreement. It sounded plausible.

"But there's still the problem of how Richard Harrison killed the second victim if he was here in the hotel. Morris was here all the time and you saw him yourself when you got back that evening. You said he was drunk."

"I know," Agnes replied. "The wretched man can't be in two places at once."

There was a long silence. Alan was the first to speak.

"Look, Agnes, I need to pop downstairs for a few minutes to bring Andrews and Morris up to speed on what the lab said about the drug found on your dress and also what we have discussed up here."

"But what if Harrison sees you? I thought you were keeping a low profile around me."

"Well, I won't be around you. You'll be up here, out of harm's way."

"So you don't want me to come downstairs and help with the case?"

"No. I need you to stay here." Alan hurried across to the door. "Once I've gone, lock the door to your room and don't open it for anyone except Andrews or me."

"But I…"

"Agnes, for once, can't you just do as I ask?" Alan interrupted. "I haven't time for any buts."

* * *

Sergeant Andrews found Morris in the drawing room. He was sitting close to the door, reading a newspaper. Out of the corner of his eye, he spotted Harrison sitting near the window.

"Well hello, John. Fancy meeting you here," he said as he walked through the door. "I can't remember when we last saw each other."

"Hello," Morris responded, guessing there must be a reason for this charade. He stood up and shook Andrews's outstretched hand. "It's good to see you again."

"Look, why don't we go into the bar and have a drink while we catch up?" Andrews said, clapping Morris on the back.

"Good idea," Morris replied, laughing heartily.

In the bar, Andrews ordered a couple of pints of beer, before pointing towards a table in the far corner. "Would you bring the drinks over there?"

The barman nodded.

"We think your cover might be blown," he said, once they were seated.

"What?" Morris gasped.

"Not so loud!" Andrews quickly looked around. Fortunately, there weren't many people in the bar and they seemed occupied with their own conversations.

"Mrs Lockwood found the listening device in her bag," Andrews explained. "However, to cut a long story short, we think it was able to pick up your conversation with her in reception."

"But I can't help wondering why he needed to plant the bug if he was going to spike her drink?"

"Good question," Andrews replied, eyeing the young detective thoughtfully. "Might you have been mistaken about seeing him drop something into her glass?"

"No!" Morris answered sharply. "I definitely saw his hand hovering over her drink before he reached further down to adjust her bag. And while he was doing that, he dropped something into it." He paused. "Harrison obviously kicked the bag on purpose to give him the opportunity to tamper with both."

"You could be right," Andrews said. "Anyway, the lab has the dress she was wearing, so we should hear something from them very soon."

The barman appeared with their drinks. Andrews paid the bill and told the waiter to keep the change. A few moments later his phone rang.

"It's the DCI," he said, flipping open his phone.

"It seems that Smithers and Jones, who were following Joanne Lyman at the shopping mall, have lost her," he told Morris, once the call had ended. "The DCI will be down in a few minutes."

Chapter Forty-Three

Once Alan left the room, Agnes sat by the window and looked down onto the quayside. The recently swollen river, wildly slapping at the sides of the quay, had subsided a little. It looked less frightening than it had a couple of days ago.

Agnes loved to look at the river from her window. There was something about watching the water as it flowed downstream which helped her to relax. She cast her mind back to when she had arrived on Tyneside. Was it really only a few days ago? So much had happened in such a short time.

It was on her first day back in the city, while taking a leisurely stroll through the park, that she had stumbled across the body in the park. She shook her head as she recalled the scene. The poor man had almost been torn to pieces. What kind of person in their right mind could do something so horrific?

The attack might have been put down to someone high on drugs, if other bodies hadn't been found in the same condition in Gateshead. Though, on reflection, they would have had to reconsider anyway, when another victim was found in the same park a couple of days later, this one being in much the same condition as the others. Then it was discovered that both the victims found in Newcastle had owned a business.

Agnes sat back in her chair and closed her eyes. Even watching the river flowing beneath her window wasn't calming enough today. What she really needed was to be outside in the fresh air, not cooped up here in her room.

She rose to her feet and began to pace the floor.

Before Alan left, they had discussed the murder case from several angles. Yet, no matter where they started, they always ended up with Joanne and Richard being involved. However, Richard had a good alibi for the night of the second murder. Detective Morris had been watching him all day. As for Joanne, despite being seen skulking in the trees that night, there was no way she could have lifted the body out of a car and carried it into the park.

Just then, Agnes recalled something Alan had said earlier. It had set her thinking back then, but, for some reason, the subject had changed rather suddenly. She was about to recollect her thoughts when there was a knock on the door.

"Hotel Security," a voice called out.

"I didn't call for security," Agnes replied. She turned to face the door.

"Yes, I know. A gentleman downstairs asked me to escort you to the drawing room."

"Oh, I see. Right, I'll be with you in a minute."

Agnes's mind was racing as she slowly made her way across to the door. Alan had instructed her to remain in her room and not to open the door to anyone except himself or Sergeant Andrews. His tone had been quite forceful, which was the only reason she had resisted the urge to go for a walk along the quayside only a short while ago. Therefore, would Alan suddenly decide to send a security man to take her downstairs without informing her first?

Now, standing by the door, she lifted the tiny flap covering the peephole and peered through. Despite the wide-angled window, she wasn't able to see the man's face too clearly as he kept turning his head to look up and down the hall. However, she saw that he wasn't wearing the uniform supplied by the hotel. Instead, he was wearing a dark suit and, though she couldn't read it through the tiny hole, there was a name badge pinned on the lapel of his jacket.

It could be that he is in charge of the security staff, she thought as she stepped away from the door.

"Sorry to keep you waiting," she called out, still unsure as to whether to open the door or not.

She suddenly decided to call Alan and check with him.

"Did you send a security man to take me downstairs?" she asked, the moment he answered his phone.

"No. Why? Is someone saying I did?"

"Well, not exactly. At least, he didn't give your name." Agnes explained what the man had said.

"I'm on my way," he told her.

A few minutes later, Agnes heard another knock on the door. However, when she looked through the peephole this time, she was relieved to see Alan and his sergeant standing outside.

"Did you see him?" she asked, the moment she opened the door. She looked up and down the corridor but the man had disappeared.

"No," Alan replied, as the two detectives stepped inside. "He must have guessed you were calling someone and fled, though we didn't pass him on the way up. Andrews used the stairs, while I took the lift. Neither of us met anyone."

"Then he must have used the staff exit," Agnes said, thoughtfully. "There's a door at the end of the corridor marked Staff Only," she explained. "I understand they have cupboards where bed linen is stored. There are also stairs and a lift to the ground floor."

"I don't suppose you got a good look at the man," Andrews asked.

"Not really." She cast her mind back to what she had seen when she had peered through the peephole.

"He kept glancing up and down the corridor," she continued. "At first, I thought he might be keeping a watchful eye out for someone Alan had warned him about. But then I wondered whether he was concerned someone might be watching *him*. Nevertheless, I think I might recognize him again if..." She broke off and clasped her hand across her mouth.

"What is it?" Alan asked, anxiously. "Are you alright?"

"Yes, I'm okay. I suddenly had the feeling I'd seen him before."

"Maybe you saw him here at the hotel," Andrews suggested. "After all, he did say he was Hotel Security. Perhaps you saw him downstairs one day while he was patrolling the hotel."

Agnes pulled a face. "Perhaps."

"But you're not convinced that's where you saw him?" Alan queried.

"No." She swallowed hard. "The thing is, I saw someone meet up with Harrison one morning, and I had the strangest feeling I'd seen him before, but I couldn't think where. Now I have that sensation all over again." She sighed heavily. "I'm definitely missing something."

"Is it possible that the man you saw today was the same man that you saw with Harrison?" Andrews queried.

"No, the man I saw with Harrison had his hair cut very short. The man at my door had rather long hair." She paused, still recalling the scene. "It looked a bit messed up – you know, uncombed. But I suppose that's the trend nowadays. He was wearing glasses and had something pinned on his jacket."

She paused. "Anyway, what about Morris? Have you left him on his own down there?"

"Yes, for the moment," Alan replied. He looked at his sergeant. "Maybe you should get back downstairs and inform Morris of what happened up here. Ask him if he recalls seeing a man in a suit with long hair. Both of you keep your eyes peeled until I get back down there. You never know, he might just show his face again."

Once Andrews had left the room, Alan blew a long sigh.

"Now then, Agnes, what am I going to do with you?"

"Well, you're not leaving me up here, that's for sure!

Chapter Forty-Four

Andrews had barely finished bringing Morris up to speed when, through one of the mirrors, he caught sight of the DCI stepping out of the lift. He was accompanied by Mrs Lockwood. The two detectives left the bar and went into the reception area to meet them.

"Harrison is still in the drawing room," Morris said. "He's alone and hasn't moved from his seat."

Before the DCI had time to reply, the door to the dining room swung open and a man walked out, closing the door firmly behind him. He glanced in their direction as he made his way to towards the drawing room. However, his eyes rested on Agnes for a few seconds before he looked away.

Agnes hadn't taken her eyes off him from the moment she had spotted him. Now, she was more convinced than ever that she had seen him before. She watched him walk into the drawing room and, through the mirrors, she saw him pull up a chair beside Richard Harrison.

"That's the man I told you about upstairs. It was him I saw with Harrison at breakfast one morning," Agnes said. "You must remember him, Morris. You were there, too."

"Yes, I do remember him," Morris replied. "I can't say I've seen him since that morning, though." He glanced at Agnes. "What about you?"

"I don't know," she replied slowly. "I'm certain I've seen him before. The face is familiar, but..." She broke off and looked at Alan.

"You've remembered something?"

"Yes, I have," Agnes replied excitedly. "I'm almost certain he was the man I saw passing something on to Harrison in the Sage a few days ago."

"*Almost* certain?" Alan quizzed.

"Does it matter?" Andrews asked. "At least we have something to hold him on."

"Do we?" Alan retorted. "So a man passes something on to another man. Is that a reason to bring in a man for questioning? It could have been anything. Some money he owed him, perhaps."

"Of course, you're right. It could have been anything," Agnes replied. "But since then, I have had time to think over everything that's happened and what if…"

"Please, Agnes." Alan interrupted. "Not 'what if' again!"

"What if," Agnes continued, ignoring Alan's interruption, "he was passing on an old photo of a man, which had been altered to make him appear to be my father?"

She looked at the three detectives in turn. "Does that make sense? I'm not very good at explaining myself."

"You explained it very well." It was Sergeant Andrews who spoke first. "However, it is a bit of a longshot. Now, think hard, Mrs Lockwood. Is it possible you might have seen him elsewhere in the hotel, before or since the morning you saw him at breakfast? It could be that he's simply a guest here at the hotel."

It was difficult to tell from his tone whether he was being serious or mocking her. Agnes decided to give him the benefit of the doubt.

"No. I'm sure I've seen him outside the hotel. I need to concentrate on his face for a few minutes and hopefully, I'll be able to pull it all together."

"Are you sure about this, Agnes?"

Alan still wasn't convinced that allowing Agnes to accompany him down here was a good idea. However, she had insisted, telling him that she might be safer with people around her than if she were stuck up in her room on her own. At the time, it had sounded feasible, especially after what had just happened. Yet there was something about the way the man had looked at her that really worried him. Even if Agnes didn't know him, he definitely gave the impression he recognized her.

"Yes." Agnes's eyes were still focused on the man's reflection in the mirror.

Alan followed her gaze to where the man could be seen talking to Harrison. At one point, the man pulled a face and shook his head. Obviously this didn't please Harrison, as he clenched his fist and struck it on the arm of the chair.

"I wish I could hear what they're talking about," Alan said.

"Me too," Agnes replied.

Just then, man swung his head towards the window and back again in frustration and something clicked in Agnes's memory.

"Oh, my goodness!" Agnes said, her eyes still fixed on the two men. "He was the man outside my room claiming to be Hotel Security."

"Are you sure?" Alan queried. "I thought you said he had long hair."

"Yes, I'm sure. It was the way he shifted his head from side to side that made me realise."

She turned to face the three detectives. "For some reason, he drops his head in the middle." She gave a demonstration of what she meant. "As for his hair, he could have been wearing a wig, or a mop out of the broom cupboard. Don't forget, those peepholes aren't perfect."

She looked across towards the dining room. The doors were still tightly closed. No one had gone in or out since the man left a short while ago.

"What was he doing in there?" she mused. "Unless that was where he ended up after he eluded you and Sergeant Andrews. Come to think of it, he was rather intent on making sure the doors were closed. Maybe he left something hidden in there."

"I get the impression that you know more than you're saying?" Alan inquired. "I think you should tell us everything."

"I have a theory," Agnes replied. "But I need to be absolutely sure that what is running around in my head is correct before I say any more."

"And when will you know?"

"When I'm sure!" Agnes winked.

Alan blew a sigh. "Andrews, you'd better take a look around the dining room. Don't leave any chair unturned."

"I hope you haven't sent my sergeant on a wild goose chase," Alan said, once Andrews headed towards the dining room.

"So do I," she replied, as she watched the sergeant close the door behind him. "My whole idea depends on what he finds in there." She lifted one shoulder. "But, looking at it from another angle, *I* didn't send Sergeant Andrews in there, you did!"

* * *

In the drawing room, Harrison scowled at his companion.

"She's only a woman, for heaven's sake," he said, thumping his fist on the chair. "She should have been a walkover! I had it all worked out. Once she signed over the department store, we could have sold the rest of the shares and made a fortune. We should have been rich by now – done whatever we wanted. The sky would have been the limit. Yet we're still stuck here."

"I never thought it would be easy," the man replied. "We should have stuck to our usual plan, the plan we both agreed to – two scams and then move on."

"But don't you see, Joe? I thought she would be an easy target – middle-aged widow, sons on the other side of the world and no other relatives in the country... none that we know about, anyway. Damn and blast the woman!"

Chapter Forty-Five

"Maybe I should have gone with Sergeant Andrews. It's a large room to cover."

It had been ten minutes since the sergeant had disappeared into the dining room and Morris hadn't taken his eyes off the door. By now, the three of them had moved across the reception area, to where they hoped they wouldn't be seen by Harrison and his friend.

"Give him a few more minutes. I'm sure he'll be out very soon."

Though Alan gave the impression he was unconcerned, deep down, he was more than a little uneasy. Who knew what, or who, was lurking behind those closed doors? If he'd had more men here, he would have sent someone with his sergeant. As it was, there were only the three detectives at the hotel. Therefore, he could only spare one.

Alan heaved a sigh of relief when the doors of the dining room re-opened and Andrews appeared.

"I found a small bag behind the door leading to the kitchen," he reported to the DCI. "I made sure that there wasn't anyone else around before I opened it. Mrs Lockwood was right. There's a dark jacket and a wig tucked inside. I put it back exactly as I found it. Hopefully, we'll catch him in the act of collecting it."

Alan took out his phone and called the station. "I want two uniformed men at the Millennium Hotel ASAP. No sirens or flashing lights."

Next, he spoke to one of the receptionists. "Is the manager in his office?"

"Yes, I believe he's alone at the moment. Would you like me to inform him that you would like to see him?" She picked up the phone as she spoke.

"Please ask him to join me here in reception. Tell him it's the police."

A few minutes later, Mr Jenkins appeared from his office. Looking around the reception area, he recognised the DCI.

"What can I do for you, DCI Johnson? I hope there hasn't been another theft at the hotel." He frowned. "Though I think I would have been the first to hear about it if there had been."

After Alan had given a brief explanation about why he was there, he asked the manager to find out whether the man with Mr Richard Harrison was staying at the hotel.

"The two men are in the drawing room at the moment. We know Harrison is staying here. However, we are keen to learn more about the other man."

Mr Jenkins took a brief look into the drawing room. By now, there weren't many guests sitting in there, so he had no trouble picking out the two men Alan had described.

"I recognize Harrison. I've seen him around the hotel. He was brought to my attention one morning by a security man before he went off duty. Apparently, he had drunk a little too much and was being a little familiar with one of the guests. I don't recall the man with him. Maybe the receptionists can help. One of them might remember checking him in."

Each of the women in turn wandered into the drawing room, pretending they were there to straighten cushions or adjust the curtains.

As it turned out, both receptionists recognised Harrison. One recalled checking him in one day, while the other had been warned of his drunken behaviour by the security man.

However, only one of the receptionists recalled seeing the man sitting with Harrison.

"The face is familiar, so I must have checked him in, though I don't think I've seen much of him since." She scratched her head before looking towards the reception desk. "Maybe if I were to go through the computer, looking at the names of the people I checked in over the last week, something might click."

The manager nodded and the receptionist hurried across to the desk.

"Perhaps, Mr Jenkins, it would be a good idea if you had a surveillance camera in this area," Alan suggested.

"It has been talked about at head office and all managers were given a vote," the manager replied. "However, I voted against the idea and I believe the 'no' votes won. I, for one, don't want our guests to be concerned that their every move is being watched."

"Not even when some people might be checking into your hotel under an assumed name, in order to scam other guests into signing away their businesses?" Agnes retorted.

"Well, Mrs Lockwood, if you put it like that…"

"Yes, I damn well do put it like that!" she stormed. "At least, with a camera pointing towards the reception desk or even the main door, you would have some idea who is entering the hotel. As it is, you don't seem to care who walks through those doors. Even your receptionists could be attacked during a quiet time of the day and you wouldn't have a clue as to the culprit's identity!"

"Mrs Lockwood is right," Alan agreed. "It would certainly have helped in this case."

"I'm sorry to interrupt," the receptionist called across, "but I have the information here."

Once they had all reached the desk, she swung the computer screen around and pointed at a name on the screen.

"Joe Barnes," she said. "That's him."

"Thank you," the manager replied.

Alan drew Agnes to one side.

"Backup is on the way. Maybe you should go back upstairs to your room out of harm's way and leave the rest to us."

"Are you kidding me?" she uttered. "Don't you think I would be more helpful down here?"

"No, Agnes." Alan's voice was firm. "I think, for your own safety, you should go back to your room."

"But I have more to tell you…"

"No buts. It's for your own good!"

Agnes stared at Alan for a moment, hardly able to believe her ears. But, from his expression, she realised he really meant it. He wanted her out of the way.

"Then, if that's what you want, so be it," she retorted, as she stormed off towards the lift. "When you realise that you *do* need me, you know where to find me."

"Maybe you were a little hard on her, sir," Andrews suggested. "After all, she's come up with most of the answers so far."

"I know that, Andrews," Alan replied, sharply. "But look what happened last year? She was very nearly killed by that MI5 man." He paused. "Though perhaps I was a little too forceful."

* * *

Agnes marched into the lift the moment the doors began to open. Thankfully, there wasn't anyone alighting, otherwise they would have collided.

"Are you okay?" Larry asked, as he selected her floor. "You don't look your usual cheerful self."

"I'm fine." She forced a smile. After all, it wasn't his fault that Alan had spoken to her so harshly. "So, how are things with you?"

"Great!" Larry replied. "Tomorrow is my day off and I'm going to look for a new car." He frowned. "Well, not a *new* car, you understand. A secondhand car, but it'll be new to me."

"I remember you telling me that you were saving for a car," she replied.

By now, the lift had arrived at her floor and the doors slid open.

"Can I suggest that you take someone with you?" Agnes added, as she stepped out of the lift. "Sometimes, two heads are better than one when looking for a car."

"Yeah, my dad is going with me," he replied.

"Let me know how you get on," she called out, as the doors began to close.

Talking with the young man had helped to lift her spirits for a short time. For an instant, it had brought back memories of when her boys had each bought their first car. Jim had gone with them on both occasions to give his advice. He hadn't wanted his sons to be taken for a ride, so to speak.

However, now the conversation with Larry had ended, her mind swung back to what had happened downstairs. How could Alan have spoken to her like that, especially in front of those other people? There were so many other thoughts running around in her head that she wanted to pass on to him... things that might have helped solve the case. Yet he had dismissed her almost as though she were a child.

Tears welled in her eyes and ran down her cheeks as she opened the door to her room and hurried inside. She threw her bag down on the bed and wiped her eyes with a handkerchief. Heaving a sigh, she poured herself a glass of wine and strode across to the window.

Maybe it was a bad idea to rush back here, she thought. *I could have got it wrong last year. Perhaps Alan and I aren't right for each other after all.*

"Well, he certainly isn't the right man for me, if that's the way he speaks to me in front of his detectives," she mumbled.

She looked up to where her three suitcases were stacked on top of the wardrobe and made a decision.

"You kept telling me to leave this hotel, Alan. Well, now you've got what you wanted. I'm going back to Essex."

She climbed on a chair and pulled the three suitcases down from the wardrobe and placed them on the bed. She would begin her packing shortly. First, she would sit by the window and enjoy her wine.

A short while later, there was a gentle tap on her door.

Her eyes lit up and she leapt to her feet.

"That has got to be Alan," she said to herself as she hurried across the room and swung the door open.

Chapter Forty-Six

Downstairs in reception, the stage was set.

The two uniformed officers had entered the hotel through the staff entrance to avoid being spotted through the mirrors in reception. They were now in the manager's officer with the DCI and Sergeant Andrews, waiting for Mr Jenkins to escort Joe Barnes in there under some pretext or other. Meanwhile, Morris had been told to hover around reception in case Barnes decided to make a run for it.

Nevertheless, when the manager walked into his office, he was alone.

"He's gone!" Jenkins said. "They've both gone."

"What the hell are you talking about?" Alan yelled. "Gone? Gone where?"

"I don't know! You figure it out, you're the detective."

"Is there another door leading from the drawing room to another part of the hotel?" Alan asked. "I certainly don't recall seeing one."

"No," the manager replied, slowly. "However, there is a door leading out onto the quayside. It's usually locked at this..."

The rest of his words were lost as the DCI and his officers rushed out of the office.

"You both look outside – check all around the building," Alan yelled to the uniformed officers. "Andrews, you look in the dining room – see whether the bag is still there. Morris, find out the room numbers of Harrison and Barnes and get a couple of master keycards. Meanwhile,

I'll check the door they escaped from. They can't have gone far. We only left them a few minutes ago."

It didn't take long for Andrews to discover that the bag had disappeared from the spot where he had last seen it. A door which led from the kitchen to the small yard outside was slightly ajar. Obviously, that was where Barnes had re-entered the building to pick up his belongings.

Andrews shook his head as he went into the reception area.

"It's gone," he told the DCI.

"Nothing in the drawing room, either," Alan replied. "Morris has the room numbers and keycards. We should get up there ASAP."

The detectives split up, with the DCI heading for Harrison's room, leaving Andrews and Morris check out Barnes.

There was no reply when Alan knocked on the door.

"Police, open the door!" he called out, knocking more firmly.

As there was still no reply, he inserted the card and opened the door. He walked slowly into the room, half expecting Harrison to leap out at him; however, that didn't happen. There was no one there. He checked the bathroom; again, no one. The DCI then checked the wardrobe and the drawers, but found they were all empty. Harrison had gone.

The two other detectives found that Barnes had also disappeared.

"I hope the DCI is having better luck," Morris said, closing the wardrobe door. "How can he have packed and left so quickly?"

A few minutes later, Andrews's phone rang.

"It's the DCI," he said as he flipped it open.

He listened for a moment.

"Same here, sir," he said, glancing around the room. "He's cleared his stuff and left."

Alan gave him a few instructions and then hung up.

"The DCI wants us to go back downstairs and find the uniformed officers," he told Morris. "He's hoping they might have something for us. He'll join us in a few minutes. Meanwhile, he's calling in to warn all officers to be on the alert for Harrison. Unfortunately, we don't have any photos of Barnes. Though, with a bit of luck, when we catch up with Harrison, Barnes will be with him."

* * *

Alan was feeling bad about the way he had treated Agnes. He hadn't been able to get the episode in the hotel reception out of his mind. Even now, when he should be getting on with the job of catching the two fraudsters, his attention was elsewhere. Why had he spoken to her like that? Why had he cut her short when she had something to say about the case? Whatever that something might have been, it could well have led to a far better conclusion than the one they had now.

Though he knew it was wrong to drop everything at this crucial time in his investigation, he felt propelled to apologize for the way he had spoken to her. After a final glance around the room to make sure he hadn't missed something, he headed towards the door.

Once he was sure the room was firmly secure, he made his way along the corridor to the stairs leading to the floor below. He was still unsure as to what he was going to say to Agnes. Obviously, he would need to apologize for his abrupt brush-off.

By now, Alan had almost reached the stairs. But that last word was floating around in his head. He stopped walking and leaned one shoulder against the wall while he thought it through.

Brush-off... He hadn't meant his comment to sound as though he was dismissing whatever she had been going to tell him as rubbish. Yet, looking back now, he knew that was exactly how it had sounded. Even his sergeant had commented on the harshness of his tone. It was little wonder Agnes had thundered off towards the lift.

Lifting his shoulder from the wall, Alan blew a sigh before continuing to walk towards the stairs. He needed to make her understand how much he cared for her. No, more than that; how much he loved her.

Now, he was making his way down the stairs to the fourth floor. Very soon he would be knocking on her door – but would she open it when she discovered who was outside?

Chapter Forty-Seven

When Agnes opened her door, she was shocked to find that it wasn't Alan, after all. Instead, she was face to face with a woman. All too late, she realised she should have checked through the peephole before opening the door.

"What do *you* want?" Agnes asked, trying to compose herself.

"You know what I want. However, just in case you have any doubts, I'll spell it out for you. I want you to sign this document," she waved a piece of paper in front of Agnes, "and then you and I are going out for a little walk."

"You're out of your mind if you think I am going to sign anything you place in front of me," Agnes retorted.

She began to shut the door. However, she was too slow. The woman pushed Agnes out of the way and quickly stepped inside.

It all happened so fast that Agnes hadn't been able to do anything to prevent it. Now, she was trapped inside her room with this awful person and potentially in danger, too. She needed to think on her feet if this was going to end well.

Making a run for it was out of the question. The woman was standing between her and the door. Besides, having felt the force behind those arms a few moments ago, there was no point in even trying to get past her.

Agnes now knew for certain that her earlier suspicions had been correct. The person standing in front of her wasn't a woman at all.

Being so close to him confirmed it. She could see beyond the hair-do and the make-up. The person claiming to be Joanne Lyman was really none other than Joe Barnes.

Suddenly, it was as though a light had been switched on. Everything was falling into place. Joanne hadn't been outside the park the night of the second murder simply to watch the police at a crime scene. She had murdered the poor man and dumped his body moments before the young couple discovered it. If only Alan had given her the chance to explain her theory, she wouldn't be in this position now and they would have their man!

A swift glance around where she was standing showed there wasn't anything she could use as a weapon to defend herself. The nearest thing was her handbag, but that was on the coffee table a couple of yards away. Even her suitcases were on the other side of the bed. The only other option was to carry on with the charade and keep Joe talking. Hopefully, someone would knock on the door and distract him.

"Joanne, why don't you stop for a moment? Think about what you're doing?" Agnes asked. "You and Harrison, if that is his real name, can't keep scamming people out of their businesses. People won't stand for it. They'll report you to the police and you'll be arrested. The two of you have already tried it on with me and I refused to be taken in then. Why on earth would I sign anything now?"

She paused, then added, "Why not just leave, while you have the chance? Before you get into any more trouble."

"I can't just leave. Don't you see? I enjoy what I do," Joanne replied, gleefully. "So, why would I want to give it up?"

Agnes frowned and shook her head. "I don't understand."

"Let me explain further." By now there was a distinct note of excitement in Joanne's voice. "I love watching people signing over their businesses to us. Seeing them squirm as they sign away their inheritance gives me a real kick. You can only imagine the pleasure I'll get when you sign the document. You'll be sick to your stomach when you write your name and I'll be enjoying every single second of it."

Joanne paused and glanced away for a second, almost as though she was picturing the scene.

"But," she continued, "that moment is short. The next thing I have to look forward to is taking over your business. That will be our greatest achievement ever. Getting our hands on all that money will be fantastic! As you can see, I love spending money." She pointed to the diamond necklace she was wearing, before running her hands down her expensive red dress.

"And, once we sell your shares in the company to the highest bidder, we'll be set up for life." Joanne grinned happily. "Yet just knowing it all came from the hard work of your parents will be the real bonus for me. That wonderful thought really makes me tick."

"Well, you aren't getting my signature," Agnes retorted. She had heard enough. "So, as far as I'm concerned, your clock has stopped ticking."

Joanne glanced towards the window and heaved a sigh before looking back at Agnes.

"I had hoped it wouldn't come to this," she said, pulling a knife from her bag. She held it out in front of Agnes and slowly waved it from side to side. "Perhaps you might like to reconsider your decision."

* * *

Alan was just about to knock on Agnes's door when he heard the sound of voices coming from inside the room. It seemed Agnes had a visitor. Maybe now wasn't the best time to call.

He was about to move away when it occurred to him that Agnes didn't really know anyone in the area. On the other hand, maybe she had made a new friend on one of her jaunts in the city. Or perhaps she had called room service and a member of staff was simply delivering her order. Nevertheless, Alan needed to know that nothing was amiss before he left.

He looked up and down the corridor and, as there wasn't anyone in sight, he placed his ear against the door. At first, he couldn't make out what was being said. However, a moment or two later he distinctly heard Agnes telling someone to put the knife down.

Agnes was in trouble. Someone was threatening her with a knife! Stepping away from the door, he pulled out his phone and called his sergeant.

"Andrews, get some officers up to Agnes's room right now." He kept his voice low as he didn't want to alert the intruder.

He knew there wasn't time to wait for the officers; he needed to do something to stall whatever was going on in the room. Recalling that he still had a master keycard in his pocket, he made a quick decision. He took a deep breath and, thrusting the keycard into the lock, he opened the door.

"I'm sorry I took so long, Agnes," he said, as he quickly entered the room. He pushed the door shut, but, while doing so, he slipped the latch to make sure the officers could enter.

Joanne was completely taken by surprise. She swung around to face whoever had entered the room. "Who the hell are you?"

"I'm staying here, with Agnes," Alan replied, eyeing the large knife in the woman's hand. "Didn't she tell you?"

Meanwhile Agnes, seizing the opportunity, took a couple of steps backwards and grabbed her handbag from the coffee table. She swung it around and hit Joanne hard on her head. The woman stumbled and fell onto the bed, dropping the knife and her handbag in the process. The contents of the bag spilled out onto the floor, revealing several knives of different sizes.

"That's for trying to take over my business!" Agnes yelled. She slammed her bag down on Joanne again. "And that's for wielding a knife at me."

Alan pulled a latex glove from his pocket and picked up the knife Joanne had been holding, just as Sergeant Andrews, Detective Morris and three uniformed officers burst into the room.

"I think we have our killer, Andrews," Alan said, showing the sergeant the knife. He gestured towards the rest of the haul lying on the floor. "Read her her rights."

"It's hard to believe that a woman could commit such atrocities," Andrews said.

"Woman? That's no woman," Agnes said. She strode across to Joanne and pulled the wig from 'her' head. "Take a closer look. It's Joe Barnes."

"But why dress up as a woman to pull a scam?" Andrews asked. He looked from Agnes to the DCI.

"Goodness knows," Alan replied, with shrug. "Read *him* his rights, Andrews."

"Do you have any thoughts on why he might have dressed as a woman to commit a fraud, Agnes?" The DCI asked, once the rights had been read to their suspect and the knives had been secured by the officers.

"I think they probably learned that a man and woman approaching someone with a scam are more like to be listened to than if a couple of men tried the same thing." Agnes said.

"You knew!" Joe said, glaring at her. "You knew who I really was all the time."

"No," Agnes replied. "Not all the time. When I saw you having break-fast here at the hotel, I got a feeling I'd seen you somewhere before. Since then, I have been racking my brain as to where that might have been. But then, quite out of the blue, two things put me onto the right track. One was something Detective Inspector Johnson said about his undercover detectives having almost fooled him with their elaborate disguises. If they could pull it off, why couldn't you? The other was when you knocked on my door trying to make me believe you were Hotel Security."

Agnes shook her head. "You could have been safely on your way out of Newcastle by now. Yet you came to my room a short while ago posing as Joanne Lyman. I quickly gathered your visit wasn't to say goodbye."

She glanced down at the knives.

"Or was it? You were going to kill me, weren't you? That was your goodbye. Whether I signed the document or not, you were going to kill me, just as you murdered those other two men in Newcastle and those found in Gateshead."

Joe Barnes glared at Agnes. "So what? Like I told you, I enjoy what I do."

"Yes, you told me how much you enjoyed watching people squirm while they signed away their businesses –" Agnes swallowed hard as shock began to make her feel shaky, "– but you actually enjoyed killing them. You told me you took pleasure in thrusting knives into those innocent people, then mutilating their bodies." She was suddenly desperate to sit down.

"Take him away," Alan instructed the officers.

"Wait!" Agnes called out. "One more question. Where is the man calling himself Richard Harrison?"

The officers nodded at Barnes, allowing him to answer.

Barnes looked at Agnes and leaned his head to one side as though deliberating about how he should answer.

"Think about it," Agnes added, encouragingly. "Do you really want him to get away and enjoy spending your share of the money, while he leaves you to rot in prison? Another thing – would he keep quiet about your whereabouts if the shoe was on the other foot?"

That seemed to clinch it.

"He knows how to get into the tunnel," Barnes replied. "You know, the one that was used during the Second World War as an air raid shelter. That's where we were going to meet up. All our stuff is there."

"Is that where you killed those men?" Agnes asked.

Barnes laughed. "Yes." He looked at the DCI. "You best warn your team. It's a bit messy in there... lots of blood and gore."

"But that's impossible!" Alan interrupted. "There's no way anyone could get into the tunnel. I know it's open to the public for guided tours, but once it's closed for the day, it is securely locked."

"Is that so?" Barnes gave a mocking laugh. "Richard can open any kind of lock. Some relation of his taught him how to do it. Now, he's a dab hand at it. Show him a lock and he's in his element. He can get into anything, anywhere. He opened the door nearest to the museum without any trouble at all."

"This relation…" Agnes began.

"Before you ask, I have no idea who he was," Barnes interrupted. "All I know is that he was an MI5 agent for quite a long time. But then something happened and he was killed. Richard really admired that man and vowed he would never forget him."

Agnes closed her eyes and thought back to her last visit to Tyneside.

David Drummond was an MI5 agent who had gone wrong. He would have got away with millions of pounds in jewellery if it hadn't been for her meddling. At one point, he had tried to have her killed. But when that didn't work, he had set about trying to kill her himself. But, in the process, he had been shot dead by someone she had yet to thank for saving her life.

Agnes looked up at the ceiling and heaved a huge sigh of relief. Now, at last, all the pieces of the puzzle were in place. Richard Harrison had hounded her, not only because she held the most shares in a large business, but also because she had been the cause of his cherished relative's death.

Agnes was now aware that she had arrived back on Tyneside too soon. Had she returned even a few days later, Harrison and Barnes would have been long gone. But then she considered whether her early return might have been an omen. Maybe she was meant to be here at this time, otherwise the deaths of the men in Gateshead and Newcastle might have gone unsolved.

"Take him away," Alan repeated firmly.

He then turned to his sergeant. "Take Smithers, Jones and as many officers as you need and head over to the Victoria Tunnel. I don't care how many feathers you have to ruffle, but you must get in there and find Harrison before he gets away."

"Yes, sir," Andrews said, before disappearing out of Agnes's room.

* * *

Once they were alone at last, Alan pointed towards the suitcases on the bed.

"Are you leaving?" he asked.

Agnes walked across to the window and stared down at the quay-side. A police car was driving away. No doubt Barnes was sitting in the back seat with an officer on either side of him. Sergeant Andrews and Morris were leaving the hotel. Morris was carrying his suitcase, while Andrews had his phone to his ear, probably dishing out orders to the detectives at the station. Everything was back to normal.

"I was certainly thinking about it," Agnes replied.

She turned around to face Alan and smiled.

"But, I haven't quite made up my mind."

The End

Dear reader,

We hope you enjoyed reading *Death on Tyneside*. Please take a moment to leave a review, even if it's a short one. Your opinion is important to us.

Discover more books by Eileen Thornton at
https://www.nextchapter.pub/authors/eileen-thornton-mystery-romance-author

Want to know when one of our books is free or discounted? Join the newsletter at http://eepurl.com/bqqB3H

Best regards,
Eileen Thornton and the Next Chapter Team

About the Author

Since finishing a comprehensive writing course with The Writers Bureau on September 27th 2001 (a Certificate of Competence proudly hangs on the wall of my study to prove it), my writing took off. Many of my articles and short stories were accepted and published in several magazines here in the UK. These magazines include *The People's Friend, The Lady* and *Scottish Life*. A couple of my short stories also appeared in *Anthologies*.

Firstly, I concentrated on writing articles. Here I enjoyed researching and writing about the towns, cities and historical buildings around the area where I live: Jedburgh, Lindisfarne and Newcastle on Tyne, to name but a few. My husband, being a keen photographer, accompanied me and took photographs of the various places of interest to go with my writing. But after a while, I decided to change my stance and set my imagination to work on writing short stories.

Strange as this may seem, I always began my short stories at the end. By that I mean, I thought of a last line, which would also become the title of the story. Only then did I begin to work on the story itself, making sure the last line ended the whole thing perfectly.

Then, for some reason, I decided I needed to move on and to write a full blown novel. My first published novel was The Trojan Project, a suspenseful conspiracy thriller. The sort of story readers can get their teeth into. Writing for magazines can be restricting. Therefore writing a novel meant I was able to really let my imagination run away with me. And it did. I let my hair down and brought all the horror and terror I could think of into the story. There were times when I couldn't believe it was me who had written it.

From there, I went on to write a fun romance, Divorcees.Biz. A novel where I was able to show there really is a lighter, more fun side to me. Here I created four divorced ladies who, when out for a few drinks together one evening, decide to set up their own dating agency in order to find new men for themselves.

Only Twelve Days was my next novel. This is a love story set back in the late 70's; a time before computers and mobile phones took over. The outline of this story had been mulling around in my head for some time before I actually got around to writing it. I really enjoyed writing it and I am so delighted I did, because of all of my three novels, this is my favourite.

Lastly, I put together a collection of twelve stories previously published in UK magazines. These are all light-hearted and so easy to read. Some are quite uplifting, if you happen to be feeling a little down.

Before I go, I should add that I am a member of the Society of Authors and have been for several years. I am also a member of the Society of Women Writers and Journalists, as well as being an Associate Member of NAWG (National Association of Writers Groups).

I have a website (http://www.eileenthornton.com/) which I hope you will visit, and also a blog at http://www.lifeshard-winehelps.blogspot.co.uk, where you will find I let my hair down and talk about everything and nothing.

Also by the Author

- Murder on Tyneside (Agnes Lockwood Mysteries Book One)
- A Surprise for Christine
- Divorcees.biz
- Only Twelve Days
- The Trojan Project

Death on Tyneside
ISBN: 978-4-86745-794-8

Published by
Next Chapter
1-60-20 Minami-Otsuka
170-0005 Toshima-Ku, Tokyo
+818035793528
3rd May 2021